MAYA RODALE

Lady Claire Is All That

KEEPING UP WITH THE CAVENDISHES

AVONBOOKS

An Imprint of HarperCollins*Publishers*

This is a work of fiction. Names, characters, places, and incidents are products of the author's imagination or are used fictitiously and are not to be construed as real. Any resemblance to actual events, locales, organizations, or persons, living or dead, is entirely coincidental.

First Avon Books mass market printing: January 2017

ISBN 978-0-06238678-6

17 18 19 20 21 QGM 10 9 8 7 6 5 4 3 2 1

For Tony, who became an American after I went through all the bother of marrying an Englishman, as befitting a Regency romance novelist.

To Emily Levine, for showing us an And-And Universe.

And for the Lady Miss Penny, whom I would never wager.

Acknowledgments

Many thanks to Caroline Linden and Josh Schwartz for help with "math stuff" and to Jody Allen for help with research. Any remaining mistakes, errors, misunderstandings are my own.

Lady Claire Is All That

Prologue

In which our hero and heroine meet and sparks do not fly

London, 1824
Lady Tunbridge's Ball

There was only one man in England whom Lady Claire Cavendish wished to meet. Only one man whom she thought it worth crossing an ocean for, sight unseen. Only one man who possessed a brain like hers, with a gift for numbers, and presumably the only man who would find a brain and talent like hers attractive rather than frightening.

When her brother, James, had shockingly inherited a dukedom, Claire had encouraged him to fully accept the role, which necessitated the Cavendish clan of Claire, James, Bridget, and Amelia traveling to England. It was the right thing to do, and opportunities to be a duke did not come along every day, et cetera, et cetera.

She might have had an ulterior motive.

Because dukes lived in England.

The particular duke she wished to meet lived in London. She had studied the Duke of Ashbrooke's mathematical papers and read accounts of the Royal Society, of which he was an influential member. Claire longed to discuss his difference engine and further possibilities for an analytical machine with him. She knew this made her somewhat of an oddity, but that didn't bother her.

But Claire had lived on a horse farm in Maryland with her brother and two sisters, literally an ocean away, and with no hope of ever traveling to London to make the acquaintance of like-minded mathematicians or to attend meetings of the Royal Society.

And yet, the stars had aligned, fate intervened, or more to the point, the appropriate people had expired, making James the seventh Duke of Durham.

And so here she was.

In London.

In a ballroom, which was likely stuffed to the chandeliers with dukes and earls, marquesses, viscounts, barons, and all their heirs and all that. Already Claire felt she'd been introduced to every peer in England.

Everyone except *the* duke.

"Looking for someone in particular, Lady Claire?" The Duchess of Durham fixed her steely blue eyes on the eldest Cavendish sister.

"Why do you ask?"

"I have my reasons," the duchess replied.

Claire had quickly learned that Josephine Maria Cavendish, the Duchess of Durham, and her aunt, was hell-bent on seeing the family—James, Claire, and her sisters Bridget and Amelia—settled in England. That meant ensuring the three sisters wed so James would stay and fully accept his new role. Cavendish men, like James and his father before him, seemed to be the only ones in the world reluctant to be dukes, preferring instead a quiet life in America. But James was too loyal to his sisters to leave them.

But that meant a debut—tonight, at Lady Tunbridge's ball—and an endless stream of introductions to the very best of society, particularly the ones deemed suitable potential matches.

"Well, do stop craning your neck as if you are on the prowl for someone," the duchess continued.

"But we *are* on the prowl for someone. Or someones, plural," Amelia cut in glumly.

"You made that list of potential gentlemen to introduce us to," Bridget added. "It's a rather long list."

"Well, a lady does not seek out a gentleman

and she certainly is more subtle about it if she does."

"Of course," Claire murmured, gaze still scanning the room, searching for the duke, not that she knew what he looked like. Beside her, Bridget appeared to be committing the duchess's words to memory. Her middle sister was trying very hard to be a perfect lady. Her baby sister, Amelia, was . . . not.

"Come, there are some more gentlemen I'd like to introduce you to." The duchess snapped her fan open and the three Cavendish girls issued weary sighs and trailed after her in their newly acquired fine gowns and delicate slippers. In spite of all their finery, these American girls were oddities in this elegant English ballroom.

Claire hoped at least one of the gentlemen would be her duke. She calculated the odds of meeting him. Tonight.

One hour later

Thus far, Lady Claire had been introduced to four marquesses, five earls, a bunch of marchionesses and countesses, and half a dozen assorted viscounts and barons and their brides. There were misters and misses and what the duchess called "fine prospects" because of what they owned, or what they stood in line to inherit, or their connections. And then Lady Claire was introduced to even more English people.

Not one of whom was the man she sought.

She bit back a sigh as yet another Lord Something—she thought she caught the name *Fox*—was bowing before her. This one, at least, wasn't some soft and paunchy fellow who had clearly spent more time in dissipation than engaged in activities outdoors, unlike most of the men she'd met tonight.

This one had an air of vitality about him. Clear skin. Dark hair. Bright green eyes.

Also, broad shoulders, a wide expanse of chest, and a flat abdomen that tapered to a narrow waist and muscular thighs. The man radiated strength and power.

Lady Claire may have devoted much of her mental activity toward advanced mathematics, but she wasn't blind. Or dead. She recognized a prime specimen of male when it bowed to her in a crowded ballroom.

"It is a pleasure to make your acquaintance," she said, for what felt like the six thousandth time that evening.

"The pleasure is all mine," he replied, following the unwritten script that everyone seemed to know. "How are you enjoying London? You must find it much grander than what you are used to in America."

Claire pursed her lips in annoyance. He was just like everyone else, reciting the same lines. But so was she.

"It is a grand city," she agreed. That was her polite response. Then, because she was fatigued and bored, she deviated from the script. There was something about this man that made her curious as to how he'd play along.

"I am keen to visit the Royal Society," she told him.

"I can't imagine anything more tedious."

"I can," she murmured. She was living it.

He gazed at her with bright eyes, but his smile faded as he realized she was an unusual young woman, and one who wasn't likely to throw herself at him.

"Right, then." He straightened and looked around for an escape. Men always did that when she intimated that she might possess more than half of a functioning brain. "It was a pleasure to meet you," he said, lying.

"Indeed," she agreed, lying.

And that was the last she ever expected to see of Lord Whatever-his-name-was.

Chapter 1

This author has it on good authority that Miss Arabella Vaughn has done something utterly scandalous and completely unthinkable.

—FASHIONABLE INTELLIGENCE,
THE LONDON WEEKLY

London, 1824
Lord and Lady Chesham's ballroom
One week later

It was a truth universally acknowledged that Maximilian Frederick DeVere, Lord Fox, was God's gift to the ladies of London. He was taller and brawnier than his peers and in possession of the sort of chiseled good looks—above and below the neck—that were more often found in works of classical art. By all accounts he was charming and universally liked by men and women alike, though for different reasons, of course. He won at two things, always: women and sport.

Fox strolled through the Cheshams' ballroom as if he owned the place. He nodded at friends and acquaintances—Carlyle, with whom he occasionally fenced, Fitzwalter, whom he had soundly thrashed at boxing last week, and Willoughby, who was always game for a curricle race.

Fox flashed his famous grin as he heard the ladies' usual comments when he strolled past.

"I think he just smiled at me."

"I think I'm going to swoon."

"God, Arabella Vaughn is one lucky woman."

"*Was,*" someone corrected. "Didn't you see the report in *The London Weekly* this morning?"

Fox's grin faltered.

That was when Mr. Rupert Wright and Lord Mowbray found him. Their friendship stretched all the way back to their early days at Eton.

"We heard the news, Fox," Rupert said grimly, clapping a hand on his shoulder.

"I daresay everyone has heard the news," Fox replied dryly.

It didn't escape his notice that the guests nearby had fallen silent. It was the first time he'd appeared in public since the news broke in the paper this morning, though Arabella had so kindly left him a note the day prior. Everyone was watching him to see how he would react, what he would say, if he would cry.

"Who would have thought we'd see this day?" Mowbray mused. "Miss Arabella Vaughn, darling of the haute ton, running off with an actor."

"That alone would be scandalous," Rupert said, adding, "Never mind that she has ditched *Fox*. Who is, apparently, considered a catch. What with his lofty title, wealth, and not hideous face."

Fox's Male Pride bristled. It'd been bristling and seething and enraged ever since the news broke that his beautiful, popular betrothed had left him to elope with some plebian *actor*.

Not just any actor, either, but Lucien Kemble. Yes, he was the current sensation among the haute ton, lighting up the stage each night in his role as Romeo in *Romeo and Juliet*. Covent Garden Theater was sold out for the rest of the season. The gossip columns loved him, given his flair for dramatics both onstage and off—everything from tantrums to torrid love affairs to fits over his artistry. Women adored him; they may have sighed and swooned over Lucien Kemble as much as Fox. One, apparently, swooned more.

To lose a woman to any other man was insupportable—and, until recently, not something that had ever happened to him—but to lose her to someone who made his living prancing around onstage in tights? It was intolerable.

"Just who does she think she is?" Fox wondered aloud.

"She's *Arabella Vaughn*. Beautiful. Popular. Enviable. Every young lady here aspires to be her. Every man here would like a shot with her," Mowbray answered.

"She's you, but in petticoats," Rupert said, laughing.

It was true. He and Arabella were perfect together.

Like most men, he'd fallen for her at first sight after catching a glimpse of her across a crowded ballroom. She was beautiful in every possible way: a tall, lithe figure with full breasts; a mouth made for kissing and other things that gentlemen didn't mention in polite company; blue eyes fringed in dark lashes; honey gold hair that fell in waves; a complexion that begged comparisons to cream and milk and moonlight.

Fox had taken one look at her and thought: *mine.*

They were a perfect match in beauty, wealth, social standing, all that. They both enjoyed taking the ton by storm. He remembered the pride he felt as they strolled through a ballroom arm in arm and the feeling of everyone's eyes on them as they waltzed so elegantly.

They were *great* together.

They *belonged* together.

Fox also remembered the more private moments—so many stolen kisses, the intimacy of gently pushing aside a wayward strand of her golden hair, promises for their future as man and wife. They would have perfect children, and entertain the best of society, and generally live a life of wealth and pleasure and perfection, together.

Fox remembered his heart racing—nerves!—when he proposed because this beautiful girl he adored was going to be his.

And then she had eloped. With an actor.

It burned, that. Ever since he'd heard the news, Fox had stormed around in high dudgeon. He was not accustomed to losing.

"Take away her flattering gowns and face paint and she's just like any other woman here," Fox said, wanting it to be true so he wouldn't feel the loss so keenly. "Look at *her,* for example."

Rupert and Mowbray both glanced at the woman he pointed out—a short, frumpy young lady nervously sipping lemonade. She spilled some down the front of her bodice when she caught three men staring at her.

"If one were to offer her guidance on supportive undergarments and current fashions and get a maid to properly style her coiffure, why, she could be the reigning queen of the haute ton," Fox pointed out.

Both men stared at him, slack jawed.

"You've never been known for being the

sharpest tool in the shed, Fox, but now I think you're really cracked," Mowbray said. "You cannot just give a girl a new dress and make her popular."

"Well, Mowbray, maybe you couldn't. But I could."

"Gentlemen . . ." Rupert cut in. "I don't care for the direction of this conversation."

"You honestly think you can do it," Mowbray said, awed.

He turned to face Mowbray and drew himself up to his full height, something he did when he wanted to be imposing. His Male Pride had been wounded and his competitive spirit—always used to winning—was spoiling for an opportunity to triumph.

"I know I can," Fox said with the confidence of a man who won pretty much everything he put his mind to—as long as it involved sport, or women. Arabella had been his first, his only, loss. A fluke, surely.

"Well, that calls for a wager," Mowbray said.

The two gentlemen stood eye to eye, the tension thick. Rupert groaned.

"Name your terms," Fox said.

"I pick the girl."

"Fine."

"This is a terrible idea," Rupert said. He was probably right, but he was definitely ignored.

"Let me see . . . who shall I pick?" Mowbray

made a dramatic show of looking around the ballroom at all the ladies nearby. There were at least a dozen of varying degrees of pretty and pretty hopeless.

Then Mowbray's attentions fixed on one particular woman. Fox followed his gaze, and when he saw who his friend had in mind, his stomach dropped.

"No."

"Yes," Mowbray said, a cocky grin stretching across his features.

"Unfortunately dressed I can handle. Shy, stuttering English miss who at least knows the rules of society? Sure. But *one of the Americans*?"

Fox let the question hang there. The Cavendish family had A Reputation the minute the news broke that the new Duke of Durham was none other than a lowly horse trainer from the former colonies. He and his sisters were scandalous before they even set foot in London. Since their debut in society, they hadn't exactly managed to win over the haute ton, either, to put it politely.

"Now, they're not all bad," Rupert said. "I quite like Lady Bridget . . ."

But Fox was still in shock and Mowbray was enjoying it too much to pay any mind to Rupert's defense of the Americans.

"The bluestocking?"

That was the thing: Mowbray hadn't picked

just any American, but the one who already had a reputation for being insufferably intelligent, without style or charm to make herself more appealing to the gentlemen of the ton. She was known to bore a gentleman to tears by discussing not the weather, or hair ribbons, or gossip of mutual acquaintances, but *math.*

Lady Claire Cavendish seemed destined to be a hopeless spinster and social pariah.

Even the legendary Duchess of Durham, aunt to the new duke and his sisters, hadn't yet been able to successfully launch them into society and she'd already had weeks to prepare them! It seemed insane that Fox should succeed where the duchess failed.

But Fox and his Male Pride had never, not once, backed away from a challenge, especially not when the stakes had never been higher. He knew two truths about himself: he won at women and he won at sport.

He was a winner.

And he was not in the mood for soul searching or crafting a new identity when the old one suited him quite well. Given this nonsense with Arabella, he had to redeem himself in the eyes of the ton, not to mention his own. It was an impossible task, but one that Fox would simply have to win.

"Her family is hosting a ball in a fortnight," Mowbray said. "I expect you to be there—with

Lady Claire on your arm as the most desirable and popular woman in London."

Nearby in the ballroom

Lady Claire Cavendish was involved in a very animated discussion with a gentleman of her recent acquaintance. To be clear: *she* was animated, whilst he looked like he was considering sticking a hot poker in his eye, just so he might have an excuse to quit this conversation.

"And so complex numbers can be represented on geometric diagrams and manipulated using trigonometry and vectors," Claire continued.

She observed that the gentleman whom the duchess had introduced her to—she hadn't bothered to remember his name—looked bored. Good. He did not appear to be in imminent danger of proposing marriage. Even better.

Claire loved math and she was truly passionate about it and all the other formulas with which one could answer questions and solve mysteries. Numbers spoke to her. She understood them. They played by the rules, always.

Claire was equally passionate about not getting married. Not yet anyway—not while her younger sisters were unwed and James was still unsettled in his new role. She had made a promise to her dying mother that she would always make sure they were happy. And Claire couldn't do that if she lived away from them, with a husband and household to manage.

Those things would also get in the way of her true passion. Deep down, Claire felt she was too smart for merely managing household accounts. She wanted more for herself.

The duchess, however, had other ideas. Or rather: idea. If she could see the Cavendish sisters wed—to Englishmen, in England—then James would certainly stay and assume his title and all its responsibilities. He wasn't keen to be a duke; the idea of returning to America had been mentioned more than once, much to the duchess's dismay and horror.

And so the duchess constantly thrust eligible gentlemen before the girls and performed one introduction after another, hoping that sparks might fly and matches would be made.

Bridget was making a valiant effort to fit into society; she even had a beau she liked. Amelia, however, was acting out by saying scandalous things or acting ridiculously and avoiding all lessons in etiquette, dance, or anything that would make her into a proper young lady.

Claire's strategy was to talk about math. Most people's eyes glazed over when she did. Most gentlemen thought it unbecoming for a woman to possess a brain and to make use of it for thoughts other than how to please men. Speaking of math kept suitors at bay, leaving her free to focus on her siblings' happiness and her own intellectual pursuits, all without giving the duchess reason to think she was deliberately trying not to get married.

Besides, if she ever were to marry—once she saw her siblings settled—it certainly wouldn't be to the sort of narrow-minded man who thought a woman oughtn't use her brain.

Anyway, she would much rather talk about mathematics instead of the weather, even if she was only talking with herself.

"I do enjoy the study of Argand diagrams," she said.

"How fascinating," he said, even though it was anything but to nearly everyone but her.

Every "exchange" was so predictable. Next she would say, "What topics do you find of interest to study?"

And then the gentleman would say, "I beg your pardon, I believe I promised this dance to someone."

And she would say, "It was a pleasure speaking with you," as if she meant it. And she did, a little.

He would say, "Indeed," and be gone and she was free to stand by the sidelines with a bland smile pasted on her face while she contemplated numbers and all the things one might do with them.

But tonight was different. Tonight she was interrupted. Tonight a man approached her, apparently of his own volition, without the duchess dragging him along. This was something gentlemen of sense no longer did. Therefore, he must not be a gentleman of sense.

"Good evening, Lady Claire," he murmured as he bowed.

He was handsome; she had to give him that. Tall, brawny, dark hair, and what could only be described as a smoldering gaze.

"Good evening. I don't believe we have been introduced," Claire said. If they had not been introduced, then they were not to speak, which did not exactly break her heart. Men as handsome as he were bound to be vapid, vain, and in love with themselves. They sought women who would reflect this back to them. She was not his girl. There was no point in wasting either of their time.

"You wound me, Lady Claire. Do you not remember?"

She blinked once, twice, trying to place him.

"I beg your pardon. I have met so many gentlemen and they are all . . ."

"Choose your words carefully," he said with a grin. "Hearts are on the line."

"British. They are all very British."

"Why do you make that sound like an insult?"

"It must be a natural consequence of my

American accent," Claire replied. "Did the duchess send you over to speak with me?"

"I come of my own free will."

"How curious."

"You'll have to explain. I'm just often slow to put two and two together." He gave her a rakish smile. And a wink. How insufferable.

Claire smiled weakly. She had immediately identified and confirmed his type: handsome in a base, elemental way. Charming, in a simple way. Accustomed to having women swoon at his attentions. And he admittedly could not put two and two together, while she did things with two and two that would make his brain melt.

This man, whoever he was, was not for her.

"But who needs to put two and two together anyway?" he continued. "Mathematics are such a dreadful bore. Would you care to dance?"

"I'm afraid this dance is already claimed by another gentleman," Claire told him.

She hadn't expected him to care, and yet she saw a flicker of something in his eyes. But then he drew himself up to his full height in that way men did when they had something to prove.

"Is that so? Well, then, perhaps later this evening."

Why was he so intent upon dancing with her? Most men asked once, out of politeness, she lied and said her dance card was full, and that was that. She'd only had a few lessons and was a terrible dancer—another reason for her to scare away gentlemen before they could invite her to waltz.

He also had to know that she was one of *those Americans*—and the bluestocking one, too. Surely he must know that there was no reason for a man like him to associate with a woman like her, unless he was after her dowry, in which case, good riddance.

"I'm afraid my dance card is full."

"For the whole evening?"

For infinity.

"Yes, for the whole evening."

"Pity, that. I'm an excellent dancer."

"I have every confidence that you are."

Truly, she did. She could tell from the way he stood and the way he held himself that he was supremely comfortable in his body and confident with himself. He was obviously strong. And exceptionally well-muscled. And now she was thinking inane thoughts about this man's muscles.

How absurd.

Mere proximity to this man seemed to lower the level of her thoughts.

"I know how to move a woman across the dance floor so it feels like she's flying. Or floating on a cloud. Or making love," he murmured in a way that was probably supposed to be devastatingly romantic, but that she found somewhat mortifying. "Not that you are supposed to know that."

"Am I now supposed to tell you that in truth my dance card is not full and that I am a liar? Am I to be exceedingly rude to the gentleman who reserved this dance, by jilting him for another? Do tell—what is the intended outcome of such a statement?"

He appeared flummoxed, but she was used to flummoxing men.

"I thought I would let you know what you are missing. I do like to give a girl something to think about."

"I assure you I have plenty to think about," she said darkly.

"Dance with me," he murmured, undeterred.

"This—" she gestured to him, in general, with his muscles and supposedly charming manner and smoldering looks "—this may work with the other ladies, but it will not work with me."

Mere moments later

Though not on the scale of Arabella's jilting of him, Lady Claire rebuffing his invitation to dance marked the second time this week—or ever—that Fox had, well, lost.

As the eldest son of a wealthy aristocrat, Fox

had been born with every advantage into a life of ease and leisure. He had people to handle the things that didn't interest him. And when it came to his two passions of women and sport, he played with the best and always won.

His natural athleticism meant that triumphing on the playing field came easily to him—and so did all the trophies and accolades.

Women usually threw themselves at him. Fox just had to smile and murmur a few choice words to the woman who struck his fancy and she was his. Such was life for a man of his rank, wealth, face, and body.

It was his expectation that life would continue in this manner.

And then, suddenly, the world had turned upside down.

It seemed everyone was witness to it.

As he made his way out of the ballroom, it proved impossible to ignore the stares and the whispers, and the fact that they were not of the adoring and swoon-inducing variety to which he was accustomed. Fox shot them all a murderous look; the subject of their conversation quickly shifted and they looked away.

Lady Claire made his head spin. But fine, most things did.

But Lady Claire was obviously impervious to his charms and she had a way of twisting things around and tying him up in knots when most women smiled coyly or laughed prettily. His attempts at banter and flirtation had fallen flat.

She did not even remember meeting him.

This was not a thing that happened.

The problem had to be with her, of course—she was a bluestocking, and so cerebral as to be unfeeling and unmoved by any man. She was not accustomed to society and perhaps did not realize what a catch he was.

Unless—here, he itched to loosen his cravat—the problem was with himself?

No. Unthinkable. He refused to consider it.

But Fox could actually put two and two together, so to speak: Lady Claire would not be easily won over by him. Winning this wager would not be the simple matter he had imagined. But he *would* win. He always won.

Besides, there was nothing that got his heart pumping and blood flowing like a challenge and the thrill of competition. Fox started to feel it now: the drumbeat of his heart, the blood roaring in his ears, his attention becoming focused on the prize. He concentrated on the inevitable triumph that awaited him: the girl, the glory, the return to the righteous way things had always been and should always be.

That was what he wanted: his world, restored to rights, where winning and women came easily.

Just as he was about to exit the ballroom, Fox turned and surveyed the room, the playing field.

My dance card is full for the whole evening.

The orchestra was playing. Dancers were whirling around the floor—men in dark evening clothes, women in white dresses with jewels glittering in the candlelight. Lady Claire was not among them.

He scanned the ballroom for her and found her standing with her sisters near the lemonade table. It went without saying she was not dancing.

They're pretty, he had thought upon meeting them. Pretty was the least of it. The Lady Claire was something else.

Chapter 2

One hesitates to use the phrase social pariah, *but of all the Cavendish siblings, Lady Claire seems like the one least likely to find acceptance in society, though that might change should her sister Lady Amelia cause a scandal as she seems destined to do.*

—FASHIONABLE INTELLIGENCE,
THE LONDON WEEKLY

Later that evening, Durham House

Late at night, the Cavendish siblings were to be found in one of two places if they were not in their beds—either raiding the kitchen for cake, much to the dismay of Cook, or in Claire's bedchamber, whether she wished to sleep or not. It was a habit developed when they were children wanting to stay up past their bedtime. Claire didn't have the heart to put an end to it now that they were all grown. With all the changes happening, she found it as comforting as she suspected her siblings did.

Fortunately, as the eldest, she'd taken a spacious room with a large bed, which Bridget and Amelia crept into. A short while later James knocked softly on the door and then pulled up a chair. They all started chattering about the events of the evening, teasing each other.

"I think I have met more people since arriving in London than I have in my entire life so far," Amelia said.

"That can't possibly be true," Claire said, starting to tally up some numbers in her head.

"Well, it feels like it is," Bridget said. James agreed.

"And not one of them is interesting," Amelia grumbled.

"I saw you speaking with Lord Fox tonight," Bridget said pointedly.

"Who?" Claire yawned, not quite following it all.

"He is Lady Francesca's brother," Bridget explained. "And he is friends with Lord Darcy."

Claire knew that Bridget was infatuated with Darcy's brother, Rupert, and angling to be friends with the popular Lady Francesca. She knew this because Amelia read Bridget's diary and related pertinent information to the rest of the family, much to Bridget's constant vexation.

Claire had met these people, of course, and hadn't formed much of an opinion of them. They weren't Ashbrooke, inventor of the difference engine, after all.

"Lord Fox was the incredibly handsome and swoon-worthy man with whom you were speaking for at least five minutes before you stalked off," Bridget said.

Ah, now Claire knew just the man. The one who thought he was God's gift to women because he had a handsome face and the body of a Greek god (or so it seemed). The one who smoldered and said ridiculous things like *I know how to move a woman across the dance floor so it feels like she's flying. Or floating on a cloud. Or making love.* She wanted to groan now just thinking about it.

"Oh, that one."

"That was an exchange between my sisters that I did not need to hear," James said.

"If that troubled you, then a word of advice: do not read Bridget's diary. She goes on and on about the handsomeness and swoon-worthiness of—" Amelia was silenced with a pillow to the face.

Claire did not chastise Bridget for that; it was the least Amelia deserved.

"Well, dear sister, how was your conversation with Lord Fox?"

"Yes, do tell," James gushed, like a girl, leaning forward and propping his head on his hands.

Claire chucked a pillow at him.

"Careful with His Grace," Amelia admonished. "He is our last and only hope for the continuation of the Durham and the Cavendish line. Which is the most important thing in the whole world."

His Grace chucked the pillow at her. James hated the formality of being a duke, was uneasy with the responsibilities that came with it, and chafed at the way it restrained him. So naturally they teased him about it endlessly.

"Please," Bridget said. "Can we focus on the fact that our sister *Claire* was seen conversing with a handsome man?"

"I do so all the time. The duchess insists on it."

"Indeed. But the duchess didn't force Lord Fox to speak to you, did she?" Bridget replied. "I saw him approach you of his own free will."

"There is nothing to focus on," Claire said honestly, deliberately ignoring how *newsworthy* it was that a handsome man should choose to have a conversation with her. She deliberately ignored a little twinge of feeling about it, too. She had long ago understood and accepted that she was not the sort of girl who attracted men; she was destined for more brilliant things. "He was one of those preening males with an inflated sense of his own charm and attractions. He asked me to dance and I begged off and that is that."

But judging by the smug, skeptical, and curious expressions on her siblings' faces, it wasn't so simple. But this—some trifling matter concerning a man—wasn't the sort of problem that excited or challenged her. As far as Claire was concerned, Lord Fox was not an equation worth solving.

The next morning, Hyde Park

Early the next morning found Hugh, Lord Mowbray, riding through Hyde Park on his second best horse. His prize racehorse, Zephyr, was presently stabled at his country estate, finishing her training for the season of races up ahead. This year, Mowbray had dreams of winning.

To be fair, he often had dreams of winning.

Whether it was a horse race, a boxing match, a rugby game, or vying for a woman's affections, Mowbray always imagined crossing the finish line first, scoring the winning goal, or getting the girl. In reality, he was always so close that he could see the sweat on his competitor's neck, feel the bruises on his knuckles, or taste a woman's kiss.

In reality, he always came in second, usually to Fox.

They'd been friends for an age, ever since their days at Eton. In sport, they always claimed first (and second) place. In class, they didn't fare as well, though when it came to academic achievement Mowbray did best his friend, not that it was much of a challenge to. When it came to sneaking out into the village tavern to flirt with women . . . Fox was first and Mowbray was right behind him.

Always. It never changed.

Mowbray had even been the one to see Arabella Vaughn first. He had held her in his arms for a waltz first. He had called upon her first, bringing a bouquet of expensive hothouse blooms. He'd been the first to claim a smile from her bee-sting pout of a mouth. For a moment there, he had been her first choice.

But then Fox came back from an extended hunting trip to Rothermere's place in Scotland and once he stepped in the ballroom, and all the new debutantes that season set eyes on him, it was all over for the other gents. Arabella promptly dropped Mowbray—handsome enough, wealthy enough, though a mere viscount—and promptly took up with Fox, who was widely regarded as impossibly handsome, ridiculously wealthy, and with a marquessate that trumped his own title.

No one was surprised.

It was the way of things.

But Mowbray started to seethe.

Why should one man always have everything?

All the prizes, all the most beautiful women? All the power, all the regard? And why was Mowbray always the one in the shadow? It wasn't fair.

And it had gone on long enough.

Mowbray urged his horse on faster and the beast went for it. The park was usually deserted at this hour—save for peers like himself, in need of solitude and clear paths for dangerous riding.

It was his turn, Mowbray thought. Arabella ditching Fox was a sign of things to come, of a change in the stars (or whatever nonsense), an indication that it was now Mowbray's turn to shine.

To win.

He had Zephyr, who would certainly win all the races. He had Fox chasing after a hopeless case—a wager which he would not only lose, but which would distract him from wooing other, more desirable women, clearing the way for Mowbray to find a stunning bride.

It. Was. His. Time.

His turn.

Fox's glory days were done.

And then, speak of the devil, there he was.

Fox was on horseback up ahead, of course, cantering gently without a care in the world while his dog ran alongside.

Even his fucking dog was perfect. A winner. The bitch was not only a top-notch hunting dog and the envy of all on hunts, but Fox had plans to breed her and gents were already jostling for one of her pups. Because of course everything Fox dabbled in had to be top notch.

Mowbray urged his horse faster until they easily overtook Fox. (Ha! He won! Not that Fox even knew they were racing.) Then he pulled on the reins, turning the horse around. Fox slowed his own horse to a walk.

Mowbray tipped his hat. "Good morning."

"Good morning," Fox replied easily.

Their mounts fell in line and walked at a leisurely pace, allowing the gentlemen to talk.

"Bit early for you, isn't it?" Mowbray teased. "Thought you might be abed with Lady Claire."

Fox's expression darkened and Mowbray felt a surge of triumph. It had been a loaded, pointed question. He had watched their interaction the previous evening and it looked like Fox's efforts to win their wager were already off to a terrible start. It appeared that if Fox had aroused any feeling in Lady Claire, it was only annoyance. Honestly, it made Mowbray even feel a bit warm toward her.

"Even I'm not known to seduce a woman that quickly. Then again, it's not really seduction, is it?" Fox gave him a you-know-what-I-mean type of look. "Besides, I still have plenty of time to woo her," he added. A touch defensively, perhaps? Mowbray dug in.

"Do tell, how fares your progress thus far?

I saw you converse with her for not even five minutes."

Five minutes in which Lady Claire looked utterly bored and totally perturbed. It had made Mowbray's night.

"'Tis not the length of time that matters, but the quality of time," Fox replied.

"I don't believe I've heard that. At least, not from women."

"Touché." Fox grinned, and Mowbray was annoyed because in his head this conversation had been a competition, and Fox didn't seem to realize or care. He let him win. "Where is Zephyr?"

"At my stables in Buckinghamshire, finishing her training. I expect her to have an outstanding season."

"Best go for it before Durham gets in the game. I'm surprised he hasn't already."

"Too busy with his dukedom, I suppose. The problems some people have . . ."

"Responsibility." Fox made a face. "I thank God every day for competent estate managers, which leaves me with time for the important things."

"Like races, boxing, drinking, and wagers?"

"And winning." Fox just grinned and kicked his horse into a gallop. The damned perfect dog ran after him. Mowbray spat out the dust left in their wake.

Chapter 3

Lord Fox has wasted no time finding a new woman after being jilted by Arabella Vaughn. He seems to have taken an interest in Lady Claire Cavendish, of all the ladies in London. This author knows not what to make of it.

—FASHIONABLE INTELLIGENCE,
THE LONDON WEEKLY

The next evening, the card room at yet another ball

Claire's sister Amelia often complained about the tedium of balls—after the novelty had worn off, Claire privately agreed, though she knew better than to encourage Amelia by admitting she felt the same. As the eldest, she had to set an example. Always. It was almost as tedious as enduring London soirees.

Fortunately, she developed stratagems to keep

herself sane in these endless social events. First, her trick with the dance card—she simply told every gentleman who inquired that her card was full and thus she was able to politely refuse her offers to dance, an activity at which she did not excel and thus did not care to partake in.

But even she came to enjoy balls when she discovered the card room. She could stand to the side and watch emotions run high as lords and ladies would win and lose fortunes at the mere turn of a card. She watched as they made idiotic wagers and foolish choices that led to disastrous outcomes that might have been avoided with some rational thought and calculations. In her head, Claire counted cards, calculated odds, and made her own private wagers on the outcome. In her head, she'd won a fortune of her own.

She yearned to play a hand herself and to *win* on the strength of her intelligence and rational judgment. Even more she wanted to play against the lords and ladies who gossiped relentlessly about her family. She wanted to beat them. Take their money, their jewels, their hunting boxes in Scotland and dole them back out once people stopped making remarks about the smell of the stables when James went by or whispers about Amelia's hoydenish behavior being embarrassing.

Most of all, she wanted an activity with which to occupy her brain.

She was too smart to simper on the sidelines of ballrooms.

Claire was edging her way closer to a table where a game was in progress and deliberating as to how she might join in when the oh-so-handsome Lord Fox found her. She thought she'd been rid of him.

Lord Fox, of the brawn and male beauty and inane conversation. Lord Fox, who was a little too certain that he was a treasure from heaven sent down for women. Lord Fox, who attracted attention when he spoke to her. She did not want attention.

"Good evening, Lady Claire." He bowed and she inclined her head slightly. "It seems we meet again."

"So it would seem." She cast him a bored glance. "Good evening, Lord Fox."

"Is your dance card full again?"

He gave her the sort of glance that was supposed to make her knees weak.

"Yes. Every last dance." *From now until Judgment Day.*

"Yet you are in the card room," he pointed out. "Shall I escort you back to the ballroom?"

Damn. She was caught in a lie. She eyed him more carefully now, not wanting to underestimate him again. She took in his green eyes, fixed on her. A lock of black hair fell rakishly across his forehead. It was the sort of thing silly girls would sigh over, but as someone who usually wore her hair severely pulled back from her face, it just annoyed her.

"Well, this dance isn't claimed," she said.

"May I have the honor of this dance?"

Claire didn't think twice about refusing him, again. She hadn't the slightest clue why he had suddenly taken an interest in *her* but she saw no point in encouraging him. Furthermore, etiquette dictated that if a woman refused a dance, then she wasn't able to accept another dance for the rest of the evening. This suited her just fine.

Sometimes, knowing the rules of etiquette could work to a woman's advantage. Not that she'd ever tell Amelia that. Or maybe she ought to. Her baby sister was willfully ignorant when it came to such matters.

But first, a rejection.

Because Fox didn't seem terrible, just misguided in his attentions, she decided to let him down gently.

"I'm afraid I cannot. For health reasons." She coughed delicately. Men were usually terrified of women's ailments.

"Of course," he said dryly. "Women have such delicate constitutions. Why, the slightest thing could gravely endanger their health—a gust of wind that is too strong or too cool, for example. Perhaps the lemonade offered tonight was not sufficiently tepid. Or your corset might be laced too tightly." He said this with a look that suggested he'd like to loosen her corset and suddenly hers did feel too tight. "There are any number of reasons why a woman would feel under the weather."

Every fiber of her being wanted to disagree with him.

"That is why it's best that I remain here, where I will be unperturbed."

"Indeed, there is nothing much to excite you here. Playing cards might be interesting, but watching others play is certainly tedious. But do take care not to overtax your lady brainbox by trying to understand the rules of the game."

This time when she coughed, it was because a hot ball of rage had lodged in her throat. *Men.* And the assumptions they made about women—especially the assumption that all women were the same.

If she weren't so determined to avoid this overbearing male, Claire would have given him a piece of her mind. She would have told him in no uncertain terms that she did indeed enjoy watching the game, far more than she enjoyed his belittling conversation. She would have informed him that her "lady brainbox" was more capable of understanding it and winning it than all the male brains in the room combined.

She bit her lip and said none of that.

"The game is vingt-et-un," Fox explained. "It's French for *twenty-one.*"

"I am aware."

"Well, I wasn't sure if they taught foreign languages to girls over in the colonies," he said with a laugh. "Wasn't sure if they taught anything other than tossing tea in the harbor."

"I assure you my education was—"

"Now the object of this game is to get one's cards as close to twenty-one as possible without going over."

Claire just sighed and rolled her eyes. This was the story of her life. Men explained things to her that she not only knew, but knew far more about.

"An ace can be either high or low."

Claire wanted to scream.

And just when she was about to throttle this man, who had for some reason developed the habit of seeking her out and annoying her, he asked, "Would you care to play?"

Claire's rage dissipated. Slightly.

"Yes, thank you, I would."

She would play, and win, and stun him into silence with the brilliance of her female brain. He would see that she was a frighteningly intelligent bluestocking future-spinster-witch and would never ask her to dance again. Which would be *fine.*

Lord Fox used his large size to intimidate

people into removing themselves from their way. Upon approaching a table, he said a few words to some gent, who immediately stood and offered his space to Claire. She took a seat, skirts swishing around legs.

Though it was normal for a woman to join a game of cards, there were murmurs around the table when she took her place. Perhaps it was her reputation as a bluestocking, or with Lord Fox, or that she was an American crashing this bastion of English high society, too. She didn't know or care.

Fox stood behind her. She was very, very aware of him.

His hands curled around the top of the chair. She felt his fingertips brush against her bare skin.

Claire went still.

It didn't mean anything, yet it was oddly intimate.

She would *not* lose her wits over it though. Not when she had the opportunity to play a hand of cards and use her brain and potentially not expire of boredom at a party for once.

Lord Fox moved slightly and she felt the wool of his jacket brush against her skin. It was fine, high quality wool. Not that she needed to know that. But now she did. Drat.

Resolved to ignore the strange effects of unintentional but slightly intimate gestures from Lord Fox, Claire turned her focus to the game.

Ever the gentleman, Lord Fox put down some money with which she might wager. She felt her lips curling into a smile at the coins glinting in the candlelight. That pile would be far larger by the time she was done.

"Are you mad, Fox? That's money you won't see again." Some fat, red-faced old lord gave a hearty chuckle. Claire resolved to crush him.

"Some of us can afford to throw money away," Lord Fox remarked casually. The red-faced boor shut up.

And then the game began. She relished the numbers, calculating the odds, taking risks, the feel of the cards in her hand, the whirring sound of a shuffled deck. And she had a good hand.

Fox leaned over to whisper in her ear. "I think you should stick. Best to play it safe."

She held a seven and a ten: seventeen. Any card from an ace to a four would improve her position. Claire watched the round proceed. One fellow took another card—a nine, causing him to grimace and turn over his cards at once to show he was overdrawn with a five, an eight, and the nine. The next player shook his head, and the red-faced boor took a six. That meant the remaining deck was full of low cards, so her odds of getting dealt an ace, two, three, or four were at least one in four, possibly as good as one in three. She could do better. And if she didn't . . . it was Lord Fox's money anyway.

"Another card, please."

"Are you certain?" His voice was a low hum, annoying her. Like a mosquito.

"Quite."

But she was also quite aware of the heat of his body radiating out toward hers. He was so close, looming behind her like that. He certainly had a view of her cards and, it occurred to Claire now, straight down at her breasts.

She didn't dare turn around to look.

There were murmurs around the table when her new card was revealed: a three. That gave her twenty. She declined another card. The odds of getting exactly twenty-one, and beating her, were approximately . . . she thought for a moment . . . one in twenty.

A moment later, the cards were then overturned and, to everyone's surprise except her own, Claire had won.

And so the scene repeated itself. She played daringly, occasionally losing, but mostly winning. The pile of money before her grew steadily with each hand, while the red-faced old toad—McConnell, she had learned after besting him twice in a row—saw his funds dwindle to a few scattered coins.

That was what he deserved for underestimating her.

Like so many males, he saw breasts and forgot that the person also had a brain.

"That's some beginner's luck," Fox remarked.

"Or I simply calculated the likelihood of certain cards being played and took calculated risks with my hand."

"In your head?"

He looked at her head as if it were empty except for vague thoughts of kittens playing with hair ribbons and that he couldn't quite fathom how kittens and hair ribbons could perform mathematical equations.

"Yes. With my lady brainbox."

"Impressive," Lord Fox murmured. She wasn't certain if he was impressed that a woman performed such calculations or that *anyone* could do such sums in their head. Or perhaps he was impressed with the mountain of winnings before her. She had won it fair and square and was proud to witness such undeniable proof of her skill and intellect. The others at the table were less enthused about it, of course, seeing as how it represented their losing to a girl, and one of the Americans as well, but there was little she could do about that now.

Claire stood and gave the merest nod of her head to the company.

"I shall leave this for you, Lord Fox," Claire said, gesturing to her winnings on the table. "Now if you'll excuse me. I believe I owe a gentleman a dance."

* * *

Fox watched Lady Claire walk away. In spite of her success at the table and in spite of their conversation, he had the sinking feeling that hadn't gone well at all, and for the life of him, he didn't understand why.

But that was women for you. How many times had he found Arabella in a mood of unknown origin? It usually required kisses and promises of trinkets to woo her into better spirits. But Fox had a hunch that would never work with Lady Claire.

He didn't understand that woman *at all.*

Mowbray then stepped into his line of vision with a big grin on his face. There was something smug about that grin, like he was relishing Fox's confounding situation. Fox found he wasn't in the mood for his friend. Or his confounding situation.

"At least you'll have a pile of money to comfort you," Mowbray said, with a nod of his head to the pile of gleaming coins on the table—the cold, hard evidence of her brilliance and his foolishness at underestimating her. "If you can't get the woman."

She'd won quite a bit—not just for a girl, or a lucky beginner, but for an experienced player. It was a cold comfort. It did nothing to restore his equilibrium. He had gravely underestimated her and she had thoroughly trounced him. *Losing. Again.*

"She's a special bird," Fox said, in what he suspected was a massive understatement. And then, because his Male Pride needed the last word, he added, "We both know that I'll get her yet."

"Hunting birds being one of the many sports at which you excel," Mowbray replied. Was that bitterness in his friend's voice? Fox felt uneasy.

"Glad I don't have to remind you."

"Speaking of which . . ." Mowbray said in way that had Fox's hackles raised. "We never did set the terms of the wager."

"I reckon you have an idea."

"I do." Mowbray paused for effect. And, dammit, it worked. "Stella."

Fox paled. He fought every urge in him to shout, *No! Never.* A knot quickly formed and tightened in his gut. Anything but Stella. The one possession he actually cared for.

"Don't think you can win, can you, Fox?"

The taunt landed like an unexpected punch to the gut and it was a second before he recovered from the shock. Mowbray didn't often challenge him; his friend was usually right by his side cheering him on. And he never went for the jugular with the terms of what Fox had assumed was a friendly wager, a little bit of ballroom sport to liven up the season and take his mind off Arabella.

He ought to cool his hot head and proceed

with caution until he got to the bottom of this. But being a man who lived and breathed competition, Fox's Male Pride took the bait and, inevitably, he rose to the taunt.

"Of course I know I can win," Fox said with a feigned ease. "I just thought you'd want something like money, or my vintage whiskey collection, or one of my un-entailed properties. Not my dog."

Stella also happened to be his prize hunting dog—an intelligent and lively pointer who was the perfect companion on any hunt. She was the envy among the peers who took hunting seriously and there was already a long line waiting for her pups.

But to Fox, she wasn't just a winning animal, she was his dog. Man's best friend, et cetera, et cetera. She wagged her tail when he walked into the room. Slept beside his bed. Joined him on hunts and long rides through the park.

And Mowbray wanted her?

It was unconscionable.

But his Male Pride had risen to the occasion and was making all sorts of promises: *You'll win. Of course you'll win. You're a DeVere and you were raised to be the best. You always win, when it comes to sport and women. Odd as she may be, Lady Claire Cavendish is still just a woman. Take the challenge. Rise to the occasion. Go. Win.*

His heart was pounding when he said, "All

right, then. But when I win, I want Zephyr. She'll be a nice addition to my stables, don't you think?"

"Fine," Mowbray agreed through gritted teeth.

The two *friends* stood face-to-face, practically choking on the tension in the air between them, all over a stupid, offhanded wager about a strange girl. There was an undercurrent of something pulsing beneath the conversation, and if Fox were the sort of man who thought deeply about this sort of thing, he might have done so. But he wasn't.

Fox clapped him on the back. "Glad that's settled," he said with a good cheer he didn't feel. "If you'll excuse me, I have prettier faces to talk to this evening."

Once he walked away, his grin faltered. Fuck. What had he done? Over Lady Claire? Fox had agreed to some supremely ill-advised wagers and gambits before but *this*—this one was already doing strange things to his heart and confounding his brain when he needed it most. For the first time, he wasn't sure he could win and something he couldn't stand to lose was on the line.

He had just stepped into the ballroom when his sister, Francesca, immediately accosted him. Her two simpering friends trailed a few steps behind, giggling about something, as usual.

"What is this I hear about you causing a scene in the card room with Lady Claire? Everyone is talking about it."

"Then do you need me to?"

Francesca ignored the sharpness in his voice.

"As your beloved sister, I would like know how to reply when people ask if my brother is courting one of the American girls. And, I might add, the sister to my nemesis."

Francesca had this idea that one of the American Cavendishes was after Lord Darcy, one of Fox's friends, whom she'd been expecting a proposal from for years now. She'd been pestering him to find out about Darcy's intentions—as if gents just sat around and drank sherry and talked about their feelings. Of course they did no such thing. If something was bothering them, they didn't discuss it, they hit something.

The next day, Horse and Dolphin pub

Most gentlemen of the ton attended Gentleman Jack's to let their fists fly and call it boxing. Fox had started there, but found his peers too concerned about black eyes and broken noses to give him a proper fight. With his skill and tolerance for pain, he swiftly moved on to regularly receive the honor of sparring with Gentleman Jack himself.

When that became too easy and too predictable, Fox ventured to the Horse and Dolphin pub near Leicester Square. The boxing academy there was set up by Bill Richardson, a former slave from America and champion fighter. His method relied on careful footwork and quick hands, and involved his wits as much as his fists. Fox loved it.

For a man like Richardson, boxing was a way of supporting himself. For most peers it appealed to their vanity. For Fox, sport was his sanity. Whether it was fighting, fencing, riding, or rowing; moving until his muscles screamed from exertion made him feel right. It made him feel alive.

Some men—most men he knew—were content to live life trapped behind a desk, to while away the hours at the House of Lords, to sit around in White's. His muscles ached with boredom if he did that for more than an hour or two. Then he needed to take his stallion out for a gallop, to feel the slick sheen of sweat from exerting himself in a fencing match, or to feel his knuckles aching and raw from a fight.

After last night, he felt the urge to hit something.

So here he was, in the ring.

Fox did not recognize his opponent, a bulky man in his mid-twenties with a bald head and, by the looks of it, a survivor of a rough encounter or two in his recent past. There were cuts. Bruises. He looked mean. Spoiling for a fight.

Yes.

Make it hurt. Make it burn. Make him sweat. Make him focus.

But there was none of that.

Fox could see the punches coming from a mile away. A left hook, a jab from the right. It was easy enough to spot and evade them. He didn't even need to move quickly.

When he did land a blow on his opponent, the man staggered back and took a moment to absorb the pain and catch his breath. Fox stood there, not sweating. His heart, not pounding.

The fight was slow.

It was too easy.

It was too predictable.

It was, he realized, not unlike how Lady Claire must have felt when watching the card game. Hell, playing the card game. Hell, conversing with him about the card game—the memory of which made him cringe now. As a clearly intelligent woman, she must have been immensely frustrated at the slow pace, the slower wits, and numbskulls like himself commenting on her beginner's luck when it was really a sharp mind pitted against lousy competition.

She must want a challenge. Something that made her heart pound and her brain whir to life. Something she had to burn and sweat for.

It was in this moment of brilliant insight—admittedly, a rarity for him—that his opponent landed a solid blow on his right eye, one which took him down.

"That was a good fight until you got distracted," Richardson said. He'd been leaning against the wall, arms folded over his chest, watching. "All it takes is a second of distraction and BOOM." Richardson slammed his fist against the wall with a fierce thump that echoed loudly. "Someone has punched you in the face."

Richardson was wrong. It had been a boring and mediocre fight until he'd been distracted with that flash of insight and spark of understanding. He understood that strange American girl a little more now and with that might come the key to winning his wager. That was certainly worth taking a fist to the face for.

Chapter 4

Lord Fox's residence

Fox returned home with a new sense of purpose. When Stella bounded up, tail wagging happily—much to the dismay of the butler, Smethport, who eschewed any display of emotion on creatures human or otherwise—Fox bent over to greet her, rubbing behind her ears the way she liked, and whispering promises that he would never, ever let anyone take her, especially the likes of Mowbray.

"I'll let your valet know you have returned," the butler said flatly, with only a hint of disapproval. "And that he should bring a remedy for your eye."

A bruise was already forming.

"Thank you, Smethport." Fox started up the stairs to his bedchamber and Stella followed.

During today's fight, he'd had a flash of understanding about Lady Claire but he had no idea how to apply this knowledge to his presently disastrous situation.

For that, he would have to call in reinforcements. An expert. A brilliant strategist with a ruthless sense of competition. Someone with a keen insight into the female mind and the collective brain of the haute ton.

Fortunately, he lived with just the person.

"And, Smethport, please inform Lady Francesca that I should like to see her in my study in an hour."

At the appointed hour, his sister, Francesca, strolled into the study. Stella, who now had made herself comfortable in a patch of sunlight on the plush carpet of his study, opened her eyes, saw it was a family member who did not reward her with food from the table, and went back to sleeping. Fox wondered idly if Mowbray had patches of sunlight at his place and would he allow Stella to sleep there?

Then he shook such thoughts from his head. He had to focus.

"Franny, if you were an American lady in London, which social event would you attend? I am asking for a friend."

"You know I hate when you call me Franny. It sounds so . . . provincial." She shuddered.

"It is my right as an older brother to annoy you in whichever way I see fit. Now tell me what I should do."

He looked down at the mound of invitations on his desk and up at the bemused glance of his sister.

"I would fire your secretary and get another before I worried about that. I hope my dowry isn't somewhere in that mess. Or rather, I hope it is."

"Darcy doesn't need your money."

"About that—" Francesca began.

Fox started to whistle as he sifted through the invitations. He sensed that she wished to pester him about what Darcy—the most reserved, inscrutable man on earth—might have said regarding his innermost feelings for her, to him, Francesca's brother, who wasn't the least interested in hearing said feelings.

After a moment of staring at him, she gave up.

"I can't believe you think I would know the whereabouts of those ridiculous Americans on any given night."

Like most of the ton, she held a low opinion of them. They were ill-mannered outsiders, upstart usurpers of a prestigious English title, and prone to embarrassing scenes and laughable lapses in etiquette. He remembered Francesca laughing for days over Lady Bridget falling in the ballroom during her debut ball.

But, like most of the ton, she also had a morbid fascination with the American family that occasionally trumped her low opinion of them. They couldn't be completely ignored for there was a dukedom involved after all. Besides, haute ton hostesses found that inviting them to parties, setting them up for causing scenes, and conversing with them provided endless fodder for gossip.

"You're friends with one of them, aren't you?" he asked. "You and Lady Wych Cross are always paying calls to them. And I see you out with Lady Bridget at balls."

Lady Wych Cross was their aunt and Francesca's chaperone. Fox avoided her as much as possible.

"Yes, but not because we are friends with them," she explained, which made zero sense to him.

"Franny, it's urgent. Desperate. Important." And when that failed to move her, he said, "I have to win a wager."

"Well, in that case . . ." she retorted. But then her expression grew serious. "What is it?"

Their family was not in the habit of losing—the previous Lord Fox ensured it and thus they were a fiercely competitive bunch. Croquet, cards, and other games as children often turned violent, resulted in simmering feuds and ruthless attempts to win. While Fox used his brawn, Francesca used her brain. Most of their games had resulted in young Fox and Francesca being sent to separate corners of the nursery until they calmed down.

But now, that fighting spirit and her devious mind were on his side. For the first time since making the bet, Fox felt like he had a chance.

"It's just a little bet with Mowbray that I can turn Lady Claire Cavendish into the darling of the ton. I wagered Stella."

Francesca looked from him, to the dog, and back again. Then she burst out laughing. He set his mouth in a grim line and waited for her to finish cackling. "Dear brother, you are an idiot. A monumental idiot."

"I know," he said wryly.

"Is this how you choose to deal with Arabella breaking your heart?"

Fox scowled as he always did at the mention of her name. "Never mind that. Franny, I cannot lose."

"Of course not. And not just because you foolishly wagered your precious dog. We are DeVeres." She placed her palms on his desk and stared at him fiercely. "*We do not lose.* We'll speak about your poor choices later, but for now you should know that everyone is planning to attend Lady Waterford's musicale tonight."

Later that evening, Durham House

It was that hour of the day when everyone retired to their chambers to be primped and preened for the evening ahead. Claire often took advantage of everyone's distraction to steal some quiet time for herself. Some days she worked on equations and sometimes she slept, exhausted from the endless social whirl.

This evening Claire was reading when her maid, Pippa, slipped into the room. She wasn't reading a mathematical paper, though one of those was lying on the bed. Today Claire read the gossip columns.

"Are you ready, Lady Claire?"

"Yes, thank you, Pippa."

She moved to the chair near the mirror. Pippa started heating up the irons to curl her hair, which was always a pointless endeavor. She had only the patience to have a few strands done, and preferred to have her hair pulled back sharply and kept entirely out of her face.

Tonight she had even less patience. She returned her attentions to the gossip columns and scanned the pages until she found the name she sought: Ashbrooke.

It is reported that the Duke and Duchess of Ashbrooke have returned from their honeymoon.

Ashbrooke: the one man she had crossed an ocean for and had yet to meet.

Well, he was back in London. That was something. She was dying to see his difference engine and to speak with him about it. They had exhibited it earlier in the season, but the duchess had kept them all so busy there hadn't been time to see any sights—something Amelia grumbled about daily. Nothing like it existed before and it promised worlds of opportunity to perform more calculations, more reliably, which had implications for so many other areas.

Not only that, Claire saw the engine as a stepping stone to more intricate machines that could perform ever more complicated problems with an unimaginable speed; that is what she wished to discuss with him and perhaps collaborate on.

But Ashbrooke was married. That shouldn't matter. She wasn't interested in marriage anyway, at least not presently, and not with him necessarily. She cared about *math,* she told herself. She cared about stimulating intellectual conversations, mechanical innovations, advanced mathematical equations. That was all. These were the things that made her heart sing.

Or so she told herself.

But a little twinge of sadness she felt told her everything she needed to know: she had secretly, in her heart of hearts, harbored hopes.

Hopes that there might be a man with whom she could share her passion. Hope that there was a man who wouldn't think her strange for her interest in numbers, and who would encourage her to pursue her studies. In other words, a man who would love her for her true self.

Hopes that were now dashed by reading the words *and duchess*.

Because if not Ashbrooke, then who?

Rather than sit idly and stare at her reflection, Claire kept reading. She knew what she looked like already: the perfectly fine, if unremarkable, features, a nice complexion. Her glasses slid down her nose as she bent her head to read. Halfway down the column she spied her name. She pushed her glasses back up so she could see the words clearly.

> *It is a sighting no one expected to see once, let alone twice: Lord Fox and Lady Claire Cavendish. Together. Once might be considered polite, but might twice be considered courtship? Everyone must agree it would be such a strange pairing. Perhaps Arabella Vaughn broke his mind as well as his heart when she eloped with actor Lucien Kemble.*

Claire knew very well what this meant and it wasn't a shock: it was very, very peculiar that the attentions of Lord Fox should be fixed upon her. Her siblings had commented on it, and she'd dismissed it as just familial teasing. But if the London gossips were intrigued by it, too . . .

With that, her curiosity was aroused. There was nothing she loved more than a problem that didn't readily make sense and that might prove interesting to solve.

Chapter 5

That evening, the musicale

Fox took more than the usual care in dressing for the evening, knowing that he had much to accomplish this evening—woo Lady Claire, make an impression upon the haute ton together, get closer to winning the damned wager. After all, the clock was ticking.

His valet, Burke, was in raptures and rose to the challenge, paying an inordinate amount of attention to the selection of the right waistcoat (midnight blue satin) and to the tying of his cravat (fashioned into an excessively intricate and stifling knot). As if Lady Claire Cavendish was the sort of woman who noticed or cared about these things.

"It's a pity about that bruise," Burke said, standing back to admire his work.

"It's fine," Fox said. The bruise from his pathetic boxing bout was a reminder of the struggle. To work for it. To sweat for it. To think of how Lady Claire must feel to want something, but to have limited options to express it.

It was a reminder of that wager. Losing was simply not an option.

He glanced down at Stella, lying at his feet, gazing up at him adoringly. He bent over to scratch behind her ears and murmured a promise to her as he strolled out, into the night.

Upon arrival at Lady Waterford's musicale, he left Francesca hanging off Darcy's arm while he sought out Lady Claire. He found her sitting upon a settee. Alone. How fortuitous.

"Good evening, Lady Claire. May I join you?"

She spared him a brief glance and a small sigh—not the dreamy sort he was accustomed to, but one that sounded a bit peevish. For a brief, fleeting second, his confidence wavered. At least that's what he thought the strange new feeling might be.

"Of course, my lord," she murmured, presumably only because to say otherwise would be impolite. He took advantage and took the seat beside her.

"Yet again you manage to make 'my lord' sound like an insult." He said this with his most charming smile, the one that made women swoon.

"My accent has not changed. Neither has my interest in dancing or conversation. I am curious about your interest though."

"Why wouldn't I be interested?"

Lady Claire raised one eyebrow. She was clearly not impressed—not with his rakish smile, his attentions, his presence. It was unsettling. Unusual. Nerve-wracking. Fox decided a compliment was in order. Women loved compliments.

"You were marvelous at cards the other night."

"I know."

"You're welcome," he said pointedly.

She turned to him and fixed her gaze upon him. Her blue eyes were magnified behind her spectacles. Her gaze unflinching.

"I take your meaning. But I know that I am good at cards and math."

"And now the ton is learning, too."

"You say that as if it's a bad thing." Then, muttering under her breath, she added, "They all say that as if it were a bad thing."

"Do you care?" When he asked the question, he was genuinely interested.

"No," she said, her smile broadening. "Not in the slightest."

"Impressive," he said softly, and as someone involved in a wager over essentially what everyone thought of him, he meant it.

"You seem to have taken an interest in me,"

she said pointedly. This must be the American directness he'd heard about.

So the match begins, he thought. She was aware their pairing was remarkable and unusual. Being a logical female, she sought a reason. His heart began to pound as it always did when he had to think quickly on his feet. Saying anything about the wager was out of the question, but he didn't have her quick wits and couldn't think of a plausible reason.

He decided to deflect her question. That had often worked when he was a green schoolboy and would hopefully work now.

"Again, with the modesty." He laughed.

"Again, with the facts. I'm curious. Why?"

Fox said the first thing that came to mind, the first thing he'd said after meeting her and her sisters, however briefly, at their first ball.

"You're pretty."

Lady Claire rolled her blue eyes. "There are far prettier girls here than myself."

"You seem to have *not* taken an interest in me," Fox replied, dodging. Evading. Turning the tables.

"Please don't take it as a personal affront," she replied. "I'm simply more interested in mathematics than courtship or marriage. Unless you are, despite your reputation, harboring a secret interest and talent in advanced mathematics?"

"As a rake, I never thought I'd say this, but I

find myself more interested in marriage than mathematics," Fox replied. Then, dropping his voice to a suggestive murmur, he added, "Or at least the marriage bed, if you know what I mean."

"I do," Lady Claire replied frostily. She was not charmed.

"Surely, there must be one man in England who sparks your passion." A pale pink flush crossed her cheeks. "One man who occupies your thoughts." The pale pink deepened.

He was forced to conclude that it wasn't all men who bored her, but perhaps just him.

His Male Pride reared its head and roared, *Who is this man?*

But as a cultivated and reserved Englishman, he merely remarked, "Ah. I see that I am right."

"What were you saying about modesty?"

"Not for me," Fox said, straightening and wanting to flex his fists. "Who is he?"

Lady Claire was quiet, as if considering whether or not to confide in him. Fox found himself holding his breath. This was progress. This pause, this moment of quiet reflection, was hope.

She finally answered, in a low voice. "The Duke of Ashbrooke."

"You do know that he has recently wed."

"Yes, of course," she replied, slightly annoyed. "And I am not interested in him romantically."

"Ah, you really have not met him, then," Fox said, leaning back in his chair. The only man considered his rival in charm and appeal to women was Ashbrooke. *Was*, as the man was married and by all accounts besotted with his new bride, a former wallflower, in fact, and not completely unlike Claire, come to think of it.

"What is that supposed to mean?"

"The Ashbrooke Effect," Fox answered. "All women suffer from it, even my sister, who has a heart of stone and is immune to flirtation or passion and couldn't care less for any man except Darcy. The only time I've ever heard her giggle is when Ashbrooke kissed her hand."

"For what it's worth, I have no designs upon his person. I wish to converse with him about mathematics. Why, his difference engine is a work of genius! He has written about an analytical machine, but I think he hasn't gone far enough with it. I have ideas for how it might perform even more complex and useful calculations, which could have profound implications for musical composition, for example, or innovations in other areas."

"Stop," Fox told her, even though her bright-eyed excitement was adorable. He had a spark of insight and knew what to do and how to woo her. "You're making my head ache. All those big words out of such a little, kissable mouth." Her lips parted, speechless. "Let's go introduce you."

"I beg your pardon?"

"If you want to meet Ashbrooke, then let us

go meet Ashbrooke. He's a friend of mine." She peered at him skeptically, assuming that a brilliant mind like Ashbrooke would never deign to associate with a lackwit like himself. So Fox explained. "We fence together."

Fox then stood, drawing himself up to his full height. He extended his hand to Lady Claire to help her stand—of course taking advantage of their positions to look down her bodice. He liked what he saw. And he liked how it felt to have her small, delicate lady hand interlaced with his as he helped her to stand.

He was glad, suddenly and oddly, that Ashbrooke was already wed.

Of all the people in England whom Claire thought might make her dream come true by introducing her to Ashbrooke, she never thought it would be this lummox. This admittedly handsome, attempting-to-be-charming-and-somewhat-succeeding lummox.

She knew Fox's type. Handsome and he knows it. His muscles developed at the expense of his brain. Used to relying on charm and flirtation to get his way, rather than wits and intellect.

He was not her type at all.

But he could introduce her to Ashbrooke.

The man she'd traveled across an ocean to meet, after late nights of reading his papers and early mornings performing her own calculations to develop his ideas further. They were strangers, but in her head they'd already spent hours together.

Before she had time to panic and compose herself, they were face-to-face.

The first thing she noticed was that the Ashbrooke Effect or whatever nonsense Lord Fox had called it was real. The man was breathtakingly handsome in the usual way—tall, strong, dark haired, perfectly formed features, et cetera, et cetera.

But there was something about him that made her knees weak.

She was glad her arm was linked with Fox's, who performed the introductions.

"Duke. Your Grace." Lord Fox bowed and kissed the duchess's hand.

"Hello, Fox!" The duke greeted him warmly. "Haven't seen you in an age."

"I believe that was because you were off on your honeymoon. You must miss losing to me during fencing matches."

"I hate to tell you but I was not thinking about you or fencing on my honeymoon," Ashbrooke replied. The ladies present blushed.

Then Ashbrooke turned his attentions to Claire. "And who do we have here?"

"A woman keen to make your acquaintance," Lord Fox said. "She traveled all the way from the colonies. May I present Lady Claire Cavendish."

"The United States of America," she managed, in something barely above a whisper.

"Whatever," Fox said, dismissively. "It's not England."

"It is a pleasure to make your acquaintance," Ashbrooke said. She felt herself become flustered.

Flustered!

Her wits, affronted by this revolt of her nerves, took their leave. And then she forgot everything else—manners, restraint, et cetera—and the words she'd traveled halfway around the world to say tumbled out.

"Your Grace, it is an honor to make *your* acquaintance! I have been following your work on the difference engine and analytical engine for some time now and I daresay your work is an excellent starting point, but there is so much more one could do. For example, have you considered that the machine might be utilized for more than simply numerical calculations?"

Ashbrooke just laughed. A friendly laugh at least.

"I have heard rumors about a young lady who speaks extensively about mathematics in ballrooms all over London," he said. "That must be you. I am very glad to make your acquaintance."

Claire nearly swooned. It went without saying that she was not the sort of woman who swooned.

Then she was introduced to his wife. Claire felt a twinge upon seeing Her Grace, for Claire recognized a kindred spirit in her—a girl of unremarkable coloring and features, a girl who wore glasses, a girl who had more sense than the usual allotment.

If only we had arrived sooner, Claire thought. She might have had a chance with him. Ashbrooke might have fancied *her.* But he was married—and very happily so, judging by the way he held his duchess close—and Claire respected that.

But still . . . this meant there might be hope for her, that a sensible, brown-haired girl with glasses might find a husband who loved her for her brains and found her beautiful just as she was. She had been so fixated on keeping everyone at bay she suddenly dared to consider someone might care for her, just as she was, spectacles and numbers and all.

It took her breath away.

"Now, as to what you were saying about . . ." the duke began, and the world ceased to exist beyond this conversation about the analytical engine with Ashbrooke.

Fox could have drifted away from this conversation about the different analytical engine and whatever numbers and whatnot powered it.

He could have excused himself and no one would have thought any less of him for it. Her Grace did just that.

"Much as I love an in-depth conversation

on advanced mathematics," the duchess said sweetly, "I see my friends. I'm going to say hello. Lady Claire, it was lovely to make your acquaintance. I hope to see you again."

With that, she took leave of the group. But Lord Fox remained.

The conversation on advanced mathematics resumed, with Ashbrooke and Claire speaking animatedly about words he didn't know and concepts he could not even try to understand.

He should go. No one would fault him for it.

Hell, no one would have even noticed.

Certainly not Lady Claire, who seemed to have recovered from the Ashbrooke Effect and was speaking rather intelligently. He could tell because Ashbrooke appeared thoughtful, nodding his head at intervals, and said things like "You're right—I'd never thought about that. But then what about—"

No one expected a man like him to stay and listen to this, whatever it was. But Fox could not bring himself to leave.

The reason: Mowbray was standing nearby, watching the whole damn thing. Hell, he was close enough to eavesdrop on the conversation, so he had half a clue what kind of hell Fox was enduring. Mowbray leaned against the wall, arms crossed against his chest. Did he really think Fox would give up and walk away? To surrender and forfeit?

Fox smiled back and slightly inclined his head. Because here was the thing: Fox had a fighting spirit. When he suffered through round after round of brutal boxing matches, still he stumbled to his feet, arms swinging, fists flying. In any other game he was the first on the pitch and the last to leave. Fox played to win. Always.

Especially when his dog was at stake. And his pride.

This . . . this was just listening to a boring conversation he didn't understand. It happened *all the time.*

"I am participating in a lecture at the Royal Society tomorrow," Ashbrooke said. "You should attend."

Ah—this was Fox's moment!

"I would be happy to escort you," Fox added. Two heads turned to stare at him, mouths agape in comical depictions of shock.

"Tomorrow is also the Exton horse race," Claire pointed out. "I am given to understand that it is an important and exciting event that those in the racing circuit keenly anticipate."

Fuck. He had been looking forward to that for ages.

He was especially looking forward to it because Zephyr, Mowbray's horse—and potentially Fox's—was running.

But he took one look at Mowbray, still skulking around and smiling at him as if the man had nothing else to do, and Fox's competitive spirit flared. His Male Pride reared its head, pawed at the ground.

He was going to the bloody mathematical society meeting with Lady Claire Cavendish if it was the last thing he did.

"If you've seen one horse race you've seen them all," Fox said with a shrug, even though the words tasted like ash in his mouth because that was *not true* at all. "But a math lecture . . . one doesn't have the opportunity to attend those every day. Especially with such a beautiful woman."

Lady Claire scoffed. Again. But he caught the faintest pinkening of her cheeks. She turned away from him to address Ashbrooke.

"Whether in the company of this ridiculous creature, or my brother, I look forward to attending the lecture."

"I should warn you that it may cause a scandal," Ashbrooke said. "On account of you not being a decrepit old male."

"I have become accustomed to it," Lady Claire replied. "Besides, what is a little scandal when compared to the opportunity to discuss mathematics with some of England's most brilliant minds?"

When the hostess indicated that it was time for the musicale to begin and everyone was encouraged to assemble, Fox expertly guided Claire away from Ashbrooke—she could have talked to him all night!—and toward the seats. She didn't have a chance to protest, for she was too distracted.

Her brain was happily humming with her ideas for the analytical engine and the questions she would ask at the lecture. Her brief conversation with Ashbrooke—she had finally met him!—gave her much more to consider. Oh, and she would have to get up early to reread his papers on the subject.

Before she knew it, Claire was seated with Fox on a very small settee.

She turned and peered at him curiously.

Lud, but he was a handsome fellow, a classical type of beauty with perfectly formed and proportioned features. But that did not account for that glimmer in his green eyes. And that stubborn lock of dark hair that drew her attention.

Her fingers twitched in the fabrics of her skirt, as if she wanted to push that lock of hair away and run her fingers through his hair. Which she would never do, of course, because that suggested an unfathomable level of intimacy between them.

And he positively radiated heat, especially when one was wedged up against him on a minuscule piece of furniture. Especially when such close proximity made the unfathomable seem somewhat fathomable.

"You stayed through that entire conversation on mathematics," she said, honestly a bit awed and surprised. "You must have been terribly bored."

"I was. But then I noticed I had a prime view down your bodice and I wasn't."

"Did you actually just say that aloud?"

"What I meant to say, very inelegantly, is that you are not without attractions. Namely, the contents of your bodice. And your brains. Admittedly, I didn't understand a word of your conversation with Ashbrooke, but it was nevertheless clear that you had many smart things to say on the subject of whatever the subject was. I was impressed."

Claire was shocked. These were not things that men had ever said out loud, or at least to her. It took her a moment to figure out what to say, such was the extent of her shock. Even then, it was pathetic.

"I am shocked."

"I have hidden shallows."

"Hidden depths, you mean."

"I have no depths, hidden or otherwise, Lady Claire. I am who I am and what you see is what you get."

He was serious. Fancy that, a person who was

who he said he was. No dissembling or posturing. How unlike every other aristocrat she'd met in England thus far. For the first time, she was intrigued.

Knowing him to be simple and direct only made her more curious about why he had suddenly deigned to seek her out and pay attention to her. She was about to question him, when he leaned in close and murmured something in her ear.

"Don't look, but your family is staring at us."

She looked.

The duchess nodded approvingly. James looked from Claire, to Fox, then back to Claire. He lifted his brow, a question.

You? Him?

She gave a little shrug. Truth be told she didn't have much to say beyond that.

Her sisters were less discreet. Both Amelia and Bridget forgot that they were grown women who had made their debut in society and instead reverted to the behavior of twelve-year-old girls bored in church.

They made faces. Rude faces.

Claire bit her lip, refusing to encourage them, as she knew she ought to do. But her shoulders were shaking from holding back laughter. Fox noticed. He couldn't not notice, given how close they were sitting.

"What is so amusing?"

"My sisters. They are making faces at me."

He gave a quick glance in their direction and caught Amelia's gargoyle smile. He chuckled softly.

"Sisters tend to do that. Mine is shooting daggers with her eyes."

Claire glanced over at Lady Francesca and she was indeed shooting daggers with her eyes, though once she saw Claire looking she quickly smiled as if nothing were remiss at all and she wasn't sending waves of dislike in their direction. Why, Claire wondered, would she care who her brother sat with at a musicale?

"Are you the eldest?" she asked.

"Yes, but Franny is the sharpest and the bossiest."

For the first time, Claire felt a pang of kinship with Lady Francesca, of all the people in London.

"You don't say that as if it were a bad thing."

"Why should I? It spares me the bother of being the sharpest and the bossiest."

As the one who was the sharpest and bossiest in her own family, she could only just imagine what a relief it was to have someone take on the burden. In fact, it was why she was glad to have come to England to submit herself to the keen intelligence and blatant command of the duchess. Claire didn't understand the rules any more than her sisters, but she was glad to know the rules were there, to be learned, and that they had someone knowledgeable to help guide them.

She glanced over at them once more. They were bickering and the duchess was wearing her I-disapprove-of-your-behavior-but-am-trying-not-to-see-it expression. She turned her attentions back to Lord Fox.

"Tell me, Lord Fox, what do you do instead of being sharp and bossy?"

"Sport, mainly," Fox said. Then grinning, he added, "Women, too."

Claire just sighed. Just when she thought that perhaps there was more to the man, he revealed that perhaps there wasn't. So much for her plan to solve the mystery of him! She would attend the math lecture with him, because it was an opportunity she would be mad to refuse, and that would surely be the end of this strange business with Lord Fox.

Chapter 6

Today promises to be an exceptionally fine day at the races. All the best stables are represented, and all eyes (and bets) are on Lord Mowbray's steed, Zephyr. Anyone slightly interested in the racing scene will not want to miss today's event.

—SPORTING NEWS, *THE LONDON WEEKLY*

The Royal Society

If there were any doubts that Lady Claire was not a typical lady, her raptures at attending a math lecture clearly dispelled them. There was no other way to describe it: her eyes were bright with excitement, her cheeks were flushed, and she was smiling like Lord Fox had never seen her smile before—like he had never seen *any* woman smile before. For that alone, he was glad to have attended with her, for it was a sight to behold.

But given that this was a *math lecture* that he was attending *voluntarily*, that might be the only reason.

Even the unwelcoming stares of so many crusty old Royal Society members did nothing to dampen her spirits, though her chaperone, Miss Meredith Green, seemed a little nervous from the attention. He noticed her pull her shawl tightly around her shoulders, as if to fashion a protective cocoon.

Frankly, Fox found the old men's faces, with deep lines of disapproval, dispiriting. In fact, they made him feel as if he were an awkward lad of thirteen, back at Eton with an enraged professor demanding to know why he hadn't completed his sums.

Because I thought it stupid and dull, so I played cricket for so hard and so long that I injured myself.

That had not been the correct answer. Punishment ensued, but the lesson was not learned. These days, he employed men to deal with sums and whatnot, while he focused on the things he actually cared about and life got along swimmingly.

But this was not about him, a marquess and peer of the realm who had managed life perfectly fine so far without a knowledge of Greek, Latin, science this, or math that.

This was about Lady Claire, who was in raptures to be at a math lecture. Of her own free will.

But eventually he saw that the collective force of their disapproval of a person of her sex gracing them with her presence caused the slightest bit of fade in her smile. Only he would notice, because he was watching her so closely.

"Is this not so exciting and fun?"

She gave his arm a little squeeze and beamed at him.

"Yes. I cannot imagine a more pleasing activity," he lied, thinking of sex, eating, sleeping, drinking, and the horse race he was missing today. *Everyone* was there—Mowbray, Rupert, Darcy, all his friends from Tattersall's and White's . . .

"It means the world to me to attend this lecture," Claire said. "Thank you for escorting me. My brother could not bear to miss the race today."

And like that, nothing else compared. Not even sex, eating, sleeping, drinking, or the horse race he was missing this very minute.

"The pleasure is mine." He meant it. For the moment.

"I don't think anyone else is excited for me to be here though," she confided to him in a low voice.

No sooner had she spoken than a little gray troll of a man stopped them. His suit was gray, his hair erupted in gray tufts from his head, and his skin took on a grayish hue—too much time inside, Fox supposed.

"Good afternoon. Thank you for attending. But you must find seats in the back," he told them as they approached the seats in the front.

"But then the ladies won't be able to see."

"The ladies don't need to see. Besides, these seats are for members of the Royal Society. Which none of you are."

Well. Then. The ladies might have been used to such treatment—he felt them tugging to turn around—but he was not. Fox did the thing where he drew himself up to his full height in an attempt to intimidate the smaller man into crying, crumbling submission. It almost always worked.

The little man did tremble as he looked around for reinforcements and found them. One or two other elders stepped over and were apprised of the issue: a woman and her chaperone wished to sit where they might see. Or more to the point: women were here!

"It is no trouble," Claire said. "We shall sit in the back."

"But—"

"We are lucky to even be here," she said softly. "At least, I am."

Because she was a woman—that was the real issue. He could bluster and pay his way in. He could put on Lordly Airs until they were begging him to sit in the front row and to say a few words to mark the momentous occasion of his attendance. But she was the one who deserved to be here and she wasn't going to pick a fight about where she sat for the lecture, as long as she was in the room where it happened.

They took seats in the back row with Lady Claire sitting between him and her chaperone. The seats were tiny, rickety chairs that were the very definition of uncomfortable. Fox foresaw a long, tedious, and painful afternoon. For him.

Not Lady Claire.

"Have I mentioned how excited I am for this?"

The aloof Lady Claire, who often appeared bored beyond belief at society functions, was nearly quivering with excitement. Even Miss Green seemed intrigued by the proceedings. He didn't understand how a body could be so passionate about a lecture, but he appreciated it all the same.

Plus, Claire was pretty with her eyes bright and her lips upturned in a smile.

"Yes, you have mentioned it, but I enjoy hearing it." *And seeing it.*

"I could only dream of something like this back home."

"No math in the colonies? I might have to go," he joked.

He stretched his arm out behind her, feeling too constrained and wanting to put his arm across her shoulders and hold her close. Not the done thing, that.

"Of course there is. But we lived too far from

a city big enough to have a group like this. Though my father did hire some tutors for me once we discovered my talent and through them I was introduced to some of the leading mathematicians in America, with whom I enjoyed a correspondence."

"Are they more welcoming of women engaged in intellectual pursuits over in the old colonies?"

Claire laughed. "Oh, no. I always signed my letters as 'C. Cavendish.' They all assumed that I was Charles or Christopher. In other words, a man. I had no desire to correct them."

"Rest assured, I don't think I shall be fooled by such a deception or confuse you with a man."

She eyed him slyly. "Are you looking down my bodice again?"

"You say that as if it were a bad thing."

She huffed something that sounded like *Gah, men*.

Before he could respond, the first lecturer took the stand. It was yet another old man—this one with a remarkably red, bulbous nose—who put Fox in mind of his teachers from Eton. Like those old professors, this lecturer seemed to be physically incapable of vocal inflection. In other words, he droned.

It was dull. Fork in the eye dull. Count the cracks in the ceiling dull. Want to bang one's head against the floor dull.

But Lady Claire was not bored. Not. In. The. Slightest.

She was nodding her head and muttering commentary under her breath. The lecture in turns fascinated her, outraged her, enlightened her.

And that was just the first forty minutes. *Forty minutes!*

As for himself? Fox was dying.

Dying a slow death of torture by tedium.

The lecturer droned.

Claire muttered.

Fox thought about the race he was missing today. Right now, in fact. He could be standing outside in the sunshine and fresh air, surrounded by jovial people, conversing animatedly on topics he understood and enjoyed (the weather, horses, gossip of mutual acquaintances). There would be drinks, wagers, winning, losing, and the thrill of the race. Fox imagined the thundering of horses' hooves and the roar of the crowd when a winner crossed the finish line.

Why the devil was he *here* instead of *there* anyway?

Mowbray.

The stupid bet with his stupid friend. His idiotic and unforgivable decision to wager his beloved dog. His relentless and reckless need to win at everything, all of the time. Look where it had led him: a lecture hall, when he could be enjoying a carefree day at the races. Consequences, that.

The droning lecture finally concluded, praise God and the infant Jesus, and Fox's heart leapt at the thought that he might be free at last. But no, now Ashbrooke stood to address the audience with additional remarks of his own.

Ashbrooke was at least a dynamic speaker, but Fox could only make sense of every other word, and certainly not the meaning of them all strung together.

He really should have gone to the races.

Another eternity seemed to pass. Ashbrooke concluded and the original lecturer—Lord Red Nose, Fox had decided to call him—stood to take questions.

Questions were asked. Questions were answered. Fox clenched and unclenched his fists. Shifted uncomfortably in the rickety chair. Half hoped the damn thing would collapse beneath him just for a spot of excitement.

Fox glanced at the delicate woman beside him, the authoress of this misery. She was no longer muttering or nodding her head. Now her hand was raised high in the air. She held it high and steady—no waving it about, like a loon—and waited patiently. Her cheeks were red.

"How long have you held your hand up?" he whispered.

"He'll see me eventually."

In other words, awhile.

Fox turned his attention back to the lecturer. The old geezer looked right at Claire with her outstretched hand and continued speaking.

"I think he already sees you."

"Perhaps he isn't ready for questions yet, but he will be soon."

"Are there any questions?" the lecturer asked, looking about the room.

"See?" She looked forward, hand held high.

"Yes, you, sir, on the left."

The sir on the left asked his question. The lecturer answered.

This was repeated with the man in the green waistcoat, the gentleman in the front, and the man with the red hair.

Still, Claire waited patiently in the back row with her hand held high. The lecturer looked straight at her.

"Thank you. If there are no more questions, then this concludes—"

"Oh, bloody hell." Fox finally understood the situation and how he could fix it. Before he could think too hard about it, he stood and, without waiting for permission to speak, declared, "I have a question."

He spoke in the booming voice of a peer of the realm who outranked most people in any given room. There was a flutter and rustle as everyone in the room turned to look at him.

"Yes, Lord Fox, how . . . unexpected of you to honor us with your presence today," Lord Red Nose stammered. "What is your question?"

He glanced down at Claire.

"Might the difference engine be induced to operate upon objects other than rational numbers, provided their relationship could be reduced to abstract, even mechanistic, rules of order?" Claire asked.

Fox cleared his throat and addressed the crowd: "Might the difference engine be induced to operate upon objects other than rational numbers, provided their relationship could be reduced to abstract, even mechanistic, rules of order?"

He sat down, having no idea what he'd just said.

The lecturer found himself in an awkward position of his own making. He had to indirectly acknowledge the lady's question. Or risk dismissing a man as lofty as Fox, which was not a done thing.

Fox began to enjoy this lecture after all.

The lecturer hemmed and hawed, and damn if this didn't feel like revenge against all his old professors on behalf of his thirteen-year-old self.

"You do have an answer, don't you? Or I have stumped your intellect?" Fox asked, relishing the moment.

"Well . . ." The man gave a lengthy reply using

words that had no meaning for Fox. He concluded with "That should answer your question."

Fox glanced down at Claire. She shook her head. It did not answer her question.

"What of musical notes, or geometric figures with prescribed patterns and relations?" she whispered to him furiously. "The rules governing these are just as precise as the method of differences!"

"What of musical notes, or geometric figures with prescribed patterns and relations? The rules governing these are just as precise as the method of differences!"

There was a murmur; she had clearly said something challenging. Or was it the fact that a woman said it?

"It's an interesting point to consider, but I'm afraid we're running out of time today," the lecturer said.

It was then that Ashbrooke stood. "With all due respect, we all know that is an evasive and incomplete answer that does not do justice to a very thoughtful and important question asked by, ahem, Lord Fox." Ashbrooke paused to cough. "I think Lord Fox deserves a more thorough answer."

"I would be curious how *Lord Fox* would explain what the method of differences even is," the red-nosed lecturer replied stonily.

Claire began to explain it.

Fox began to repeat it. Then he stumbled over a word and forgot what she had said. "What was it again?" he whispered.

Lady Claire stood and, in a strong clear voice, began to explain.

Before anyone could shush her for the grave sin of being female and speaking in public, Ashbrooke broke in with a response that seemed to be both thoughtful and challenging.

Lady Claire replied.

The duke and she exchanged volleys about the rules of harmony in music, relative pitch, and how one might turn musical composition into a science—shocking, since music was long considered an art form, not a science. And even more than that, how an engine such as Ashbrooke's could be constructed to produce original music.

Fox sat back down.

His work here was done.

There was nothing left to do but bask in the glow of her brilliance. And she was brilliant—every comment was met with a quick reply, a thoughtful challenge, and another question.

Not that anyone else acknowledged this; that is, until Ashbrooke repeated it. Then there were nods and murmurs and more discussion.

But Fox saw.

He saw a young, scrappy fighter fiercely taking on her challengers, who were more resistant to the form of her body than the contents of her brain. He recognized a competitive spirit—whatever she was saying was too important for her to back down from obstacles and detractors. He knew the rush of adrenaline she must be feeling now—the pounding heart and racing pulse. He knew the exhilaration she must be experiencing from winning by her own strengths and talents, developed over hours and years of diligent practice.

It was how he'd felt winning his first fencing match after practicing a parry and riposte for hours on end. Like he'd unlocked some secret power for all the world to see.

Fox didn't understand eight-tenths or seven-eighths or whatever was a significant amount of what she was saying. But he was starting to understand *her*.

After the lecture had concluded, after they quit the hall and made their way outside, Claire's heart was still pounding. It felt like everything—*everything*—in her life had been building to that moment.

All those late nights poring over mathematical papers, afternoons scratching equations on scraps of paper or with chalk on slate, countless letters signed "C. Cavendish" in which she had to hide her sex so she could share the contents of her thoughts, the teachers who taught her anyway, James unexpectedly inheriting, leaving home to journey across an ocean, and Claire herself overcoming her initial resistance of Fox . . .

Fox. What a handsome, chivalrous lummox.

She was too happy to be here, so enraptured by the way he championed her, that she didn't want to spoil the mood by pondering why the likes of him had attended a mathematical lecture with her. It was curious, of course, and worthy of study, but . . . later.

He had clearly been daydreaming about sticking forks in his eye. She knew the look from Amelia. But nevertheless, he had stayed. Because of that, something shifted in the way she regarded him. She gave him more credit.

Once in the carriage, the man seemed to take up a significant portion of the space, with his broad shoulders and his long legs. His head nearly brushed the roof. There was hardly room for Claire and Miss Green seated opposite.

They had only just closed the carriage doors when—

"Oh! I forgot my shawl," Miss Meredith Green exclaimed. "Do you mind if I dash back for it?"

She and Miss Green shared A Look—Claire certainly should not be left alone with a man. But it was only for a minute. How could one possibly be ruined in such a trifling period of time?

"Go," Claire said. "We will wait right here for you."

The carriage door closed behind her.

All the air in the carriage seemed to go with her.

Claire was left alone with Fox. He was impossibly large, impossibly handsome. Surprisingly . . . surprising. He had championed her in public. James had always encouraged her and stood up for her when the situation warranted, but Fox had brought her into the arena, shone a light on her, and cheered her on.

And, oh, what an arena it had been. What a matching of wits, too. She'd sparred with the Duke of Ashbrooke himself! And she'd shown that smug, red-nosed old man—and all the other Royal Society members like him—that she was not to be ignored.

Her heart was still racing from the thrill of it all.

"That was brilliant. Maddening, infuriating, exhilarating. But overall, it was brilliant."

Fox gave her a lazy smile.

"I never thought I'd say this of a math lecture, but it was mighty entertaining. Not the whole thing, mind you. For most of it I wanted to slam my head into the wall repeatedly. But I did enjoy watching you take on those old windbags."

"I have waited my whole life to engage in debate with the leading minds and experts. Did you see the look on Ashbrooke's face when I asked if his engine might be able to operate on objects rather than just rational numbers? I dare-say he never considered it."

"You certainly shocked him."

"Of course, my simply being in attendance was a shock. Foolish old men and their absurd notions of women's intellect."

"That lot doesn't seem accustomed to having skirts in their company. Now, I'm not the sharp-est knife in the drawer but I got the sense that it was what you said that really had their unmen-tionables in a twist."

Fox grinned and leaned forward, resting his elbows on his knees. Gah, he was close. In this private space.

Claire could feel herself beaming. Like her sister Bridget, mooning over the boy she liked. She felt like her eyes were starry and bright and her skin glowed and her heart was doing a la-di-da dance.

But how could she feel any other way? This man gave her the opportunity to be her true self; she had seized it and it had been wonderful.

"This would have never been possible without you. Thank you."

"My pleasure—"

Impulsively, Claire leaned forward and kissed him.

She meant to lean forward and kiss him on

the cheek—a polite, chaste kiss of thanks. But he turned his head and their lips collided.

She didn't move away.

Neither did he.

In fact, he reached out to hold her arms steady. Not gripping like he would maul her, but gently holding as if to say, *Please stay.*

She felt herself soften. That was the only way to describe it. All the hard edges and sharp corners that held her back seemed to melt away.

Before she even realized it, the kiss deepened, a quick turn from shallow waters to unknown depths. He teased the seam in her lips, urging her to open. Softening further—what was happening to her?—she opened to him, let him in, tasted him, let herself be ruled by feelings rather than reason, and let herself get lost in this kiss.

There was no logic or sense to this, just a curiosity and a slow dawning feeling of desire. She'd never felt this before—not just a man's touch and taste—his large hands holding her, the faint stubble on his cheek that she felt against her own, the way he tasted, like trouble. But this desire of hers was new. She'd never wanted these sensations, had never known to want them, and now her wanting felt insatiable.

And yet, her brain exploded with thoughts: *Wait! Fox! Kissing* him*! What? I cannot—! This can't be—! But,* oh . . . Like a firework, there was an initial explosion, a burst of light and energy, following by little stars of light falling softly to earth.

Fox kissed her, slowly, surely, *expertly*. Thoughts fled; the whirring machine of her brain ground to a halt.

For once, Claire began to feel, just feel.

Her senses took over. His lips, firm but softening against hers. The taste of him. She breathed him in. She ached to touch him, thread her fingers through his hair and pull him closer. So she did, and he didn't resist and it was a strange new pleasure to share such intimacy. Her heart began to beat in a calm, steady, driving rhythm. Her breath turned shallow.

Her brain had been on fire earlier. And now the rest of her was enjoying the slow burn.

And then, as quickly and unexpectedly as it began, the kiss was over.

There was a perfunctory knock at the carriage door.

"I have returned," Miss Green announced as she pulled the door open and climbed in, carefully averting her gaze from the two of them hastily setting themselves to rights, with the shawl wrapped around her shoulders. "My apologies for detaining us when I'm certain you must all be so eager to return home after the lecture."

"Oh, it's quite all right," Fox drawled with a charming grin that did nothing to hide what they were up to.

"Don't worry, Miss Green," Claire said, reaching up to fix her hair. "It was no trouble at all. I'm glad you have your shawl back."

"Well . . . some trouble." Fox gave her a wink.

Wits addled, Claire agreed. "Just a little."

"I do apologize . . ." Miss Green murmured, with a smart smile on her full lips. She seemed to sense they were not speaking of her, or her wayward shawl at all.

"But a little trouble never hurt anyone?" Fox lifted his brow.

"No. A little trouble might do a girl some good. From time to time," Claire said. She was aware of Miss Green looking perplexed, then shaking her head and deciding not to pursue a greater understanding, probably because she was smart and knew exactly what they were talking about. Fortunately, Miss Green was also discreet.

"Just once in a while?" Fox asked. *He was asking to kiss her again!* Claire forgot all about Miss Green.

"A lady shouldn't make a habit of it," Claire replied. Because it was absurd enough that she had kissed him once, never mind again. Repeatedly. He was a rake and she was a bluestocking and that combination rarely added up to anything.

"Pity. I like to engage in a spot of trouble regularly. Before breakfast, in the afternoon, late at night . . ."

"That sounds excessive."

"Just wait until you experience it to pass judgment." Fox gave her one of those grins, like a rake thinking utterly wicked thoughts in the company of an innocent. But Claire wasn't *that* innocent. That grin did things to her—stoking the fire inside, making her cheeks turn pink, making her think of kissing him again.

"You give a girl ideas," Claire murmured.

"Among other things, I hope."

Her lips parted, a perfect O shape of shock, and a little gasp escaping. That cad! That was a bit much. But her brain . . . oh, her brain started imagining and calculating the possibilities.

The next day, Durham House

Breakfast at the Cavendish household consisted of the same items each day: strong black tea, toast, eggs, bacon, and the gossip columns. Plural.

The duchess sat at the head of the table, impeccably dressed and styled, even at the early hour. She sipped tea out of a pale blue china cup decorated with gold leaf. Everything about her was elegant and collected, even the way she turned the pages of the newspapers—an assortment of which were always freshly ironed by the butler, Pendleton, and left next to her place—stopping only to read the society gossip.

Claire took little interest in this. After all, it

almost never concerned her, and when it did, it was to criticize her: her card playing at balls, a dismissive reference to her as an odd girl from the colonies, the occasional linking of her name with Fox's. But there was never anything dire.

That was reserved for Bridget, who did things like fall on her backside in the middle of a ball and thus immediately became known as The Girl Who Fell. Or Amelia, who intimated that she wore the stable hand's breeches when riding astride—that had caused more than a few matrons to reach for their smelling salts. Or Arabella Vaughn, who scandalized everyone by eloping with an actor—and ditching a marquess to boot.

Nothing Claire did ever compared to any of that.

Thus, she had no expectation that there would be anything reported about her. She pushed a wayward strand of hair behind her ear, adjusted her spectacles, sipped her tea, and carried on with her serious thoughts about how exactly the analytical engine might be programmed to create musical compositions.

But she had kissed a man.

She had kissed Lord Fox.

A man to whom she was not betrothed.

She would never pledge her troth to him. What a preposterous idea.

It had been in a closed carriage.

It hadn't meant anything. No one saw.

In an unfashionable neighborhood.

In another reality, really.

At an event that was essentially the opposite of scandalous or interesting, and that certainly did not attract those prone to gossip. Lectures at the Royal Society were not exactly hotbeds of scandal.

She had attended a math lecture with Lord Fox! In what world did that occur? Why on earth would anyone even care?

It had been a mathematical lecture, for Lord's sake.

Why, she could have ripped off her dress and dashed around the lecture hall and the haute ton wouldn't learn of it.

His kiss had made her think about ripping off her dress.

His kiss had made her thoughts stray to him, once or twice, here or there. Or, more specifically, in bed, late at night when the house had gone dark and quiet and she was alone with her thoughts and memories and desires.

Claire felt her cheeks reddening at the memory. The breakfast table was not the place to think of such things. Perhaps it would be best if she focused on sipping her tea and buttering her toast. Priorities. She had them.

"Well, this is interesting," the duchess murmured. She attracted no attention; the Cavendish siblings did not usually share her definition of interesting.

"What is it, Your Grace?" Miss Green asked.

"It concerns Lady Claire."

"Well, now I am intrigued," Amelia said, setting down her knife and fork and giving the duchess her full attention, which is something that almost never happened.

The duchess read aloud from *The London Weekly*:

A young lady scandalized the Royal Society not only by daring to attend the lecture, but by engaging in what was called a "fierce" debate with one of the society elders, abetted by none other than the Duke of Ashbrooke. This author has a distinct lack of interest in a debate over math; however, she is very intrigued by the young lady's companion. He is the last person on earth anyone would expect to see at a lecture of any sort. Or in this young lady's company. Of course, I'm talking about Lord F—.

Claire exhaled a sigh of relief when her siblings showed no interest. Of course she went to a math lecture and engaged in a debate; it was like breathing to her. They had known that she went with Fox—since they all refused to attend with her—and teased her endlessly about it.

But Claire caught Miss Green's eye and saw a sparkle there.

The duchess sighed. "Another day, another Cavendish in the newspaper for all the wrong reasons," the duchess lamented. "Though at least you were linked to an eligible gentleman, Claire."

"Not in *that* way," Claire pointed out. "He is not my sort of gentleman. He wasn't courting me."

"He is a marquess, wealthy, and easy on a woman's eyes. That should be any woman's sort of gentleman."

"Josie, I am shocked," Claire replied evenly. Josephine frowned; she did not like being called Josie.

"Perhaps you are shocked because you are spending all your time at mathematical lectures," the duchess replied, her insinuation clear. There was soft choking laughter from Bridget and Amelia. James, at the far end of the table, just groaned. "I daresay your threshold for interesting is excessively high and your consideration of other qualifications of a potential spouse woefully inadequate," the duchess replied.

"I am proud of Claire for her ability with math," James said. "I am glad that she now has an opportunity to further her studies. It is one of the benefits of coming to London."

"Thank you, James."

Her thanks were mainly for his attempt to change the subject.

His attempts failed.

"This is not about her ability with math," Amelia said, smirking. "It is about our dear, respectable, bluestocking older sister being linked with a handsome and eligible gentleman. Repeatedly."

"I'm so proud," Bridget said, beaming.

"You ought to follow her example, Lady Amelia," the duchess replied. "I'd be delighted to read your name linked with an eligible gentleman's instead of whatever scandalous thing you said or did."

"What if my name were scandalously linked with a gentleman's?" Amelia questioned.

"Then I would start planning a wedding," the duchess replied. "You'll be marching down the aisle and saying your vows before you know it."

"Ha. Watch out, Amelia. She'll see you wed yet!" Bridget crowed.

"She'll see all of you wed," Miss Green said, with a knowing glance at all the sisters.

James gave Miss Green a long look from the other end of the table. "Even me?"

"Even you, Duke," Miss Green replied evenly, holding his gaze with her dark eyes. "The duchess will settle for nothing less than perfect matches for each and every one of you."

"That's right." The duchess punctuated this with a harrumph.

James looked away. Miss Green sipped her

tea. Claire pushed food around on her plate and worried about their vastly different ideas of a perfect match.

After the kiss, she had considered the situation and decided that as pleasant—*pleasant* being a woefully inadequate word for it—as it might be, it would not be repeated. It was a spur of the moment thing, when they had been swept up in the spirit of . . . a math lecture . . . and it would likely never happen again.

This was fine, of course. It wasn't as if they were courting. That would be an exercise in futility because they would make a terrible match.

She was . . . *her*. Cerebral, intelligent.

He was . . . *him*. More brawn than brain—and content with that.

The two of them together added up to nothing and it went without saying that she was an expert in something as basic as addition.

But something nagged at her . . . why a man like Fox would seem to have even a passing interest in her—and to take her to a lecture hinted at more than a passing interest—to say nothing of his intentions. He could have had any woman, he and the gossips would have her believe.

But why *her*?

Something in this equation did not add up and despite her halfhearted attempts to discover why, she hadn't a clue. But she would have to either avoid him completely or attempt to discern what and why before the duchess got more Ideas.

"Now that Lady Claire has found a suitor," the duchess said, "I can turn my attentions to you, Amelia. And you, Duke."

And then there was that: the duchess's relentless dedication to ensuring they all wed. Soon. To perfect, prestigious matches. To men who were wealthy, titled—ease on eyes optional.

Claire saw quickly that her ruse to push away all suitors would only work for so long. Once the duchess secured matches for her little sisters, her full attentions would be fixed on Claire's prospects.

In the meantime, better the devil you know, Claire rationalized. Better the devil who is easy on the eyes and at least knew how to kiss a woman. And who took her to mathematical lectures.

Chapter 7

The most anticipated event of the season is not to be found in the ballrooms of London, but on the outskirts of town: the long awaited boxing rematch between Barkley and Kearney.

—SPORTING NEWS, *THE LONDON WEEKLY*

Later that afternoon, the duke's study

Claire had been working on a vexing math problem in James's study when Pendleton interrupted with a letter for her. She had barely skimmed the contents before James quit his own work, crossed the room, and snatched the paper from her hands.

"He invited you to join him for a boxing match?" James glanced up from the letter he had so rudely stolen. Duke or no duke, he was an older brother who made a habit of annoying his sisters. Stealing one's correspondence was just one way to do that.

Especially when one's correspondence was from a man.

Especially when one's correspondence from men was almost never a personal invitation.

"He suffered through a mathematical lecture so apparently it is only fair that I suffer through a boxing match. And then I'm certain that shall be the end of that."

Was this because of the kiss? Claire dismissed the thought as soon as it popped into her brain. It had been a good kiss, she supposed, but not the sort of deep, ravishing kiss that required another outing—especially to a boxing match, of all things. It was hardly a proper and customary destination.

This made her mind wander to the sort of deep, ravishing kiss that *would* require another outing, and would such a kiss take place at a boxing match?

"This is not normal," James pointed out.

"I never had the impression that it was."

"It is not a normal courtship," he clarified.

"Perhaps because it is not a courtship."

"Then what is it?"

"Devil if I know." She shrugged her shoulders and turned back to the calculations before her. She was attempting some equations to support her idea for the analytical engine. In other words, a more interesting problem and one that was actually solvable rather than the matter of why Lord Fox was interested in attending a boxing match with her. Surely he had friends for that.

"Will you attend?"

"I doubt the duchess will give her blessing. Something as rough as a boxing match is hardly a respectable outing for the sister of a duke."

"But you heard the duchess." Then in his best British accented falsetto, James said, "He's titled, wealthy, and easy on the eyes."

Claire rolled her eyes. True on all counts. And yet . . .

"He is her definition of a perfect match," James continued annoyingly. "And you know she will stop at nothing to see you all wed."

"He is a hulking lummox of limited intellect. As such, he is hardly a man I could wed."

But one who expertly knew how to kiss a woman. That had to count for something.

"Is this where I say 'the lady doth protest too much' or whatever it is?"

"It is where you remain blessedly silent and go tend to all your important ducal matters." Claire waved an arm in the direction of his ducal desk on the other side of the ducal study.

"As head of the family, *this* is one of my ducal matters requiring my attentions. I must approve of my sisters' suitors."

Claire scowled at him and fixed her attentions

on her calculations. She had come here to work, expecting to be free of distractions. But now her brother was looming over her. Staring at her. Annoying her.

"I think you should accept," he said.

And giving her unsolicited advice.

"Because I fancy attending," he added.

"The invitation was not extended to you."

"I volunteer to attend as your chaperone."

"Miss Green is my chaperone. Which is beside the point, because I have not accepted Lord Fox's invitation. What do I care for a boxing match?"

"Oh, bloody hell, Claire, stop being so difficult. Let's just all go and have a fun time *not* going to calling hours. Honestly, for a smart girl you think you'd recognize an opportunity to avoid making small talk for hours while sipping buckets of tea when it sends you a damned invitation."

Claire set down her pencil. She had not considered the problem from that angle. She had simply seen the impossibility of her and Fox as man and wife and that was that. But this was merely an invitation to a boxing match, which was hardly an invitation to wed. James certainly had a point. There were worse things than privately enjoying Lord Fox's appearance and company while *not* enduring more calling hours.

"You do have a point."

"I know," James said.

"I just don't understand why he's asking."

"Does it matter?"

She supposed that it did not matter. In fact, she supposed a man like Fox could not possibly consider her as a prospect or have some other ulterior motive, for an ulterior motive seemed too complicated for a straightforward, plainspoken man such as he was. He must simply be the sort of man who thought nothing of inviting an unwed female to attend a boxing match with him.

Very well, that did confound logic and boggle the mind.

But the alternative to his invitation was sitting at home, enduring calling hours, with all the busybody matrons and obsequious fortune-hunting suitors and Bridget trying to sneak dozens of biscuits when she thought no one was looking, the duchess managing everyone, and Amelia . . . the less said about her behavior, the better.

Yes, Claire could do with an afternoon away from social calls.

"I shall accept," Claire finally agreed.

"I will join you. As your chaperone."

"Miss Green is my chaperone."

"We can *all* attend."

The boxing match

The duchess was led to believe that Claire, James, and Miss Green were joining Lord Fox for a picnic outside of London. She was not to know the real reason the foursome gathered in Fox's large carriage for a little adventure.

"Well, aren't I a lucky man to attend a boxing match with two beautiful ladies?" Fox remarked.

Claire and Miss Green exchanged wary smiles; they weren't the sort often called beautiful. James coughed.

"And a duke," Fox added hastily. "But really . . . beautiful ladies."

"Why do I fear this is going to be a long afternoon?" Claire replied.

"But if I may be so bold, I'm certain it will be more exciting than calling hours," Miss Green pointed out. "And I beg you—do not tell Her Grace I said that."

"You know your secrets are safe with me," James said to her, causing a blush to rise in her cheeks.

"But this won't be nearly as exciting as a mathematical lecture," Claire replied. "Ashbrooke will soon be presenting a paper, if anyone is interested."

"No one is interested," James said. Fox did not disagree.

"If last week's lecture didn't excite you, then I'm afraid you won't find others entertaining at all," Claire said. "That was quite a debate I had with Ashbrooke."

"I'm afraid I'll never have the opportunity to

know about any others," Fox replied, looking right into Claire's eyes.

"Afraid or hopeful?" she countered. Then he turned on the charm.

"For you, Lady Claire, I would attend a thousand mathematical lectures."

"Now you're just being ridiculous," she replied. But she felt the telltale creep of a blush revealing that some small part of her actually cared.

She expected James to point this out and mock her for it, because brothers were hideous creatures like that. But for once, he did not. He was making eyes at Miss Green. Who was here to chaperone Claire.

"Who is fighting today?" James asked after a lull in the conversation.

"Barkley and Kearney. Which may mean nothing to you, but it is of great significance to the thousands of people likely to attend today."

"Do tell us why this is so exciting," Claire said.

"Barkley and Kearney last fought five years ago, and Kearney triumphed in a match everyone expected Barkley to win. Today, they meet in the ring again."

"Ah, a rematch."

"But it's more than that," Fox said, now growing animated. "It's a battle between two different fighting styles. Kearney has a more scientific style, which relies on nimble footwork and correctly judging the distance of a hit. But Barkley, on the other hand, relies on the brute strength of his entire body, a little too much, if you ask me."

Intellect and calculation version strength and passion—for the first time in her life, thanks to Fox, Claire could relate to the battle. With one deep kiss, Fox had tempered years of logic and reason with a hot jolt of passion.

Fox carried on explaining the differences in their fighting styles and the long tortured history between these two opponents. Neither men had fought since that initial battle, and this one had only come about due to a challenge issued in the pages of *The London Weekly*. Unprecedented sums were being wagered today. This was, according to Lord Fox, a potentially historic occasion, at least in the world of sport.

By the time they arrived at the match—a mob scene in a field on the outskirts of London, essentially—even Claire was actually keen to see it and eagerly anticipating the outcome. Fox's passion for the sport, his descriptions of the players, and explanations of the stakes had actually sparked her interest.

She had thought it was merely grown men grunting and hitting each other, with more brute force than grace and strategy. Based on Fox's explanation, she learned there was so much more to it—skill, precision, even intellect.

It so happened there was also *less* to it. As in,

it happened to involve grown men with minimal attire. No wonder it was frowned upon for gently bred ladies to watch.

The fighters wore breeches. Just breeches.

That meant that there were wide expanses of bare chests, rippling muscles glistening with sweat.

Claire fanned herself, discreetly.

She had seen farmhands on a hot summer day making adjustments to their attire to better stand the heat, and inadvertently revealing parts of themselves young ladies were not to see. She had not seen grown men live, in the flesh, circling each other, gazes locked, attention fixed, tensions high.

She had not been standing next to Lord Fox.

Lord Fox, whom she was quite certain probably gave these men a run for their money when his own jacket and waistcoat and shirt were removed and set aside. Or cast on the floor in a fit of passion.

She could easily imagine it. Frantic kisses, mouths crashing against each other, the wrenching off of a jacket, a linen shirt being ripped in two. In fact, she was imagining it right now. In public. In this seething mob of humanity.

"Are you all right?" Fox asked, leaning close to murmur in her ear. She trembled. Not because she was chilled—not in the slightest—but because her nerves had become overexcited and the low hum of his voice and his nearness was just too much.

"Yes, perfectly well. Why do you ask?"

Oh, damn, her voice was shrill.

"You seem overheated. The crowds here are intense. Perhaps it is too much for a lady. Shall we loosen your bonnet strings? Or find some shade? Perhaps you'd like a respite from the crowds."

It wasn't the crowds. But she could not admit it was the sight of sweaty, naked men (how elemental!) and the fevered imaginings of her brain that was having a profound effect on her temperature. She did want to loosen her bonnet strings, and corset strings, and find some shade—in private, with Fox. She was a civilized, intellectual woman, naturally inclined toward logic and reason; how could this be happening to her?

She resorted to her usual calming tactic of repeating as many digits of pi as she could: 3.14159 . . .

The crowd roared and she was spared from answering.

Barkley and Kearney circled each other, fists raised, in the square that had been roped off. There were supporting men nearby to pass out water to the fighters, or oranges for a burst of energy. Umpires stood at the ready.

Fox placed his hand on the small of her back, urging her forward, in front of him, where she might enjoy a slightly better view. It was a polite, chivalrous gesture, not a caress.

But tell that to her nerves.

Every last, tingling one of them.

3.1415926 . . .

But then Barkley lunged and Kearney expertly dodged the advance, then took an opportunity to swing. His fist connected solidly with Barkley's jaw. The crowd roared and she found herself focused on the fight before her and not the internal one waging between her brain and her body.

She gasped when Kearney swung and missed.

She cried out, "No!" with the rest of the crowd when Barkley landed a fierce blow on his opponent.

Whereas before she might have just seen two brawny, sweating men brawling like Neanderthals, she now saw a pitched battle between two disciplined fighters, two fighting philosophies, two personalities sweating it out in the ring to emerge victorious.

Looking beyond the fighters, she saw the passionate faces in the crowd, shouting, reeling, and cheering with each move. James among them, standing awfully close to Miss Green, who also appeared riveted.

It became clear to Claire that this wasn't just a brutish fight, but something more. To say nothing of all the money wagered today; some men would emerge rich, others broken.

Thanks to Lord Fox, she saw all these things

she would not have noticed otherwise. He had taught her something and showed her a more nuanced view of the world. Perhaps he was not the dolt she had originally thought.

Perhaps there was more to him than muscles and kisses. This was not something she wished to contemplate, so she turned her attentions back to the fight before her, a mass of physicality, of blood and guts and skin and bones. And sweat. And muscles. Pure, unadulterated *male.*

Just like Fox, her brain whispered.

Shut up brain, she whispered back, for the first time in her life.

The fight continued for some time. These two nearly naked men, duking it out in the ring, circling and waiting for the perfect moment. Fists flying, connecting, cracking against bone. Roars and punches. Sweat.

Eventually, the crowd grew impatient. And drunk. And rowdy.

En masse, the seething group of mostly stinking-drunk men surged toward the ring. Claire, accustomed to quiet afternoons in drawing rooms, or reasoned discussions with refined and educated persons, began to experience the physical manifestations of panic: a racing heart, a shortness of breath, an overwhelming desire to escape.

There were too many, the crowd was too strong, she was surrounded. She could see herself being trampled underfoot by this unruly mob. Escape. She had to escape.

And then she felt a strong arm around her waist, pulling her close, and keeping her safe from the crowd.

Lord Fox.

Her physical manifestations of panic did not subside. Her heart still pounded. Heat suffused her limbs. Breathing was impossible. But the crowds? She forgot about them. She felt Fox's chest hard against her back.

Strong, like a wall that would protect her from anything and everything except the desire to melt against it.

Claire saw that James had pulled Miss Green close as well. The men were making every effort to protect the women from the crowd.

It was basic chivalry. It was nothing to swoon over. It certainly didn't signify anything. She didn't want it to signify anything.

Her body had a mind of its own, it seemed.

She delighted at the touch of his hand.

She, Lord help her, actually welcomed the feeling of his arm around her, holding her close and protecting her with an intimate embrace. They had kissed in the carriage, but he hadn't held her. Now she knew both and the logical thought was to add them together and long for that experience.

"Shall we take leave of this scene before it turns into mayhem?" Fox suggested. "The duchess would never forgive me if anything were to happen. Besides, I'm not scared of much but I'm terrified of her."

"That is so touching," Claire replied.

"What kind of man would I be if I failed to protect the female entrusted to my protection?"

"And here I thought you cared about me."

"Didn't say I didn't." Then he winked at her.

Lud, he was the sort of man who winked at women. He relied on a twitch of the eye rather than words. But then again, a wink from his green eyes was far more effective. Claire was certain he knew it, too.

In the carriage ride back to London, Fox carried on an exuberant discussion about the fight with the duke, reviewing and analyzing the key moments and choices that led to Kearney ultimately triumphing. Claire and Miss Green occasionally chimed in as well, but eventually the group fell silent.

In the silence, Fox was left with his own thoughts.

He realized too late that the boxing match had probably been a stupid idea. He had wanted to show her his world, as she had shown him hers. Perhaps he also wished to put himself in a position to show that he was knowledgeable about certain things, though he had perhaps shown that he was *too* knowledgeable about the entire history and philosophy of competitive boxing in Britain.

How this would help him win the wager, he knew not. He suspected it was the doing of his Male Pride, wanting to impress her.

But Claire had seemed only vaguely interested in all the men sweating and brawling like animals. Which was to be expected by anyone who had even considered whether a woman like Lady Claire Cavendish would be interested in attending such an event full of hulking masses of humanity with the likes of him.

Fox, being Fox, hadn't considered it. He just knew he had to capitalize on the success of that initial meeting of the Royal Society of X = Boredom and keep up the momentum of his developing relationship with Lady Claire. At some point, now that she was speaking to him, he would have to start making her popular.

The wager was never far from his mind.

The challenge of transforming her—and reclaiming his position as leading charmer of the haute ton—haunted him. He knew he had to do it—one dog and his Male Pride depended on it—but he wasn't quite sure how to go about it. His random thoughts on the matter added up to *more Lady Claire* and that was it.

Which is why when, over a fencing match the other day, Ashbrooke mentioned a gathering of Royal Society members at his home, Fox actually paid attention for once. He even made an effort to secure the information into his brain.

The information retrieved itself and communicated itself to the Lady Herself as they were parting ways after the match.

"There is another meeting of the Royal Society of Boring People to Death with Numbers, on Tuesday. I shall come 'round at two o'clock for you," Fox told her as he held her hand when she alighted the carriage at Durham House.

The duke and Miss Green had already gone into the house; he had this brief moment alone with her to make something happen.

"Oh!" Her lips parted in surprise. Then he kissed her palm. He was gone before she had a chance to say no.

Though it would be a certain torture for him, it would give them another opportunity to spend time together. Perhaps by then he would have figured out how to make her popular—though he had a suspicion that encouraging her studies in mathematics wasn't the best tactic.

After the fight, the Bull and Bear pub

Hours after the match, Lord Mowbray was to be found in the crush of people in the Bull and Bear pub, mug of ale in hand, the promise of more and plenty of blunt in his pocket.

He had won!

He had wagered on the outcome of the match and had picked the winner! This is what triumph felt like. This, surely, was a sign of more winning to come.

Hours passed as he and his friends merrily (the winners) and grumpily (the losers) drank mugs of ale and animatedly discussed, argued over, and occasionally reenacted every facet of the fight—that one move of Barkley's in the fourth round, and the way Kearney dodged that left hook in round eight, or was it twelve? Et cetera, et cetera, et cetera.

And then someone had to go and mention Fox.

"Did you see Fox there?" someone asked. Mowbray hadn't. And he felt a pang, because attending a fight like this was something they would have done together if things between them weren't so fraught. "And did you see who he was with?"

Mowbray took a sip of ale while the speaker paused dramatically.

"Well, come on, then, tell us," someone said, impatient.

"Lady Claire Cavendish."

Mowbray spit out his ale. Sprayed it all over the damned table.

"Bloody hell, Mowbray! What the devil?"

His first thought: this did not bode well for winning his wager. This was no mere social call. If Lady Claire were accompanying Fox to a boxing match, it indicated a certain level of intimacy and friendship had developed between them, which signified that Fox was in a position to change her, to make her popular, to win.

Or not.

His second thought: this might be a lucky bit of information to have at his fingertips. If word got out that Lady Claire was in attendance at a rough and tumble event like the Kearney versus Barkley match, it certainly wouldn't help her reputation as an odd and unconventional lady who struggled to fit in with all the other young women of society. He decided to file this information away for potential future use.

Mowbray took a long swallow of his ale, draining the glass. When he looked up, he couldn't believe his eyes.

Arabella Vaughn. That radiant beauty and society darling was *here*, among the brutes in the Bull and Bear after a boxing match. She looked like an angel out of place on earth. Mowbray watched, stunned, as she surveyed the room anxiously. When her gaze fell on him, her eyes lit up.

His heart swelled.

His heart pounded as she crossed the room toward him, threading her way through slack-jawed men, shocked and awed at the angel in their midst. She was here, she was coming to him. He must be drunk. Or dreaming.

"Mowbray. I cannot tell you how happy I am to see a friendly face," she said, smiling. But there was a sadness in her eyes he'd never seen before.

"Miss Vaughn, what are you doing here? Are you alone?"

Was she still Miss Vaughn? He didn't know. She didn't correct him.

"My maid is about somewhere. So is Lucien."

She glanced over her shoulder, and he followed her gaze. Famed London actor Lucien Kemble was demonstrating his ability to down multiple pints of ale in quick succession as a rousing crowd cheered him on.

Beer dripped down his chin, onto his clothes.

He slammed the mug down and roared and the crowd cheered.

Arabella looked pained, then looked away.

"You're a long way off from Gretna Green," he said. "Either that was a quick trip or . . ."

Or she hadn't wed Lucien Kemble after all. Mowbray's mind reeled with the implications of that possibility.

"We are on our way." She said this forcefully, as if she could make it true. "And true love is forever, right? What is one more stop here or there along the way?" Here, she forced a lilting laugh and Mowbray remembered hearing the genuine version in happier times. "He wanted to see the fight."

But she couldn't keep up the show for long.

Quickly, she added in a low voice, "I suppose word is out about us."

"You know how the ton loves to gossip," Mowbray said, reluctantly confirming her worst suspicions. "And the papers love nothing more than to report on the scandals of beautiful young ladies."

"Well, there goes my hope that my absence had been unremarked upon, perhaps allowing me to slip back into society and claim I had been visiting an aunt in Bath."

She heaved a sigh and batted her dark lashes quickly, as if trying to keep tears from falling from her big, blue eyes. This was a version of Arabella Vaughn that Mowbray had never seen: she was vulnerable, remorseful, and no longer at the top of the world.

She had never needed him or anyone before—not with her beauty, her dowry, her family connections, her influential friends. But now, in the Bull and Bear, she was a fallen angel looking for a savior, or at least a protector.

Mowbray would be that man for her.

This was his chance to woo her, to win her, to redeem her.

"How can I help you, Arabella?"

"I don't think you can. I don't think anyone can. I have made a foolish choice that I shall have to live with for the rest of my life." She blinked hard, fighting the tears. She bit that bee-sting mouth that he had once kissed. "Don't you dare tell anyone I ever said that."

"Your secrets are safe with me. *You* are safe with me. I promise."

"Thank you, Mowbray. You've always been a good friend."

Friend. Was there a worse word for a man in his position?

Never mind that now, there was an opportunity here. He just had to seize it. He could continue his new winning streak. He could be her savior. He could be the one who got the girl.

"Would you like to return to society?"

"It's a moot point, isn't it? I'd never be welcomed after this—" She waved at Lucien, now doing an embarrassing improvisational jig to the musical stylings of an inebriated fiddler. "I must face the facts: I am ruined and shall no longer be welcomed in society. The best I can hope for now is to wed Lucien." She made a face. "That is, unless Fox were to take me back."

Mowbray swallowed hard. Fox. Always Fox.

But not today, and not any longer, if Mowbray could help it. Not that Arabella needed to know that now. First, he would earn her trust and help her return to London. When she saw that Fox had taken up with Lady Claire, perhaps she'd turn to her savior, Mowbray, for consolation.

"Perhaps that's not impossible," he said. "Perhaps I can help."

"Will you?" Her eyes brightened. Her lips upturned into a smile.

"Of course," Mowbray promised. And he meant it.

"But why would you help me? Especially now? And after we . . . ?"

After they courted and kissed and she jilted him for his friend, whom she later jilted? It was a fair question. Though he had his reasons, Mowbray knew better than to share them, so he simply said, "I want you to be happy," even though it wasn't that simple at all.

Chapter 8

Arabella Vaughn and renowned London actor Lucien Kemble were sighted at the Kearney-Barkley boxing match, which is of note since it is not exactly en route to Gretna Green, where they are assumed to be traveling. If a young woman is going to run off with a man, the least she must do is marry him.

—Fashionable Intelligence,
The London Weekly

A Royal Society meeting at the home of the Duke of Ashbrooke

On Tuesday, just before two o'clock, Lord Fox collected Lady Claire and her chaperone, Miss Green, for the exciting prospect of a gathering of Royal Society members at the Duke of Ashbrooke's residence.

Exciting being a relative term.

But Fox found he was in a state—he was anxious to determine if taking her to the boxing match had been a good idea or a terrible one. But mostly he was just keen to see Lady Claire.

She was not at all like any other women he'd known—she wasn't fussy, delicate, or simpering. She was sharp and smart, so self-assured and unbowed by him. He was starting to like her, he found, but he hadn't forgotten he had to transform her into something more acceptable to society. More delicate. More simpering.

He noticed that she wore a perfectly fine gown—the duchess would hardly let her out in anything less—but she wore it with such little care. A button near her wrist was undone, her shawl was awkwardly draped, and her hair was simply and severely pulled back and restrained, as if she ran out of patience with having it done. Her glasses were perched on her nose.

"The duchess is hardly encouraging of my studies," Claire was saying in the carriage. "But then I mentioned we were meeting with Ashbrooke . . ."

"A duke trumps everything," Miss Green said. "Apologies, my lord."

"No offense is taken. Poor me, I am only a marquess."

"Well, as an American I couldn't care less about any of this business with titles." Then, changing the subject, she said, "By now you must be familiar with Ashbrooke's work on the analytical engine."

"No, but I feel like I am about to be," Fox said. Miss Green stifled a laugh.

Lady Claire was already chattering about her idea for the analytical engine—of course he didn't comprehend a word of it. Miss Green turned to look out the window and Fox did his best why-yes-I-am-paying-attention-to-you expression. Meanwhile, he stole glances at her mouth. And lower, at her breasts.

Lady Claire did have a nice figure.

She didn't flaunt it, which may have been why he and the rest of the gentlemen of the ton hadn't exactly noticed. Arabella had certainly known she had an excellent figure and made sure that everyone knew it by the dresses she wore and the poses she adopted.

Fox felt he probably ought to persuade Lady Claire to wear more revealing dresses and stand around in positions that showed her figure to its best advantage. But then, strangely, he didn't care for the idea of anyone else seeing her thusly.

If he were a man prone to deep thought, particularly on the subject of emotions and women, this might have concerned him. As it was, it did not. Yet.

* * *

Fox continued to notice her fine figure while the ladies took tea with the Duchess of Ashbrooke. They seemed to get along exceedingly well. And then Lady Claire and he traveled down a vast corridor to the room where the Royal Society of People Who Were Immune from Death by Boredom of Numbers were gathered around a small machine in the center of the room.

"This is the prototype of the difference engine, which, as you know, was recently completed," Ashbrooke explained. Fox had vague recollections of talk of its debut at the Great Exhibition recently.

While the others conversed, Fox, feeling restless, sauntered about the room, looking at things—books, globes, little automatons, biological specimens—to distract him from listening to the conversation he didn't understand or to avoid thinking about *why* he was even subjecting himself to this.

Because Arabella had jilted him (by any definition, a catch) to run off with an actor (by any definition, not a catch) and in doing so had greatly disturbed his understanding of the world and his place in it.

But oddly enough, Fox hadn't thought of Arabella in quite some time now, other than a passing comparison of her to Lady Claire, who surprisingly came out higher in his estimation.

Not being a man of deep thinking or emotional soul searching, Fox did not delve into what that might suggest about how much he had truly loved Arabella, or how suited they really were, or what this all might mean for his feelings toward Lady Claire. He was too focused on the wager.

Fox was also here—poking around in Ashbrooke's study while things he didn't understand were discussed—because of Mowbray.

Fox hadn't seen his friend in days, but he couldn't erase the image of Mowbray's smirk at the musicale. *You can't woo her. You're not smart enough. You're nothing without Arabella and I'll unmask you as a fraud before the entire haute ton.* That's what his smirk said. That's what Fox rebelled against—people not believing in him. Not believing in himself. Not being able to see another role for himself other than *winner.*

He and Mowbray had always been competitive—from rowing races at Eton, to seducing women at Oxford (instead of attending classes, naturally), to whatever pursuit came their way as adults—but it had always been friendly.

But something seemed to have changed.

Fox didn't care to delve into whether this change in the tenor of their friendship was real or imagined, or what it might be owing to, or what he ought to do about it. That was something best done alone with brandy, if at all.

Fox resumed perusing the shelves. Ashbrooke

had quite a collection of books and other little curiosities. He picked up one little automaton—a dancing lady—and started to play around with it, trying to get her to move. He was not known for being gentle. Occasionally he forgot his own strength.

Of course he ended up breaking off a bit of it. Little bits of metal fell to the ground. He swore. Loudly.

A few heads turned in his direction, saw nothing of note, and then carried on with their discussion. Claire gave him A Look.

And then, a distraction. Some little pipsqueak burst into the room, breathing heavily from the exertions of walking at a brisk pace down the hall. The kind of activity, it had to be noted, that wouldn't get Fox winded in the slightest.

"Apologies for my tardiness," he said breathlessly. He shuffled the folio he held in his hands and papers drifted out and fell to the floor.

Fox knew the type: pale, small, bespectacled, and underdeveloped from sitting around with books and papers all day, rarely venturing into the sunlight or exerting their limbs. Fox's opposite.

"How good to see you," Ashbrooke said, greeting the latecomer. "Though you missed the most fascinating insights from our esteemed guest today. Lady Claire Cavendish, may I present Mr. Benedict Williams?"

Fox leaned against a bookshelf and smirked

while Williams turned red when presented with a human of the female persuasion.

"Lady Claire, I have heard great things about you and I was much impressed with your questions at the recent lecture," Mr. Williams said, bowing.

"Mr. Williams is the author of the paper on polynomial equations," Ashbrooke explained.

"Oh, that was a brilliant article. The way you built on the groundwork of our predecessors was remarkable," Lady Claire started to gush. "I do have some questions for you—"

"It would be my pleasure to discuss them at length with you," this Williams fellow said, and it was Claire's turn to blush.

Fox coughed, loudly, reminding everyone of his existence.

"You know everyone else, of course," Ashbrooke said. "But I must also introduce you to my friend Lord Fox."

Mr. Benedict Williams nodded briefly and his head swiveled completely and immediately back to Lady Claire. And really, how could he not? Finally, a young, attractive woman who shared his interests and might actually be interested in him.

Fox saw too clearly how this would play out. Williams was already a goner. Lady Claire's brain would become overexcited by his talk of numerical this and polynomial that. Her passion for discussing math and equations would be confused as passion for the little man himself. She'd find herself wed in a marriage of minds that would not make for a happy marriage between the sheets.

Women who were not happy between the sheets were not truly happy, in Fox's opinion.

But that was beside the point. A courtship with a wheezy academic like Williams would hardly enhance her popularity with the ton, which meant he could kiss his dog and pride goodbye if they continued to make eyes at each other and have long, hard, and intimate conversations about polynomial equations.

Fox would have to remind her that there was more to life—more to her—than numbers and logic. Now bored, anxious, and restless, he waited for the first opportunity to awaken Lady Claire's passion. It presented itself shortly, though by God it felt like an eternity.

A short while later, in the gallery

Finally, finally, finally the meeting concluded and the participants dispersed and Fox had officially survived a few more hours of listening to discussions of advanced mathematics. The things he did for Lady Claire . . .

The introduction of Williams was an annoyance, but Fox had a plan to make Claire forget all about him: he would kiss her until she was senseless. This plan excited him.

"That was just brilliant," Claire gushed as they strolled through the corridor on their way back to the foyer, where they would find Miss Green for the carriage ride back to Durham House. "I cannot believe I had the opportunity to debate with Ashbrooke himself! Not to mention all the others, particularly Mr. Williams. He has an exceptional mind."

"You're quite pretty when your cheeks are pink with excitement like that," Fox said. "And your eyes are bright. They sparkle."

"Thank you. I hope you weren't too bored."

"Not at all."

"Really? Even I thought Mr. Williams went on a bit too long—" *me, too* "—about such a basic principle." *Not me, too.*

"Have you ever seen Ashbrooke's gallery?" Fox asked, changing the subject. "We fence here, though he has also displayed some portraits of dead relatives. As one must do, somewhere about the house."

"I have not—this is my first time at his home, although he has invited me to return and collaborate with him and Mr. Williams on a paper explaining his work and its significance. I can hardly wait to begin. Back home I could only dream of opportunities like this."

"Hmm," Fox murmured. He found what he

hoped was the right door, tried the knob, and the door swung open to reveal the room he sought.

It was blessedly and wonderfully empty and dimly lit. Late-afternoon light streamed through windows at the far end, but there was no other illumination. It would be difficult to fully appreciate the portraits of Ashbrooke's dead relatives in such a light; fortunately, Fox had no intention of doing so.

"Ah, here we go." Fox pushed the door open and stepped aside.

Lady Claire swished in past him, her skirts grazing his boots.

In truth, Fox did know some math—the kind a man used in real life.

*A brush of hands + a quick backward glance + a coy smile – an audience * heart pounding desire = a kiss.*

He wasn't sure who started it.

He already knew he wasn't going to end it.

Fox barely had a moment to pretend to show her a statue or a portrait or some other bit of art when she had whirled around to face him instead.

Her hand touched on his sleeve. She had reached out to him, and that meant everything.

The thing about the spectacles she wore is that they magnified things, like the desire in her eyes. It was the invitation he needed and badly wanted.

Fox closed the distance.

His mouth found hers, or hers found his, and

the slow burn began. Tentative at first before desire made them bold. The kiss deepened.

He needed to hold her closer.

Fox placed his big hand on the small of her back, exerting the slightest pressure. She took one, two little steps until he could hold her close, and she pressed herself up against him, leaned into him, let him support her.

She didn't despise him after all.

Around and around the world spun; he kissed her or she kissed him, his heart pounding in an ever increasing strength and rhythm.

He feared it might explode.

Because Lady Claire kissed like Lady Claire talked about numbers—passionately, with her whole being. With a similar result, too: she twisted him in knots and confused him, made him lose his mind, made him excited and desperate to hang on and to stay with her. The taste of her, the scent of her, the feel of her commanded all his senses, and all his attention. He didn't understand what was happening, but he was content to be swept along by it.

Fox leaned back against the wall, tugging Claire closer. She straddled his leg. There was a tangle of skirts and limbs and mouths and it was hard to tell where he ended and she began.

Closer, closer, but still not close enough.

He slid his hands through her soft hair, mussing it up before skimming his hands lower to explore the swells of her breasts and then the delicious curve of her backside. One curve after another, each one dangerously tempting.

He was hard now, with wanting.

Her hands stretched across the broad expanse of his chest, exploring the ridges and planes of his muscles—or what she could feel with his stupid shirt in the way. Women always did that; coo and caress his muscles and giggle over them. This time he was especially glad of them.

He heard a soft little sigh from her wicked little mouth.

She writhed up closer to him and pressed herself against the hot, hard length of him. He groaned. She moaned. He entertained visions of them, like this, with more privacy and fewer clothes and no reasons to slow down or stop.

More. He wanted more with her.

This was supposed to be just a kiss to awaken her passion and to show her that Williams wasn't everything and that Fox had talents of his own. Just a kiss to help win a wager and as a reward for enduring two math lectures. There was a whole list of reasons for kissing her, but only one mattered and only one drove him now.

Because he wanted to.

It was a long, lovely, intensely pleasurable moment before it dawned on Claire that they could be discovered. And if they should be discovered like this—in the throes of some mad, wonderful passion—it would mean wedding bells as sure as $e^{i\pi} + 1 = 0$.

Her brain finally resumed functioning and reminded her of this fact.

Her brain rarely took a little holiday, but when Fox kissed her, Claire's brain packed its bags, closed the house, and left town. Her feelings took over: he was handsome and hard and hot and she was drawn to him like a magnet; that is to say, as if it were an inviolable natural law and who was she to break such rules? He may not know the things she prided herself on, but he damn well knew how to kiss a woman.

Before Lady Claire even knew what happened he was leaning against the wall, mussing up her hair, and she was draping herself all over him like a wanton, simpering slattern.

And loving every blessed second of it.

But they might be caught. And every lovely second of this would come to an end, with consequences.

Her brain, returning to duty, performed some calculations. It was most likely that, if they were to be caught, it would only be by Ashbrooke or his wife and they seemed more likely to be amused than appalled; they would make no mention of this.

Passions of her body trumped the considerations of her brain.

Claire wrapped her arms around him, shimmying up closer, feeling her breasts against his chest, reveling in the strength of his that held her up. She felt her heart pounding, blood pulsing through her veins, and her skin had suddenly become more sensitive. Her every nerve was quivering with anticipation of more. All these physical feelings were new to her and she wanted to revel in them.

Logic intruded again: Miss Green would find them momentarily, surely. But Claire highly doubted she would say something to the duchess; and as long as the duchess didn't know, there would be no consequences.

Claire could indulge in one more moment of this man.

Then Fox deepened the kiss.

She breathed him in.

There was something about his scent that drove her wild—it wasn't any fragrance or whatnot that she could identify, but breathing him in felt like a drug. It reduced the whirring machinery of her brain to producing simple, elemental thoughts: yes to this man, yes to this kiss.

There was something about the way he touched her that was just . . . everything. Men didn't usually touch her, of course, because it was hardly the sort of behavior one engaged in with polite company. She didn't get the sense that any of them hungered to, which was fine, because the feeling was usually mutual.

Fox cupped her bottom with his big, strong hands and she groaned and writhed up closer against him, feeling the hard length of him pressing urgently against the vee of her thighs. Hardly ladylike behavior but it felt right.

When he kissed her, when he touched her, Fox unlocked a part of her that was new to her. Passion, desire, feeling, lust . . . she experienced them all for the first time with Fox. And how powerful these feelings were—even her brilliant, ever-working brain couldn't rein them in.

In the end it was Mr. Benedict Williams who reminded her of who she was, where she was, what she was doing, and with whom. She heard his voice in the hall, just on the other side of the door. "So absentminded of me, I forgot my folio . . ."

Claire pulled away from Fox.

Williams's folio . . . notes for the paper she was to write with him . . . her opportunity to share her thoughts and insights with the world . . . everything she had ever dreamt of . . .

Fox pressed one finger to her lips as if to shush her and prevent her from drawing attention to them. And then she playfully nipped at his finger, which made him grin.

"The butler will show you back to the foyer," they heard a maid say.

"I daresay, has Lady Claire departed yet?"

Fox tugged her close again and kissed her deeply once more. She closed her eyes and leaned into the wicked, wonderful sensations of this strong man giving her pleasure and this desire pulsing inside her.

"I'm not quite certain," the maid answered.

"I do see that her chaperone, Miss Green, is waiting in the foyer. Thus Lady Claire must still be here."

"Good day, sir," the maid said firmly. Claire sent up a prayer of thanks to her, whoever she was, for protecting her reputation and, just as much, not ruining this moment of pleasure.

But was it enough pleasure to risk the consequences?

"This must remain a secret," she told Fox in a whisper. "No one can know about this or else . . ."

The consequences were obvious and need not be spoken aloud.

Marriage.

She was quite fine with kisses and touches and stolen moments, but it couldn't be *more* than that. Because she needed more than kisses, touches, and stolen moments from her future husband. She needed a meeting of minds as well as bodies and she was afraid Fox wasn't the man for that, or the man for her.

For a second, Claire thought he looked

wounded. But why, and since when did men like Fox care about anything more than stealing a kiss and a quick feel of a woman's bottom? She dismissed the thought and started to put her appearance to rights as best she could without a mirror.

"Your hair looks pretty all mussed up like that. You usually have it all pulled back, but those tendrils soften you."

"Since when are you an expert in women's coiffures?"

"I have two interests. Sports and women," Fox said with a grin. "I'm an expert at both."

"Never mind that, you'll get me in trouble. Everyone will know what we've been doing," she replied as she still tried to fix her hair. She hated the feeling of these wispy tendrils in her face. They were distracting, which is why she usually preferred her hair sharply pulled back.

"Everyone will know that I can't keep my hands off you." He grinned.

"Oh, who would even think that of you and me," she said with a laugh as much at herself as at him. Because honestly, he was the stud of the ton and she was known as an odd young lady best avoided at parties.

"I must go before we are discovered or—"

"Before we get into any more trouble?"

"Particularly the kind of trouble that lasts a

lifetime." She stared up at him fiercely. "Truly, Fox, no one must know about this. Or us. Promise me."

His gaze darkened, his lips pressed into a firm line, and he didn't say anything for the longest time. Finally, in a low voice, almost reluctantly, he said, "I promise."

Later that afternoon, Durham House

Claire and Miss Meredith Green returned to Durham House to find that her sisters and the duchess were still out, paying calls and visiting the modiste. It was decided that they would take tea in one of the smaller parlors.

"You seemed to have enjoyed yourself this afternoon," Meredith said as she handed Claire a cup.

"Yes, tremendously. But I hope it wasn't a terrible bore for you. I do appreciate that *you* are my chaperone, though it hardly seems appropriate since we are both unmarried and the same age."

"Yes. Well." Meredith paused and sipped her tea rather than say the truth of the situation that they were both aware of and that Claire now felt uneasy about alluding to: Claire was sister to a duke and Meredith was companion to a duchess. They were of different ranks, and there were different expectations. Claire was to marry well, and it wasn't expected that Meredith would marry at all, or any time soon.

"'Tis fortunate for you that it is I, rather than, say, the duchess," Meredith said, lightening the moment.

"You must have worked a miracle to secure permission from her for me to visit with Ashbrooke and the Royal Society. You have my eternal gratitude."

"You are too smart not to attend those meetings and to continue your studies," Meredith said. "For what it's worth, I may have intimated to the duchess that your attendance at such meetings keeps you happy in England, which means you might encourage your siblings to stay."

"There is definitely truth in that. You are quite clever."

"I also said you might find a suitor there."

"You mean Mr. Williams," Claire said, smiling coyly. She had never imagined her Mr. Right, but if she had, he would be someone like Mr. Williams—a brilliant mind and boyishly handsome. She smiled more, thinking of his lean but muscular frame, his big brown eyes behind spectacles like hers, and all the intelligent things he had said.

"Actually, I meant Lord Fox."

Claire choked on her tea.

"Oh, he's not courting me," she replied. "He's

just . . . well . . . I have no explanation for why he pays attention to me, but courting is certainly preposterous."

"For a smart, logical girl, Claire . . ."

"Very well. Perhaps he is courting me, for what else could it be? But you must admit it's a strange pairing. He's so brawny and I'm so . . . brainy."

"They do say opposites attract."

"They do say that," Claire murmured, feeling a surge of heat course through her and a telltale warming of her cheeks thinking of their stolen moment this afternoon. The attraction between them was so potent it took only a second alone before they were throwing themselves at each other.

"Is there something you care to tell me?" Meredith teased. Then, seriously, "In the strictest confidence, of course."

"Do I need to?" Claire lifted one brow. Surely, Meredith must have a clue.

"Your secret is safe with me. I understand the appeal of some private time in the portrait gallery," Meredith said with a glimmer in her eyes.

"Visiting the portrait gallery with Lord Fox certainly has its appeals. In fact, I find it to be a very enjoyable activity. And yet, he is not the sort of man I imagine myself with. So I hesitate to encourage him but . . ." Claire let her voice trail off, not quite ready to admit aloud that she simply wanted to dally with him.

Meredith smiled knowingly. "What will you do?"

"I don't know. I'm afraid of the risks and consequences that come if I continue to explore this attraction with him. Marriage or ruination are hardly trifling things."

"I suppose there is a simple solution until you are sure," Meredith suggested.

"Do tell."

"See him in secret. It is fine enough, I suppose, to continue to see him at your mathematical events such as you are. But when out in society, take care not to be seen with him. If you are sighted together, it will attract notice, the papers will report on it, people will find it curious and then pay more attention."

"I did make him promise secrecy."

"Good. It is one thing for society to *read* that Fox has been frequently seen with you. It is quite another to see you together. Because there is something about the two of you together."

"What do you mean?"

"In spite of your differences, or perhaps because of your differences, you complement each other. I wouldn't write him off just yet, Lady Claire."

Claire's heart leapt—leapt!—at the thought of just a little more time with him. And by time, she meant all those stolen moments of pleasure.

"I suppose I could continue to see Lord Fox in

secret, just until I have a better sense of things. And we shall see what develops when Mr. Williams and I work on that paper together . . ."

"A perfect plan."

"Avoid Fox in public, indulge with him in private. I quite like it."

Chapter 9

The rumor mill is buzzing with the news that Arabella Vaughn—or is it Mrs. Lucien Kemble?—has returned to town.

—FASHIONABLE INTELLIGENCE,
THE LONDON WEEKLY

The following day

Each day, Fox required some activity that made his muscles burn with use, his heart pound with vigor, and his breath hard and heavy. He needed to sweat. This was the only way he stayed sane.

It was also, he feared, the only thing that Lady Claire *liked* about him. Or rather, the result of it. His muscles. His strength. The swagger that came from knowing he had the physical and mental strength to overpower and outlast any challenge. The way he could hold her forever and kiss her almost senseless.

That she fancied him for his hard-earned strength shouldn't have bothered him at all, and yet here he was, fencing with Rupert and trying a little too hard to kill the man.

"You are skittish today," Rupert pointed out.

"I am *not* skittish," Fox said, annoyed. "Men do not get skittish."

"Touché. Allow me to rephrase. You are irritable and unfocused."

Rupert was wrong. He wasn't unfocused, just focused on something that made him irritable. But he didn't want to get into any of that. Fox just shrugged. "I suppose."

"Arabella's rejection must be hard for you. To be jilted, so publicly. I can't imagine it." Rupert made a sorrowful face and Fox lunged toward him.

To be jilted was one thing; to have one's equilibrium disturbed was quite another. Fox didn't know himself in a world where women didn't just throw themselves at his feet. First Arabella, now Lady Claire.

"To be honest, I haven't really thought about it," Fox said, lying. Then, correcting himself: "Her."

"Is that so?"

"I'll admit that my pride was slightly wounded," Fox said, which was a vast understatement.

"And was it your slightly wounded pride that led you to agree to that wager?"

"That, and being an English gentleman, means that I live to make impossible wagers."

"Is it so impossible? The papers have linked you and Lady Claire together. And people are talking and the ton is paying attention."

"I'm making progress," Fox said. That was the truth—at first she wouldn't even speak to him and now they were stealing kisses. Not missish little kisses, either, but ones that were deep and passionate and that tortured, confused, and confounded him. After the kiss the other day, Fox had been surprised by the intensity of his desire for her, the way lusty thoughts of Lady Claire had begun to intrude on his thoughts, both waking and sleeping. As if he wanted her anyway, regardless of the wager.

This was confusing to him. Because she did have a point; they were a strange pairing.

"But how much progress?" Rupert asked, and it took a moment for Fox to return his attention to their conversation and the sword his friend was wielding. "Will you have the ton raving over her within the week, or is that precious dog of yours going to live with Mowbray?"

"I'm going to win." Fox surged forward forcefully, trying for a point.

But Rupert easily evaded him, then attacked, and Fox was too distracted to put up a proper fight.

Because he wasn't sure he was going to win.

He did not have "a way" with her, as he did with just about every other woman he'd met in his three and thirty years. She had hardly been impressed with him, and his God-given good looks that so often charmed the petticoats off most women were ineffectual with her. He'd never worked so hard to woo a woman before, and by such unconventional methods, too.

And yet, he had her aroused and cooing the other day. She had wanted him, he was certain of it. But then she stepped away, straightened, and begged for them to keep everything a secret, lest they find themselves publicly linked or in a long-term entanglement. How could he keep courting her and pursuing his plans to make her popular when she didn't wish to be seen with him?

And yet, what could he do but agree, even though it thwarted his plans?

His Male Pride had been offended, too.

Or had that been his feelings indicating they were . . . hurt?

He just needed to win a wager.

Keep telling yourself that, fool.

Banishing thoughts of women and wagers, and the confounding Lady Claire, Fox dragged his attention back to the matter at hand: Rupert, sword gleaming, trying to kill him.

Rupert feinted toward his chest and Fox parried to *quarte*. However, his parry was too aggressive, letting Rupert disengage, avoiding Fox's blade, and lunge toward his unprotected side.

"Point," Rupert said. "Damn, Fox. You are unfocused."

"Shut up."

"And irritable."

"No, *you* are far too cheerful."

"It's not every day I see my friends laid low by love."

"I am not laid low by love." Fox had never been so sure of anything in his life. He was confounded by a woman, but that was due more to the mysterious workings of her brain than the occasional feelings of his heart. He had loved Arabella, and that had been a pleasant feeling. He was tortured by the impossible situation he found himself in with Lady Claire, that was all.

"If you say so," Rupert muttered. There was little talking after that, until the end when Rupert said, "Good luck with the girl."

Later that afternoon, at White's

Fox didn't need luck with the girl. With *any* girl. He had half a mind to go out and seduce some other woman just to prove something. Instead he went to White's, where he expected not to be plagued by women problems.

He'd forgotten about Mowbray though.

He settled into White's with a drink and the latest issue of *Gentleman's Sporting Quarterly* when a figure emerged, blocking his reading light.

"Good afternoon, Fox."

"Mowbray."

He looked up and saw his friend and experienced mixed emotions. Ever since the wager, things had been different. Their easy camaraderie had been diminished by an undercurrent of tension that seemed out of proportion with the fun little bet, one of hundreds they'd made standing around a ballroom over the year.

"How goes our little wager?" Mowbray asked, leaning against the wall, drink in hand. Fox remained seated.

I endured two math lectures and nearly ravished her. No one saw and she hopes for secrecy on all fronts. In fact, she made me promise not to say a word.

"Good. Excellent. Fantastic."

"Your vocabulary is impressive," Mowbray replied. "But I daresay your progress is not. Escorting her to a mathematics lecture and helping her make a fool of herself? Taking her to a boxing match? How that helps her become a darling of the ton, I know not. But then again, it suits me just fine if that's how you wish to spend your time with her."

Fox scowled because Mowbray had a very valid point. These activities had endeared Fox to

Claire, but it did nothing to improve her reputation, nothing to make her popular. He was encouraging her in her strange, unfeminine, unfashionable ways.

Fox didn't have a quick, witty retort at hand. That was not his strong suit. A good punch to the nose—yes. But he didn't really feel like standing up at the moment, not after that fencing match with Rupert earlier. And he didn't fancy punching his friend in the face, either.

So he just said, lamely, "This is all part of my plan. I have time yet."

It went without saying he did not have a plan.

"Aye, but the clock is ticking. And she's running around in her glasses and unfashionable styling, discussing obscure mathematical theorems no one cares about, and fleecing peers at the card tables. If she keeps that up she won't even be welcome there."

Fox thought back to Lady Claire *besting* everyone at that card game so expertly. She defied expectations and demonstrated her brilliance and skill—especially to him, after he had patiently explained the game to her in simple terms. It was kind of marvelous of her, really. Seemed a shame to tell her to keep that part of her under wraps.

"But then again, what do I care if you trade one dog for another?" Mowbray asked with a shrug. "This might be the easiest wager I've ever won."

And *that* was too far. Good-natured needling

Fox tolerated—it was part of the game. But Lady Claire was not to be insulted.

"Mowbray?"

"Yes."

"You're an ass."

"So clever, aren't you," Mowbray taunted, folding his arms over his chest.

It was Eton all over again. It was some pipsqueak mocking him for his intellectual capabilities, or lack thereof, feeling safe because they realized Fox was really a gentle giant—capable of immense force and power, but not really inclined to use it.

There was only one tried and true way to make it stop and to ensure that any mockery of Lady Claire did not continue. Fox was compelled to haul himself up to his feet. He downed his brandy in one swallow, setting the glass down firmly.

Dramatics, that.

Then he stood, slowly, allowing his bulk and his height to grow and overshadow Mowbray.

"Sorry, what did you say?"

"You're so clever, aren't you?"

"I do apologize but I cannot hear you from *all the way up here*."

Mowbray was not nearly as tall as Fox. Not nearly as handsome, charming, rich, or powerful, either. Fox made sure Mowbray felt keenly aware of it. Even though he considered Mowbray a friend, Fox was so mad at the slight toward Lady Claire that he wasn't inclined to let it slide.

"You'll have to shout to be heard," Fox said.

They were in a quiet room.

"All right, Fox, I see what you're doing. You want me to shout out how clever you are."

"Oh, good, I was afraid my cleverness was a bit much for you," Fox said. "Oh, and congrats on Zephyr's winning race. I look forward to her joining my stables."

Mowbray gave him a dark look and stalked off. Fox settled back into his chair and motioned for another brandy.

Then he plotted.

Even later that afternoon, Fox's study

The problem was that Fox was not a plotter. Or a focuser. His intentions to sip brandy at White's and sort out how to win his wager were derailed first by an interesting article in the *Gentleman's Sporting Quarterly* about some new training techniques Lord Giddings was using with his hounds—something he might try with Stella and her future pups, should he be so lucky. Then he had a conversation with some gents about the horse race he'd missed earlier that week, which was followed by a quick card game, which he lost, which reminded him of Claire, which reminded him of his dilemma.

He went home.

He locked himself in his study, because his aunt and chaperone to his sister, Lady Wych Cross, left him alone there. Francesca, on the other hand, thought nothing of strolling in, uninvited.

"What are you brooding about?"

Lady Francesca could be the soul of sweetness and amiability when she wished to charm someone. Her older brother was usually not that someone.

"None of your business."

"I don't suppose it's about your American girl," she said with a sigh as she perched on the corner of his desk. "Honestly, I don't know why everyone is so taken with them. They're just so . . . forthright, and cheerful."

Here, she shuddered.

"I'm not taken with them," Fox muttered. First Rupert, now Francesca. Why were people thinking he was *taken* with her?

"Oh, just the one?"

"It's just a wager, that's all."

Maybe if he kept repeating it, it would be true. But it wasn't just a wager; it was his Male Pride, his understanding of himself in the world, and his precious dog—who sat watching the conversation as if she *knew*—and it was Lady Claire, whom he had to change. But he was starting to think that would be akin to wrecking a great work of art.

"Dare I inquire about your progress?" Francesca asked.

"I have taken her to a mathematics lecture, a boxing match, and a visit to Ashbrooke's to discuss his difference engine with yet more boring Royal Society members."

For obvious reasons, he did not disclose the kissing. But he wanted to, if only because Francesca was laughing mightily. Cackling, really.

"Dear brother, you call that progress?"

She was laughing so hard Stella trotted over to see what was happening. When it was nothing, she rested her head on Fox's leg and gave him that adoring look with her large brown dog eyes. He *had* to win.

"How are those activities supposed to endear her to the ton? Why, you might be only making things worse!"

He mumbled something about "earning her trust and favor" but Francesca wasn't buying it. She confirmed what Mowbray said, and his own worst suspicions. In the process of developing a relationship with her, he was encouraging her in the activities that made her unpopular with the ton in the first place. But Fox didn't see any other way to proceed.

"Look, I've often said you got all the brains in

the family and we both know it's true," Fox said. They both regarded this as a statement of fact, rather than a compliment. "Why don't you tell me what to do?"

One would think Francesca had given the matter extensive consideration, given how quickly she spoke.

"She wears her hair too severely, which suggests she doesn't have any interest in fun or pleasure, which is off-putting to those who do, which is nearly everyone in society. You also need to do something about her spectacles," Francesca said. "They make her look too . . ."

"Smart."

"Aye. And gentlemen don't want to be confronted with a woman who is smarter than themselves because it makes them feel inadequate, which makes them question the validity of their position of authority in society. It calls into question the entire social order. 'Tis a troubling line of thought," Francesca explained. "Also, spectacles are just plain unfashionable. Have you ever seen a fashion plate in a magazine wearing spectacles?"

"Can't say that I'm in the habit of perusing fashion magazines, even though you leave them lying about the house as if you were the only one who lived here."

Francesca ignored that.

"Her clothes are quite finely made and the

current fashion—that's the duchess's doing, surely—but Lady Claire doesn't wear them well. She wears them as if she didn't care at all. With her plain styling and those spectacles, it all suggests that she can't be bothered making herself pretty and presentable."

"So?"

"That says she's not interested in fitting in. That she's not interested in playing the game. That she thinks she's better than everyone else because she is concerned with 'more important' things."

Fox stared at his sister, somewhat in awe and somewhat terrified. What she said had a ring of truth to it. Claire did care about more important things and she didn't care who knew it. But perhaps there was a way to make it seem like she cared for society's good opinion of her, without compromising what made her *her*.

"Are you telling me that all she has to do to be popular is change her hairstyle and lose the spectacles?"

"Well, she also needs to stop talking about math," Francesca said bluntly. "She has gained a reputation as one to be avoided at all costs, lest one find themselves on the receiving end of a lecture when one wants only to gossip and dance."

"Ashbrooke talks about math."

"Yes, but not at soirees and balls, and certainly not as incessantly as she does. Also, he is a man.

He is allowed to display his intelligence. It's unbecoming in a woman."

This Francesca said with no small amount of bitterness. Even he noticed it. Even he took a second to consider that his fiercely smart sister might have to hide her intelligence behind a pretty smile, or simpering laugh, just so it wouldn't hurt the delicate sensibilities of some nitwit peer of the realm.

And there was, within the recesses of his chest cavity, a pang. Because it seemed wrong to ask Lady Claire—or any woman, really—to shut up about the thing she loved just so she could be popular.

"All that sounds impossible, Franny. How am I supposed to get her to change her hair and lose her spectacles and speak only of the weather?"

"Now that you have earned her favor—or at least her attention—make suggestions when the opportunity arises. How nice she'd look in blue, how pretty she'd look with her hair curled. That sort of thing. But you must do so delicately," Francesca said with a pointed look suggesting that was beyond his abilities. "Or at least change the subject when she mentions her studies."

"I'm not sure I can manage that without gravely offending her." Fox was not keen to undo all the progress he'd made just to get her to speak with him in the first place. He still felt so uneasy about it, too.

"Well, there is also popularity by association. It's what Lady Bridget is attempting with me."

"What the devil do you mean?"

"You need to be seen together, publicly. Even better, you need to be seen together in a manner that suggests that you two are courting. Or even better, in the throes of a wild romance. Then let the force of your popularity and good favor with the ton shine on her."

"I'm afraid my reputation at the moment is hardly such that an association would be beneficial to her . . ." Since Arabella jilted him, he hadn't noticed as many adoring glances and sighs from young ladies whenever he walked by.

Or had he simply not noticed because he was so focused on Lady Claire?

And because he'd lately been attending boxing matches and math lectures, where there was a dearth of young, swooning women?

It was something to think about, if he thought about things.

"Nonsense," Francesca said. "You are a renowned rake. She is, admittedly, not the sort of woman people would associate with you. This will cause gossip and speculation. Women will be curious about what you see in her—men, too. Both of your profiles will be raised. People will seek you both out for conversation in order to attempt to discern the truth. This will give you both an opportunity to charm them."

"I see." And he did. Just be seen with her publicly, in a manner that suggested they were linked romantically. This was a brilliant but simple course of action that he could follow.

"The Cavendish family will be at Lady Winterbourne's garden party. I trust you can put two and two together."

Chapter 10

The most important element of any social event this season is the presence of the Cavendish family. One never knows what this scandalous batch of Americans will do next . . . or with whom.

—FASHIONABLE INTELLIGENCE,
THE LONDON WEEKLY

Lady Winterbourne's garden party

Fox was a man on a mission: be sighted with Lady Claire and avoid the temptation of stealing off with her for another one of those devastating kisses. He'd never imagined that a woman like her would arouse him so much, but there was no denying she did. Seducing her, however, would hardly solve his problems.

Shortly after arriving at Lady Winterbourne's garden party, he sought out Lady Claire, who stood with her family at an awkward distance from the other guests. He noted three dark-haired sisters decked in pretty white dresses with bonnets and parasols; the duke standing idly by, looking like he'd rather be elsewhere; and the duchess, trying to herd them all in the direction of the other guests.

Fox bravely ventured toward the pack of Americans. He overheard comments and conversations on his way.

"Do my eyes deceive me, or is Fox seeking the company of the Americans?"

"I heard he has taken up with Lady Claire, the especially odd one."

"Well, it's not as if anyone compares to Arabella Vaughn."

"But really . . . one of the Cavendish girls?"

Fox swaggered past, refusing to acknowledge what he'd overheard, and paid his addresses to the object of his attentions.

"Lady Claire, it is lovely to see you today."

"Good afternoon, Lord Fox." She gave a slight curtsy.

"My day is brighter now that I have seen you." He treated her to his most dazzling smile. The one that usually elicited a starry-eyed sigh from the ladies.

Was everyone watching? He hoped they were watching.

Lady Claire leaned in, nearly stabbing him in

the eye with her parasol as she did so. "You don't have to do that, you know."

"Do what?"

"Flirt."

"Who says I am flirting with you?"

She straightened immediately and blushed tremendously. "I beg your pardon, I just thought . . ."

He grinned. Flustering her was such fun actually.

"I confess. I *was* flirting with you."

"You have made me doubt myself." She was not pleased with this. He wondered if she would smack him with the parasol.

"How terrible of me. Would you care for some lemonade?"

"That's so kind of you to offer, but—"

"She would love some lemonade," the duchess said, practically pushing them together and off in the right direction. Her Grace was doing him a favor and yet she still managed to terrify him; but that was the Duchess of Durham for you.

He and Claire linked arms and he found himself standing straighter, taller. It was a way of commanding attention, in the event that guests weren't already agog by the unexpected sight of him gallantly paying his addresses to Lady Claire, the "especially odd one." He wanted everyone milling about at this garden party, under a blasted hot sun, to see them together and to think of them as together.

A part of him might have also wanted to impress her with his towering strength. She seemed to like that about him.

Lemonade was procured.

Lady Claire sipped her drink, seemingly oblivious to the other guests' curious looks. He was all too aware. This was part of the plan, and yet he found himself uncomfortable because people were watching them awkwardly standing there, mute.

He struggled to think of something appropriate to say. The only questions he could think of were about Ashbrooke, the machine, and math—all topics Francesca had told him to avoid. But the more he thought of inappropriate topics, the more he became aware that time was passing in which they were not conversing, and she was drinking her lemonade like she would get a reward upon finishing it, and the whole garden party seemed to be watching them.

Say something. Ask her a question. Good God, man, it's not like you haven't spoken to a woman before. You're not some green schoolboy. Ask her a bloody question!

Finally, Fox seized upon a topic.

"It's a lovely day, is it not?"

"Indeed."

"Fine weather for a garden party."

"Ideal, even."

"Yes."

Was he really going to be the first English person to run out of things to say about the weather?

Fox was aware of people still watching. And now whispering.

"Tell me, Lady Claire, what do you like to do besides math?"

"Why do you ask?"

"Can a man not just make conversation?"

"Of course. But. Well. I just . . ."

Flustered. He had flustered her. That was good, yes? People would see her blushing and think he was charming her. If they thought she was the sort of woman who became flustered and blushed from the attentions of a rake, it would help win the wager.

"I enjoy playing cards, as you know," she said. "And riding, as you might expect."

"That's right, you grew up on a horse farm," he said, piecing together all the gossip about the family. They had a horse farm in one of the former colonies. Maryland, was it? The haute ton thought it shameful, but he thought it must have been rather nice—and probably not much different than growing up on an English country estate. "That must have been a wonderful place to grow up."

"You know, you are the only person I've met to think it fun and not embarrassing," she replied, genuinely smiling at him. "There is a very slight but important distinction between a peer's estate where horses are bred and raised as an expensive hobby and a farm in America where horses are bred, raised, and trained for money."

"We're a lot of snobs, aren't we?"

"Whatever you say, my lord," she murmured. Smiling. Agreeing with him.

"Well, I think it sounds like fun. I'd much rather be out riding and even mucking about in stables instead of sitting around inside, doing whatever it is lords do inside all day. Account books, correspondence, et cetera. We have some good stock in our stables at Norwood Park. Perhaps you and your brother might like to visit sometime."

"That would be nice."

Their conversation faltered. People were looking. Even better, people were commenting to one another about it. This was excellent. Francesca's plan was working.

Or was it?

"It's a very bright day, is it not?" she remarked. "I would just love some shade."

His brain sounded an alert: Why was *she* speaking of the weather?

"What about your parasol?"

Or her bonnet. For that matter, why was *he* the one to point out the logical remedy to her perceived problem?

"Oh, this hardly provides sufficient coverage," she said with a laugh, which begged the question of why women always carried them.

She linked her arm in his and urged them to walk in the direction of the hedges and shrubbery. The green things that provided shade, yes, but also the privacy he was trying to avoid.

It gave him wicked ideas.

It wouldn't necessarily help win the wager.

It might even get him leg-shackled.

"You're not one of those women worried about freckles, are you?"

"Hardly," she scoffed. But before he realized what had happened, she had expertly maneuvered them both to the area behind the hedges, where it was cool and shaded.

They were alone.

No prying eyes.

He wanted prying eyes, for Fox was afraid of what he might do without them to keep him in line.

Lord Fox solved all sorts of problems for Claire. Since the duchess had deemed him an eligible suitor, she ceased thrusting Claire into the path of other, more tedious and, honestly, less attractive men. She even allowed Claire quite a bit of freedom with Fox. Freedom to do things like attend events or visit with Ashbrooke or even to stroll behind the hedges.

She had all sorts of reasons for leading him behind the hedges.

For one thing, while the duchess had her hands full keeping Amelia out of trouble, she lost track of Bridget. While sipping her lemonade, Claire had spied her sister strolling this way with the man she fancied, one Mr. Rupert Wright. Claire was not at all opposed to them making a match, but she was opposed to her sister causing a scandal by, say, being caught in a compromising position in a shrubbery.

Scandal meant they would have to be on their very best behavior, which did not include attendance at lectures or mathematical studies. It meant additional pressure to wed—and to marry for reputation and prestige, not necessarily love. They would be separated. They might not be happy.

Claire had promised her mother to ensure her siblings were happy, above all else. It was that simple.

Claire had also given the matter of Lord Fox, her desire, and hedges some consideration. Her brain was finally beginning to recognize the demands of her body.

She had long thought of her body as a mere vessel for carrying around her brain, but ever since that kiss Fox seemed to have woken her up from a long slumber, with hungers and demands.

She craved his kiss, the strangely wonderful sensation of souls and bodies melting into one as the whole world fell away. Her brain wished to know what his body looked like unclothed; her body wished to know what his bare skin felt like against hers. It was intimacy she craved, lots of caresses and gentle kisses and solving the mysteries of what two people did in bed. She'd never really given much thought to it before—well, other than in the abstract. The truth was, she'd never met a man with whom she wanted to explore all these things.

Until Fox.

She had no illusions that they would be a good match in any meaningful way, but there was no denying a potent attraction between them. Meredith had given her the idea to dally with him in secret. Perhaps she might, while ensuring her sister stayed out of trouble, get into a little bit of trouble of her own.

Hence, the hedges.

"Ah, this is better." She fanned herself. Even though she now stood in the shade of hedges. Fine English hedges. There was a garden party in the front and a promise of wickedness in the back.

"Indeed," he remarked, gazing at her. "You at least aren't wearing a wool jacket."

"You could take it off," she suggested coyly.

Oh, dear Lord, when did she become a woman who made coy suggestions, let alone coy suggestions about the removal of attire?

"Are you flirting with me?"

"No. Please." She gave a nervous laugh. The words had been out of her mouth before she could stop them. She hadn't meant to flirt with him. But her thoughts about him were of a romantic direction, there was no denying that.

He lifted one brow, questioning.

"Perhaps," she mumbled.

"I don't mind if you flirt with me," he murmured, stepping closer.

"I bet you don't," she replied.

"At any rate, I can't get the damn thing on or off without the assistance of my valet. And he's nowhere to be seen. Obviously."

This reminded them both that they were very alone.

"'Tis the same with my dresses and corset," she added. Why, why, why did she have to mention the removal of her dress and corset to him? What the devil had happened to the filter that had previously existed between her thoughts and her mouth? Honestly.

The man addled her wits.

"Careful, Lady Claire, of the ideas you put in a man's head," he warned softly.

"Were they not already there? I thought men thought about undressing women all the time."

"Not *always*," he replied, grinning like a naughty schoolboy.

"Oh? I am intrigued. What else do men think about?"

"Sport. Beer. Food."

"How positively barbaric."

"And lifting up a woman and carrying her back to our lair."

"Truly?"

"No. Women would make such a fuss. All that screeching and pummeling of tiny fists and wriggling about like a trout on a line. That is not the way to get a woman to bed."

"Neither is comparing a woman to a trout on a line."

Fox laughed. "Good point."

"Either way, we should not be speaking of this."

"Says the woman who speaks of equations and numbers and whatever they all do together. Some say women shouldn't speak of those things, either."

"Ashbrooke speaks of mathematics all the time," Claire pointed out.

"Aye, but not in ballrooms, and besides, he's a man."

That heat she was feeling cooled considerably. And quickly. She knew what people said and what they thought. She just hadn't realized *he* shared their opinion. She hadn't realized she cared until this moment.

"I didn't think you shared the ton's sentiments about that," she said acidly.

"I don't. I mean . . . That is to say . . . I'm just . . . saying."

"Well, don't say it," she snapped. "I couldn't care in the slightest what the haute ton of morons thinks about a woman of intellect and sense. But you—" She gazed up at him. Strong jaw, noble profile, confused dark eyes, darker hair. The shoulders, the chest, the arms she wanted wrapped around her, and his mouth . . . "I thought you were different. But honestly, you are such an idiot."

"It's not my—"

"I dragged you back here so you could kiss me and you just have to go and insult me. Well, I nev—"

The thought was unfinished, the sentence unconcluded. The kiss happened. His mouth crashed down on hers.

She yielded to him, or he yielded to her. She didn't know, it didn't matter. In this, they were of one mind. Connected.

Tasting, his mouth opened to hers. Touching, his hand upon the small of her back, tentatively caressing higher. She did not say no in any way, at all.

He kissed her neck; she sighed.

She slid her hands along his chest. He kissed her again.

His palm closed over her breast and he teased the center with his thumb. She shivered, even though it was a hot sunny day and even though a marvelous heat was pulsing through her. It was a shiver of awakening. She hadn't been touched like this before.

Claire leaned into the pleasure. She threaded her fingers though his hair and kissed him deeply.

Oh, God, this was better than her idle daydreams.

But her daydreams weren't interrupted by garden party guests. Their kiss slowed at the sound of people walking and talking on the other side of the hedge.

"I heard a rumor that Arabella Vaughn was coming back to London. Alone," someone said.

Fox, to his credit, kept kissing her.

"Alone? You mean she didn't actually elope?"

"That is the rumor. I heard she and that actor only made it as far as Alconbury before realizing their mistake."

Fox lavished kisses along her neck. His fingers splayed at the edge of her bodice and she ached for his touch to go lower. But she also listened.

"I wonder if Lord Fox will take her back."

"Of course not."

"Because he has taken up with Lady Claire?"

"No," the woman said with a laugh. "Because of his male pride."

"Still, Arabella is a much better match for him."

And whoever they were, two nameless and faceless gossiping matrons, they carried on their way while listing all the ways in which Arabella Vaughn was a better woman for Fox than Claire, presumably ignorant of who had overheard them and what they'd been doing while listening.

Fox claimed her mouth with his and she kissed him passionately, hoping the pleasure of it would drown out her troubled thoughts. But it didn't.

He kissed her like she was the most desirable woman in London but that couldn't possibly be true. She faced facts. That was one of them.

Of course Claire would find him so arousing—every woman in London did, it seemed. But she wondered why he seemed to find *her* so desirable? Because he kissed her like he wanted her, badly, even though she was an eccentric bluestocking, a future spinster, always the odd girl out. Even though she hardly compared to the likes of Arabella Vaughn.

It was odd.

Something didn't add up.

She couldn't concentrate on her thoughts and she couldn't let herself get swept up in this kiss. She just knew that this—whatever *this* was—couldn't continue until she knew more. The risks were too high, the consequences too permanent.

"We have to stop," she said. Gasped, really.

"Yes. Right. Whatever the lady wishes." His voice was rough, too. He wasn't unaffected, which she noted with some surprise and satisfaction and confusion. Perhaps she had expected he wouldn't be affected because this was an act, a game, a lark.

Even though they kissed like they had a perfect connection, in truth, the two of them together as a couple did not make sense. Until she knew more, she would have to keep her distance.

"We cannot keep doing this. People might see us."

"Right." His mouth, which had just a moment before been kissing hers, pressed into a firm line, as if he were disappointed. It was the logical, sensible thing, so his reaction hardly made sense.

Hearing more voices, Claire did not stick around to debate the point.

Someone had decided that a garden party would not be complete without rowing in the lake. Fox, for one, was glad of it. Rowing was an activity at which he excelled; it also allowed him to showcase his strength and brawn.

Women loved strength and brawn.

He was about to ask Francesca's giggling friend Miss Montague if she wished to join him in a boat. That girl could always be counted on to flirt with a man, and his Male Pride was in the mood for a simple female to fawn over him.

But then Her Grace, the Duchess of Durham, interfered. She did so in a way so expert and elegant that no one quite realized what was happening until it was done.

Fox watched as she arranged things to her liking—Darcy found himself rowing a boat containing Lady Bridget and hardly looked happy about the situation. Rupert set off in a boat with Lady Amelia.

Lady Claire was matched with him. Even though he was troubled by Claire's hot and cold behavior behind the hedge, he recognized that this fit into his plan, because now he would be seen with Lady Claire by one and all. They would be seen as a pair. As a couple. Encouraged by the duchess herself. People would talk.

And he would have a chance to talk to her, alone. Fox didn't like how they parted earlier this afternoon, what with her running off and leaving him behind the hedge, with a hard arousal. Deuced awkward, that.

Some part of his brain wondered why she didn't want to be seen with him publicly. Most women save for, until recently, Arabella would have swooned at the chance to have their names linked with his—to say nothing of a more intimate connection. But then again, Lady Claire was hardly most women.

Confounding creatures, women.

Fox dug the oars into the water and pulled.

The boat glided through the water. He repeated this action, taking note of the way Lady Claire watched him move. She seemed to like what she saw.

Women always did.

And yet. The fact that *she* did made him suddenly more aware. More keen to please her. More anxious to know why she didn't wish to be seen with him.

Lud, but the woman tied him in knots.

He was all brawn, just enough brain and *feelings.*

"Where are you taking us?" she asked.

While he had been dealing with his own inner turmoil and trying to read her thoughts via staring into her eyes, he had rowed them quite a bit away from the others.

"I am absconding with you to my lair. Obviously."

"That's not funny. People will see."

There it was again: people will see.

"What will they see?"

"They will see two unmarried persons without a chaperone. They will hear wedding bells."

"We are in full view of at least a hundred people. We are hardly unchaperoned. As a woman of sense, you must agree. And as for wedding bells and holy matrimony, I hardly know where you got that idea from."

"It is the only idea that women are allowed to have."

"Like that would ever stop you from all your brilliant thoughts."

"Please stop, I might swoon."

"Please don't. I shouldn't like to have to fish you out of the water."

"But wouldn't you like the opportunity to demonstrate your strength?"

"I'm doing so right now. Without getting my clothes wet and risking the ire of my valet."

"Are you really such a dandy?"

"Not at all. I just live in fear of upsetting my valet."

She was looking at something off in the distance. Fox followed her gaze toward her sisters, off in boats with Rupert and Darcy. Amelia was standing and waving her arm dramatically, rocking the boat in the process.

Without a word, Fox started rowing them in that direction.

"Thank you," Claire said. "They are a constant bother. As the eldest, I must claim some responsibility for them."

"What are your sisters doing?"

She sighed and, once they got closer, strained to listen. "It seems that they are reciting poetry."

"It's a very dramatic recitation."

Lady Amelia was certainly projecting. And now Lady Bridget was joining her to stand in the boat, which was a terrible idea, one that offended both laws of etiquette and physics.

Fox chuckled at the murderous expression on Darcy's face. God, the man must be dying.

"Yes, well, Amelia never does anything in half measures and Bridget never could restrain herself from an excess of fun."

Fox waited to see something like annoyance or resignation in Claire's countenance. But she spoke of her sister's behavior as fact, and thus something to simply accept. It was in a way, oddly loving.

Before he could say more, there was a crash and a splash and a female shriek. The boats had collided, launching the occupants into the water. There was Rupert and Amelia, laughing. Lady Bridget thrashing about, Darcy hauling her out of the water and *not* looking happy about it.

"I suppose you'll be wanting to return to shore in anticipation of an immediate departure," he said.

Claire just laughed and said yes. It was the prettiest sound he'd ever heard. She was confusing and a challenge, but, he realized, she was a game he didn't want to stop playing.

Chapter 11

This author does not even know where to begin with recounting the adventures of the Cavendish sisters at Lady Winterbourne's garden party. The sooner the Duchess of Durham marries them off, the better.

—FASHIONABLE INTELLIGENCE,
THE LONDON WEEKLY

The breakfast room, Durham House

There were three somewhat contrite Cavendish sisters at breakfast the following morning. Bridget and Amelia's exploits at the garden party would certainly be covered at length in all the papers, but Claire hoped that her time with Fox had gone unnoticed.

Her hopes were quickly dashed by the duchess, or rather the newspaper she read from:

"If it weren't bad enough that every paper is reporting on Lady Bridget and Lady Amelia's spill in the lake, *The London Weekly* is suggesting that Lady Claire and Lord Fox were spotted behind a hedge together."

"How shocking," Lady Amelia declared, with a mischievous glimmer in her eye.

"How improper," Bridget murmured, while smirking.

"How absurd," Claire scoffed in the uncharacteristically illogical hope that she could convince everyone the report was false by pretending it was.

"No, it's excellent," the duchess declared. Claire choked on her tea.

"How do you figure that, Your Grace?"

"How many times must I tell you that he's a catch?" the duchess asked impatiently. "And I would rather the ton gossip about a potential suitable match than . . . whatever one would call their behavior." Here, she waved in the general direction of Bridget and Amelia, the ladies of the lake.

"Entertaining," Amelia said.

"Outlandish," the duchess replied.

"Or charming," Bridget suggested.

"Scandalous," the duchess declared. "And the last thing this family needs is more scandal."

The conversation was interrupted by the arrival of Pendleton, the butler.

"There is a caller for Lady Claire. Are you at home?"

"Who is calling at such an early hour?" the duchess inquired.

"Mr. Benedict Williams."

"I am not aware of him," the duchess said, which is all she needed to say in order to convey that he was not a person of consequence and thus not a suitable caller. Just wait until the duchess learned the reason he was calling . . .

"Who is this Mr. Benedict Williams?"

"He is an esteemed mathematician and academic. The Duke of Ashbrooke introduced us and suggested that we collaborate on a paper for publication detailing the intricate workings and immense possibilities in the design for his analytical engine."

"I'm not certain that ladies of your station write papers for publication."

"This one will," Claire replied.

"Perhaps as long as your name isn't on it . . ." the duchess said thoughtfully.

Claire pursed her lips, as she had seen the duchess do when confronted by a situation that did not please her. The thought of all her hard work being credited to someone else—even Mr. Williams, whom she liked—made her heart rebel. She realized in that moment that she didn't just want the liberty to indulge her interests, but she wanted to share her ideas with the world and receive acknowledgment for them. But at the breakfast table with a caller waiting was not the time to argue the point.

Besides, she didn't want to waste a minute arguing when she could be discussing more intellectually stimulating subjects with Mr. Williams.

"Perhaps we might talk about that later," Claire replied, thinking that never might be a good time. "I should go see to Mr. Williams now."

In the drawing room

When Claire stepped into the drawing room, door left slightly ajar behind her, her heart was beating quickly and she felt no small amount of anticipation for the visit—and visitor—awaiting. This is why she'd wanted to come to London and why she'd encouraged her family to seize this opportunity. This is what made suffering through all the rules of the ton and the social whirl worth it.

"It is so nice of you to call, Mr. Williams."

He smiled warmly at her. He did have a rather nice smile, and fine eyes—bespectacled, like hers—and a boyishly handsome face. He didn't quite compare to Lord Fox in terms of masculine strength and beauty, which Claire was horrified to find herself thinking, but that didn't matter to her.

"The pleasure is all mine, Lady Claire. Ever since we discussed the prospect of collaborating on a paper together, I find that I cannot wait to get started."

She grinned. "I've already started taking notes."

"How excellent. And I must say I'm not surprised. You have a gift and your dedication to the study of mathematics is very admirable."

"Thank you."

Finally! Someone who appreciated that about her!

Her heart swelled and, under the warmth of his gaze, she wondered if perhaps he could be the one for her. If she wasn't mistaken, by the way he was looking at her, his thoughts might be straying in a similar direction.

"Do you have a moment now? Shall we begin?"

"I would love to," she replied. "I'll ring for tea."

By the time tea had arrived, Claire and Mr. Williams were deep into discussions. Her mind was buzzing with thoughts. Mr. Williams challenged her, questioned her, and made her brain explore new options. This . . . this is what she loved and was meant to do. How lucky of her to find a partner for it—finally, for the first time in her four and twenty years.

He wasn't at all like Fox. Once the thought of him popped into her head, Claire started comparing the two men. She'd never have a conversation like this with him. But then couldn't quite imagine Mr. Williams teasing her, tossing their papers aside, and kissing her until her knees were weak.

"Lady Claire?"

"My apologies. I got distracted by a thought."

"Do tell. I'd love to know what is happening in that brilliant brain of yours."

She quickly thought of something to say that had nothing to do with being ravished in the drawing room by a man she had no intention of marrying.

By the time his visit concluded, Claire felt a new enthusiasm for their project. Even better: it was agreed that she would take the lead on writing it, and Williams would be available for assistance and to consult. She couldn't dream of a more ideal situation . . .

. . . except for the distracting thoughts of Lord Fox that kept flitting through her head . . . and the thought that perhaps she might need to part ways with him.

If her sisters thought they might interrupt a kiss or romantic moment—or even eavesdrop on a conversation they'd find interesting—they were sorely mistaken. But that didn't stop them.

Claire fully opened the drawing room doors to show Mr. Williams out and was treated to the unsurprising sight of her sisters lingering in the foyer.

"What a surprise," Claire remarked dryly. "My sisters. Lady Bridget, Lady Amelia, this is Mr. Benedict Williams."

Bridget swept into one of her well-practiced curtsies. Amelia embarked on one of her deliberately ridiculously extravagant ones—an extra deep bow, extra flourishes with her hands.

Beside her, Mr. Williams cleared his throat nervously.

"I am honored to meet you both, Lady Bridget, Lady Amelia. It is quite a sight to see *three* Cavendish sisters all together."

Amelia gave him her excessively broad smile, the one that made her resemble a gargoyle. Claire shot her A Look.

"It is also quite a sight to see someone as interested in math as our dear sister. We never thought we'd see the day," Bridget said.

"Well, except for Lord Fox," Amelia remarked.

"He is hardly—" Claire said.

"He escorts her to lectures, among other things," Bridget said in a rather suggestive manner that really needed to be corrected . . .

"Yes. I have—" Claire began, but she was cut off again.

"We are going to call on Lord Fox and his sister, Lady Francesca, this afternoon," Bridget said.

"Oh, I had quite forgotten . . ." Claire said. Lady Francesca had left her card, which apparently meant that they owed her a return visit.

"Well, I shall leave you to it," Benedict Williams said. He bowed, and kissed Claire's hand and took his leave with a promise to be in touch regarding their work. She wasn't sure if he meant *just* their work or if he might be a potential suitor.

Once he was gone, Claire turned to her sisters. "What was that all about?"

"Just assessing his competitive spirit," Amelia replied.

"I don't think he has one," Claire said. "He's not that sort of man."

"What sort is he?"

"The sort who is reasoned and logical. The sort with whom I could share a meeting of minds and a passion for our shared work."

Bridget shrugged. "I think Fox is a better match for you."

There was no denying their compatibility in certain ways that she did not discuss with her younger sisters.

Certain ways that made her forget all about the finite method of differences and Mr. Williams. Ways that made her skin tingle in anticipation. Ways that made her thoughts stray to kissing, just to start.

"Well, then, you pursue him," Claire replied quickly. "The duchess thinks he is a good match."

"But he's already after you," Amelia pointed out.

"What are you going to do about him, Claire?" Bridget persisted. "Are you going to keep encouraging him or tell him once and for all that he is not the man for you?"

It was a fair question, and it was the sort of question that required rational, logical thought. Fortunately, this was something at which she excelled.

Lord Fox was a catch, if one cared about things like title, wealth, the way a man filled out his jacket, or the way breeches lovingly clung to his muscular legs. Claire did not care about these things.

Mostly.

She was now distracted, thinking of the way clothes fit taut across his strong frame, and imagining him merely flexing his muscles and the clothes splitting apart, falling away, and revealing what promised to be a glorious specimen of the male figure.

Mr. Williams would certainly not be the duchess's idea of a suitable match. Claire had ascertained that he did not have rich, titled relatives, nor wealth or a title himself. He did have a fine situation teaching at Oxford, a prospect that delighted Claire. She could be quite happy as an academic's wife, spending her days assisting him in his work—or focusing on her own. They would socialize with fellow thinkers and scientists and have thought-provoking and important conversations around the dinner table, rather than gossiping at balls. And at night . . . well, she couldn't quite imagine Mr. Williams bursting out of his clothes and kissing her until she wanted to rip off her own.

She knew she couldn't imagine it, because she tried. Every time she closed her eyes and thought of kissing Mr. Williams she found herself envisioning a kiss, and then more, with Fox.

That handsome, hulking lummox who, despite all logic and reason, decided to pursue her one evening. The man who made her think less, and feel more than she'd ever felt before.

Usually she walked around thinking of numbers. Dry, cold, predictable, rational, understandable numbers. But because of him, she was beginning to feel. Full stop.

For the first time in her life, she felt lust—pure, molten lust.

She found her thoughts wandering toward erotic scenes that were maddening and wonderful all at once. When he was near, or when she thought of him, she found herself more aware of how the silk fabric of her dress caressed her skin; she noticed a strange heat that began deep inside her, making her feel feverish. Her nerves tingled, sometimes pleasantly, sometimes agonizingly, in anticipation of something.

Because of him, she was torn between her brain and her body—and now, when it was never more important that she be focused and brilliant. This was her time to shine, to share ideas that might change the world, to show everyone what women could do, what Lady Claire Cavendish could do.

Fox was tempting. Oh, so tempting. But not tempting enough.

Chapter 12

Later that afternoon, Lord Fox's residence

The Cavendish women had only just arrived for their social call to Lady Francesca and her frightening chaperone, the tea had only just been poured, and the pleasantly malicious small talk had only just begun when Claire excused herself to go to the ladies' retiring room.

The butler popped out of his pantry just off the front door and pointed her in the right direction. When he had returned to his closet, she wandered the halls, peeking into rooms, in search of Fox. She had no idea if he was at home or wished to see her if he was.

Her heart was pounding.

This was ridiculous.

This was the behavior of a lovesick schoolgirl, when in fact it was the logical course of action of a reasonable woman. Claire had decided on what to do. She wanted—needed?—to have a rational conversation with Fox. They had to discuss this *something* between them—what it was, why it didn't make sense, why it had to come to an end.

There was not to be any more kissing—not in carriages, or behind hedges at garden parties, or wherever they might happen upon each other. Kissing was dangerous, and as much as she might want to indulge, she needed to play it safe.

But perhaps a small, insistent part of her did simply want to see him and kiss him, to hell with the consequences. With every stolen moment and illicit kiss they shared, she wanted more. Blast. That was confounding. But still, enough logic and reason remained in her brain that the more time they spent together, the more they indulged, the more likely they were to be caught.

If she could keep her wits about her, she might ask the right questions, guide the conversation and relationship to its logical and inevitable conclusion: they didn't suit, not in any real long-term way, and it was best they part now.

Claire opened a door, only to close it when she saw it was a lady's private parlor. There were a few more doors to try.

She felt color rising in her cheeks—was it anticipation or embarrassment? Probably embarrassment, as she was snooping through the halls, opening this door and that. In the end, she did find him in a study.

She was treated to the unexpected sight of Lord Fox . . . reading.

He had dressed informally—breeches and boots, a shirt open at the neck, and a waistcoat. He was seated informally, too, with his heels kicked up on the desk as he sat back in his chair. She noted his forearms, tan and muscled and exposed from his rolled shirtsleeves. Gah, she was mooning over his forearms.

There was a dog sleeping at his feet. Some sort of pointer or retriever that seemed like it should be more at home in the country than the city.

"Well, this is a sight I didn't expect to see," she said, by way of hello.

He looked up, surprised. And, if one could judge by the light in his eyes, not an unwelcome one. The dog also looked up at her, then at Fox, as if awaiting his direction on how to greet the visitor.

"I could say the same," he said, standing. The dog did as well—what a loyal and obedient creature. "To what do I owe the honor, Lady Claire?"

"My family is calling on your sister. I got lost on my way to the ladies' retiring room."

"Oh, it's just down the hall." He closed the

distance between them—mostly. And the dog followed, then trotted all the way over to her to sniff her skirts.

"And who is this?"

"The best hunting dog in England. Otherwise known as Stella."

"She's a beauty." The dog beamed up at her and wagged its tail, as if she understood she was being praised and adored. Claire held out her hand for the dog to sniff and then, when she'd been approved, she pet her.

"And she knows it," Fox said, with pride. "What she won't tell you is that she's also the best hunting dog in the country and the envy of all my friends. I raised her from a pup and trained her myself."

Claire glanced up at him, noting Fox beaming with pride and something else she couldn't quite place. So much for the idle lord she'd assumed him to be. She knew from her brother what dedication, patience, and kindness was required to train an animal.

"She's a country dog, of course, but I like having her around too much to leave her at Norwood Park," Fox explained.

After a moment, the dog trotted back to a spot on the carpet in a patch of sunlight and made itself comfortable, though she kept her eyes on Fox. What a life that Stella must lead.

"She seems like she prefers to be with you," Claire replied, and Fox made a noncommittal noise.

There was an awkward moment of silence when they seemed to have run out of things to say.

"Apologies for the distraction," he said. "I'll show you the way."

She was acutely aware of the distance between them. He was near, but not near enough. Was that . . . longing she felt?

"No, silly," she explained. "I *'got lost.'* If you catch my meaning."

Lud, but she felt ridiculous. And then something in her stilled at the way Fox gazed down at her.

"Am I to understand that you have sought me out? Where we might not be seen?"

That burned.

"I came with some idea of apologizing to you about that," she said, nervously adjusting her spectacles. "And to speak to you about us being seen together."

"You shouldn't. You ought to have a care with your reputation."

"Of course. Which is why I wanted to say that perhaps it is for the best if we took care not to be seen together so much."

There, she had said it.

Even though looking at him now she wasn't quite so sure.

"Why is that?"

"The consequences of a rumored liaison . . . would be . . . dire."

"Dire?"

"Life-altering, surely."

"And you sought me out in private to tell me that?"

"You do agree that we ought to take care not to be seen together, then."

"Well, we certainly shouldn't be caught together in private."

Oh. Well, then. That was that. They were agreed. They should not be seen together because of reputations, et cetera, et cetera. This one last risk should end quickly before it turned into a life-altering encounter. She could turn and go and carry on with her life.

Why, Mr. Williams had called on her; what a lovely visit they'd had. Perhaps he was The One for her.

"Then I ought to go," she said, "before anyone recalls I am missing and discovers me here."

But she didn't move. Couldn't bring herself to leave, really. Claire was a smart girl but she could not understand why she just wanted to be near the man. He was wrong for her, she told herself. She was too smart for him, she told herself. A man like Mr. Williams was right for her, she insisted to herself.

I want to kiss Fox.

That was her brain and her heart's only response.

"I am glad for the interruption though," he said, gazing down at her. His slight smile caused slight crinkles around the corners of his eyes and she thought it adorable. "I'd much rather see you than attend to all this correspondence."

Without taking his eyes off her, he gestured to a mountain of paperwork on his desk.

"I am touched, truly. You do know how to compliment a girl. I should go."

She waited one more beat just in case he, oh, wanted to pull her into his arms and ravish her on this very plush, but hideously patterned, carpet.

No, Claire, be reasonable!

"It was good to see you," Fox said. Then he nodded. She was dismissed, which was for the best. So she turned to go.

Heaven forbid that she do so *elegantly*. Her slipper caught on the leg of a chair, causing her to lurch forward, limbs flailing, glasses jerked off her face and flying across the room.

Claire was caught before she hit the ground—one strong arm snaked around her waist and hauled her against a rock-hard chest.

"Oof," she said. *Oof*?

Once again, Fox's lightning-quick reflexes and strength served a purpose: Lady Claire tripped and nearly went sprawling and he saved her, of course, because he was the kind of man who saved women from such situations. The reflexes. The strength.

Then there was the small matter of the woman he held pressed against him. For safety. Yes, that was it, safety. It had nothing to do with actually wanting her. His palm splayed across her belly. Her head rested against his chest. He felt a wanting so profound it went beyond mere lust.

He held her close because he didn't want her to go—not now, and not forever, as she'd been trying to suggest. If he really thought about it, it was his heart rebelling at the thought and not the part of his brain reserved for that wager.

So Fox held on to her longer than necessary, to preserve the moment as he tried to make sense of it. He tried addition, as she might do: Lady Claire + him + intimate moment in study = little cracks in his heart and soul being filled up. Fox wasn't the sort to be bothered by those little cracks and bruises—that was just life and a result of playing the game and nothing to get all frothy and emotional about. But damn if everything didn't suddenly seem right and better.

"Are you all right?" He asked this gruffly.

"Yes." She turned to face him.

And all the air rushed out of his lungs.

Her glasses had gone flying and now Fox gazed at Lady Claire as he'd never seen her before.

She looked . . . softer. Without them, and with tendrils of her hair escaping her coiffure, she looked more girlish. Lady Claire without her glasses was altogether a different creature, one who was less imposing, more fragile.

If only Mowbray could see her like this.

He never wanted Mowbray to see her like this.

The wager would be won if he could just get the ton to see her thusly. Francesca had been right—Franny was always right.

"I can't see much at the moment—just enough to discern that you are agog at my appearance without my spectacles."

"Yes. Essentially."

"Might you instead look around for my glasses? I should like to regain my vision."

"Can you see without your glasses?"

"Of course not." She gave one of those peevish lady expressions that was oddly adorable. "That's why I wear them."

"Because you are . . . you look . . . without them you look . . ."

"I know. I look less like an intellectual bluestocking destined to become a spinster and more like some delicate girl."

The mouth, still the same. Her brain, still sharp. Fox smiled, not that she could see it.

"I was going to say beautiful," he said. "But that, too."

"Spare me." She rolled her eyes but he could

have sworn that, first, there was the merest, briefest flash of a smile. "Just help me find them."

"Very well. Stand there and don't move."

She obeyed and he located her glasses a few feet away. They'd landed on the carpet and thus did not sustain cracks in the lens or other damage. Fox was ashamed that he thought of damaging them before the ball, so she might appear in public without them, and everyone would see what he saw and the wager would be won, the world would return to rights, and then what? Lady Claire would stumble around blind, probably doing herself an injury just so she could be popular?

He handed her the glasses, taking one long last look at this secret version of her. Their hands touched.

He could not unsee what he had seen.

Suddenly Fox felt possessive. He wanted no one else in the world to see her like this. Just him, alone.

Lady Claire slipped the spectacles back on.

He still wanted to kiss her.

"You are beautiful," he blurted out. As if he had just realized this. As if he wasn't an expert charmer of women. As if she hadn't just told him they weren't to see each other anymore.

"You're not terrible to look at, either. But I suppose you already knew that."

He couldn't help a little smile because of course he did. "Shh. Just smile. And say thank you."

She smiled and thanked him.

"I should go," Lady Claire replied. "My family is waiting. I am missing a visit with your sister and aunt."

"Yes, you absolutely must go," he said, not meaning a word of it. "One would not want to miss the opportunity to socialize with my female relations."

He stepped closer to her.

"I shall go right this minute."

"This very second," he murmured, standing very close now. He noticed she didn't move away. He noticed, because his heart was starting to pound because of her nearness.

"I should never have come to seek you out," she whispered softly.

I could say the same, he thought quickly. Then he wouldn't be in this mess of a wager. But right now, alone in his study with Claire, the air between them thick with lust, he was actually glad of it all.

"You fancied a little bit of trouble," Fox murmured. "But a little trouble never hurt anyone, right?"

No, a little trouble never hurt anyone. One stolen kiss was a great pleasure in life, not to be missed, and it needn't be a harbinger of doom, or marriage, or whatever.

Fox kissed her. His mouth finding hers, claiming hers. She was so sweet and passionate all at once and he was overcome with wanting. He scooped her up in his arms and held her, taking one or two steps until she was up against the bookshelves.

Support was necessary. She made his knees weak.

This wasn't a gentle kiss, but one that was fraught with tension and loaded with passion.

Stopping now was simply not possible. Not when he needed to drink her in completely. Every kiss with her felt like it might be the last, which meant it felt like he needed to make it everything. It wasn't a hard thing to do. He gave and she gave and together they tangled so perfectly, like they were made for this.

Their families were just down the hall.

That sobering fact should have diminished his passion but it only fanned the flames. The risk of discovery heightened his pleasure in the moment.

What would someone see?

Their mouths, connected. Their bodies, touching. Discovering how her full breasts and round hips fit perfectly in his big hands.

What would they hear?

Soft sighs of pleasure, a low groan of wanting more, the steady thump of pounding hearts.

In the far recesses of his mind, he had to

wonder: What if he wanted to be caught with her? What if he secretly, deep down in the unexamined corners of his head and heart, wanted the consequences of discovery in a compromising position?

For a second his heart stopped beating.

Then Claire writhed against him and his cock hardened even more, if such a thing were possible. All other thoughts ceased.

There was just him and her and a passion that was so easily sparked.

There was nothing to prove with this kiss—it wouldn't help him win the wager or help her solve a math problem—nothing other than that they could not keep their hands and mouths off each other.

Fox did not care to consider what it signified that their every interaction resulted in a mad kiss, frantic with passion. The sound of her breaths, his groan, and his cock strained at his breeches, her little hands roaming all over, feeling him, learning him, knowing him.

Fox pressed his arousal against the vee of her thighs and her moan of pleasure nearly undid him. He sank his fingers into the mass of her hair, holding her so he could kiss her deeply.

Don't go away, came a whisper from some hidden depths of his heart.

Then, daringly, he softly traced his fingertip from her lips, down the curve of her neck, then lower, toying at the edge of her bodice. She peered at him through those eyes; the spectacles only made the truth clearer. She was not saying no. She was saying *yes*. YES.

First, he pressed kisses along the edge, where the lace caressed her pale skin. Then he tugged the fabric out of the way and pressed kisses there, upon her breasts.

Lady Claire gave no doubt as to whether this pleased her. She clasped his head, holding him close. He took a dusky pink center in his mouth, teasing her.

"Oh, God," she whispered, arching her back and exposing herself to him.

He lavished attention on the other perfect, plump breast until her breaths were quick and shallow. And then even he was lost in a frenzy of kisses wherever he could find bare skin—her neck, her breasts, her mouth—and a frenzy of touch, as he wanted to know her.

So he explored, and she did the same. So many women had adoringly run their hands over his muscles, cooing over all that strength. But this was the first time he felt a shudder, a shiver. Like he cared, especially, that it was Lady Claire doing the adoring.

Her small hands slipped underneath his shirt, caressing the ripples of his abdomen and the planes of his chest. She teased his nipples, causing him to suck in his breath.

"I wish I could see you," she whispered, and he wanted to reveal himself to her. He wanted to see her, too. Wanted like he'd never wanted anyone or anything.

"I can't get enough of you," he said in a hoarse whisper.

She arched into him and he dared to slip his hands under her skirts, skimming higher and higher, tracing his fingers lightly along the soft, sensitive flesh of her inner thighs until she shuddered.

"Tell me to stop," he whispered as he dared to reach higher, closer to the sensitive folds between her legs.

"I should," she murmured.

"But you won't."

She just kissed him. Drank him in. Arched up to him. Fox took that as a *yes* and it was confirmed when she gasped, "I can't. I want . . . I need . . ."

Claire meant to say, *I can't stop. I want more. I need you.* But the words were lost between her lips and her head or her heart or that delicate, sensitive place he was stroking, gently and relentlessly. She let her head fall back and he pressed kisses along her neck. It was all so much, almost too much. But she wanted it all: the feel of his fingers on her most sensitive place, the feel of his lips on her skin, the feel of his body against hers, radiating heat . . .

All of it. She wanted all of it.

So much for the conversation she'd come here to have. Something about no more of this.

More of this. She wanted more of this. It wasn't a thought—her brilliant brain had laughed and run away. Her body was in control now, taking over, giving in to the desire and encouraging Fox to fan the flames.

Claire loved it.

She tried to tell him all this, the only way she knew how: with a kiss. A frantic, imperfect kiss. She felt it everywhere. Or perhaps that hot, shimmery feeling was from the way Fox teased and touched the sensitive bud of her sex.

The pressure—the intensely pleasurable pressure—was building. He expertly stoked that fire within. She knew what would come next. More pleasure than she thought she could take. So much that she would shatter. Time would stop. Pleasure would overwhelm her.

This is exactly what happened. But it was more, so much more, than it had ever been before.

Fox knew she was close, so he kept up his steady rhythm, kept up the kisses, kept up everything she seemed to like until he'd brought her to the brink and then beyond.

She cried out and he caught the sound with a kiss.

Fox held her as she drifted back to earth. He

listened to her breathing return to normal. His pounding heartbeat started to slow. His cock was still straining for her, more than ever, but that would have to wait until . . .

. . . until, possibly, never. The thought of never making love to her suddenly struck him as impossibly sad, and not because of a sense of sport, or competition or that damned wager. Sad because he yearned for that connection with her. He wanted to be the one to give her pleasure and to bring her to climax again and again. He wanted her to do the same for him.

This sudden rush of feelings suggested that perhaps it was something he ought to give considerable thought to, later, when his brain was fully functioning again.

But for now, he held her and breathed her in and just wanted her.

"That was . . ."

"I know," he murmured his agreement.

Any other further conversation was interrupted by the sound of voices in the hall. Familiar voices. Plural.

"I must go," she whispered. Did she sound forlorn? Or did he want her to sound thusly?

He pressed one last kiss on her lips. *What if it was the last one?*

"How is my hair?" she asked.

"A disaster," he said frankly, and she laughed.

"I do love an honest man," she murmured.

She did her best to set it to rights, but pins had been lost, she hadn't a mirror, and, he suspected, she didn't have much practice or interest in styling hair in any circumstances. He had a hunch that if it were up to them both, she'd leave it undone, tumbling around her shoulders, her breasts . . .

"You have to go," he said. Because he really, *really* wanted her to stay. He wanted to remove that green dress and lay her down on the carpet and bury himself inside her. He wanted to bring her to orgasm again and again and listen to her crying out, not smothering the sound with his kiss. He wanted to find his own release with her and show Claire just how much she affected him. Lord knew he didn't have the words to explain it.

But there was no time for that now.

She gave a quick nod, a slight smile, and then she was gone, hurrying down the corridor to catch up with her family.

He paused outside the door, leaving it open just a crack so he could listen.

"There you are, Claire, we're ready to leave," he heard Lady Bridget say. She sounded *very* ready to leave. He knew his sister could be a trial; what had Francesca done now?

"I'm sorry. I wasn't feeling well. I was light-headed. I had to lie down."

"Your cheeks are flushed." He recognized the duchess's voice.

"I might be feverish." And he heard a little catch in her voice.

Feverish indeed.

Fox sagged against the door, willing his heart to stop pounding and his cock to relax. Was it only days ago, weeks ago, that he thought her a social pariah and a future spinster, best avoided and an easily won wager?

The woman did something to him.

Fox wondered if his feelings for Lady Claire went beyond winning or losing. He had a sneaking suspicion that when he wasn't paying attention, the rules of the game had changed.

Chapter 13

Wednesday evening, Durham House

Claire's bedchamber door burst open to reveal Bridget, all dressed up in a pink gown for that night's event—a soiree, or Almack's, or some other thing with hordes of people in a ballroom. It was all the same to Claire—hair to be done, delicate frocks to don, manners to be minded, gentlemen to be avoided.

Fox included. Fox especially. After what happened in his study, it was clear that she could not trust herself near him.

"Well, good evening to you," Claire said to her sister.

Bridget looked her up and down. "Claire, you're not wearing pink."

"Obviously not." Bridget looked concerned. "Does it matter?"

"You know that Lady Francesca says we are to wear pink on Wednesdays, to Almack's."

"Is it Wednesday, then?"

"Claire! Lord save me from absentminded sisters," Bridget said, rolling her eyes. "Yes, it is Wednesday. Tonight we are going to Almack's. And we ought to wear pink."

Bridget punctuated the reporting of these facts with a beseeching gaze. The kind that revealed how desperate she was for their family to fit into society, how she despaired at what little effort everyone but her was making, how she hoped that Claire would be the one to be sensible and see why it was vitally important that they all wear pink (except for James, presumably, though she wouldn't put it past Bridget to have a pink waistcoat made up for him).

Claire was not wearing pink, but not deliberately. She had let her maid select one of the dresses that the duchess had picked out for her. She cared little for clothes; she had more important things to occupy her thoughts; though, admittedly, her thoughts of late had been almost completely devoted to what had transpired between her and Fox in his study the other day.

Just thinking about it brought a *pink* blush to her cheeks. That didn't seem to appease Bridget now, who was giving Claire her most pleading look.

"Are you asking me silently with your eyes and in your heart to change so that you can impress your friends?" Claire asked. Did she even own something pink?

"Yes," Bridget gushed.

Amelia chose that moment to burst in.

"Is she trying to make you wear pink as well?"

Claire noticed that Amelia had been badgered into a having a pink hair ribbon woven through her large mass of dark curls.

"Go away, Amelia," Bridget said with a wave of her hand. "Go . . . read my diary or something."

"If you wish to bend over backward to impress a lot of simpering, scheming, vapid creatures, I will not stop you," Claire said. "I will wish you the best. But I couldn't care less about what any of them think of me."

"Yes!" Amelia gushed. "What Claire said!"

Claire turned to her youngest, most trouble-prone sister. "You, young lady, still need to mind your manners."

"Except for the rule that a lady is only supposed to talk about the weather and how much she is enjoying the ball even if she is so bored she wishes to stick forks in her eye," Amelia replied. "But you, Claire, talk about math *all the time* to anyone who will listen."

And even some who won't.

"First Lord Fox, and now you," Claire muttered. She hadn't forgotten his suggestion that she talked about math too much. It rankled, even though half the time she did it to deliberately scare off gentlemen. It wasn't fair, though, that Ashbrooke should be admired for his displays of intelligence while it made her an outcast.

She wondered, idly, if she should save such conversation for her visits with Ashbrooke or Mr. Williams.

Claire also hadn't forgotten what Fox had said about her spectacles. She looked at herself in the mirror, adjusting her glasses, wondering what reaction she would get if she left them at home. Even without them, she could tell that Fox was awestruck at the sight of her. What would the rest of the ton's reaction be? She decided she would be too blind to see, it wouldn't be worth risking an injury, and it was best to wear them.

"I don't care what you talk about," Bridget huffed. "As long as you wear pink."

In the end, Claire added a pink shawl to her ensemble, *not* because she gave one whit about impressing Lady Francesca or anyone in the haute ton. She did so because it mattered to Bridget and Bridget mattered to her. It was that simple. Or so she told herself.

Almack's assembly rooms

The Lady of Distinction was not the only one who wondered at the unlikely pairing of Lord Fox and Lady Claire. As she strolled through the crowds at Almack's with her family, Claire happened to catch pointed looks in her direction and to overhear a few choice snippets of conversation.

"I don't know what a handsome charmer like Lord Fox sees in her."

"She certainly doesn't compare to Arabella Vaughn."

"Not with those spectacles."

"I can't believe she's wearing pink."

Claire wanted to turn to that woman and say, "I can't believe it, either, but it mattered to my sisters, so there." And then perhaps stick her tongue out. While she was at it, she might also say that Fox didn't mind her spectacles and severe coiffure the other day while nearly ravishing her in his study. But of course such things were not said and that type of behavior was frowned upon.

It was also entirely beside the point. In spite of what happened afterward, and what she still daydreamed about, Claire meant what she said to Fox: they could not risk being seen together.

Fox was not the sort of man that she had ever imagined herself becoming involved with, in part because Claire was not the sort of girl who ever imagined herself with boys or suitors. She had more important, lofty things to do with herself and her brain.

But what about the rest of her? The rest of her body that Fox had so lovingly explored and pleasured just the other day? What about those kisses that made her knees weak? What about the adventures he'd brought her on?

When she had, vaguely, considered the prospect of marriage she had expected a meeting of minds; someone with whom she could enjoy intellectual conversations with at the breakfast table, who would encourage her work, challenge her, teach her. Someone like Mr. Benedict Williams.

But Claire had forgotten to factor lust into the equation.

Until Fox reminded her that she was not merely a brain, but a living, breathing woman with a body that had feelings, desires, and needs.

Those feelings, desires, and needs had, of late, been overpowering her logic and reason. The other day was the perfect example: she'd gone to him with every intention of putting an end to this madness and instead he'd brought her to the peak of pleasure and sent her off with flushed cheeks, lips full from kisses, her hair in disarray, and her thoughts preoccupied.

Which is why she would have to avoid him at all costs tonight.

Lady Claire was wearing pink on a Wednesday, Lord Mowbray noted with disdain—though not as much as he reserved for the fact that he knew that young ladies of fashion and some social standing wore pink on Wednesdays to Almack's.

But there it was: proof of her effort to fit in. As

far as Mowbray was aware, this was the first time she'd even deigned to try to align herself with the young, unmarried ladies seeking societal approval and husbands. One pink shawl carelessly flung about her shoulders revealed this.

What was next? Mowbray wondered. Would she lose the spectacles, too?

He sauntered closer to her, morbidly curious to learn more. As he lingered nearby, he overheard the duchess wrangling a young man for an introduction, a polite conversation between two utterly disinterested parties, an obligatory invitation to dance, and then . . .

"I do apologize but my dance card is already full."

Shocked, Mowbray watched as she flashed a dance card, apparently full of names.

A full dance card. Pink on Wednesdays. Her name in the newspapers, linked with Fox's. There was no denying that she was making progress and there was still time for her to complete the transformation from hopeless spinster and frightening female to society darling.

Fox would win. Again.

Mowbray would lose. Again.

Lady Claire's resolve was tested almost immediately. She'd had just enough time to fill in her dance card herself, so as to have an excuse if any gentleman dared to ask her to dance, and find a spot near the wallflowers when she noticed Fox.

He was there, of course, with his sister. Predictably, Bridget joined Lady Francesca and her cohort of simpering young ladies and they all wandered off to be holier than thou elsewhere.

When the duchess saw Lord Fox approaching, she mentioned something about introductions and practically dragged James and Amelia away.

Ah, subtlety.

Remember your resolve. The reminder was necessary. Watching Fox make his way through a crowded ballroom, in her direction, with his gaze fixed on hers, and his intentions clear, was something else. He was resplendently dressed, and he was large, and the crowds parted for him.

Her heart began to beat faster. She thought, *I have kissed this man. Tasted him. Felt him.* He had made her heart beat faster, her breathing become shallow, her thoughts focused only on him. The fact that she should not have done only made it all more delicious.

"Good evening, Lady Claire." He murmured her name like they shared a secret. Which they did. Which she would do well not to think about.

"Good evening," she replied, smiling, because it wouldn't do to be rude. And because she did, actually, like him. She had to admit that now. She had to admit this yearning was real; it could not be disregarded or ignored, so she would have to account for it somehow.

"On Wednesdays you also wear pink?" He gave a lift of his brow and a teasing smile. Her heart did a little pitter-pat thing that embarrassed her. "I didn't think you were that sort of woman."

"Apparently I am," she groaned. "The things I do for my sister."

He reached out and touched a corner of the soft, pale pink silk shawl.

"The color suits you." Then he leaned in close and whispered, "It reminds me of your lips when I've been kissing you."

The color reminded her of sunsets and blushes and kisses. It also reminded her of Bridget and Amelia and the reason she was wearing it—to help her sisters become settled in this new life in this new world. The color reminded her that they would have to come first and her needs and desires could wait.

"May I have the honor of this dance? Or is your dance card all full again?"

If she danced with him, they would be seen by one and all. It would be reported in the papers.

If she danced with him, one of his hands would be on the small of her back and his other would hold hers. It would remind her of all the wicked loveliness that had happened in his study. It would make her want him more. She would gaze up into his eyes and wonder what he was thinking (anything, other than what she looked like naked? Was that wrong?) and it would make her confused and bothered, the way a good math problem did, but this one would have no solution.

If she danced with him, it would feed this mad desire of hers, which would distract her just when she needed her wits the most.

And above all, everyone would start those questions again: *What does he see in her? She's no Arabella Vaughn. She's just so . . . and he's just so . . . Who does she think she is? How smart is she if she can't even manage the steps to a waltz without being so embarrassingly clumsy?*

"I'm afraid my dance card is full," she said truthfully. Mostly. Out of fear, mainly.

"Is that so?"

Before she could protest he lifted it up, squinted at her handwriting, and began to read.

"Ah, I see the first waltz is promised to Lord Denominator. And the next to Lord Rhombus. And then the Duke of Pythagoras." He paused and adopted a quizzical stare while she wished the floorboards were opening up beneath her and she was falling, falling, falling. She should be so lucky. A hot flush of shame enveloped her. "I have not made the acquaintance of these gentlemen."

"They are new to town," she whispered.

"Is that so?"

"Yes."

But her cheeks flamed pink because she had thought him foolish, but he wasn't. He had discovered her ruse and obviously did not find it amusing. It was just something she did, to get rid of all the gentlemen. This wasn't the first time. Was he hurt? she wondered. He seemed hurt. Why did that make her feel a swell of shame and an ache of her own?

She could see him thinking now of all the other times he'd asked her to dance. It was one thing to lie to him then, before they had shared kisses, and before he'd brought her to climax, before they'd ceased being strangers to each other. At some point between then and now, things had changed between them.

He was not having it. He would not tolerate being lied to.

She had thought him a dolt, but now he made her exceedingly aware of his integrity, his good heart that she had wounded, and that he was sharper than she had supposed.

Fox was large; she had known this. But now she felt it. He towered over her, radiating a quiet strength and power, and making her feel small.

Fox grasped her wrist and stepped aside, tugging her into a private alcove.

She stumbled after him, not exactly resisting.

He was close. Fox leaned down so he could speak softly in her hear.

"I may not know what a denominator or a rhombus is or what they do when they are together. But I do know when a woman is lying to me."

"I am so sorry. Truly."

"Don't apologize," he said, annoyed. "A woman as logical as you must have a reason. And a man as stupid as me obviously cannot grasp it unless you explain. And please, use small words."

Wasn't that a knife to the heart. She could see that he was emotional in that male way—an internal battle to identify an emotion, wrestle it into submission, and put it away in the locked box inside so one might never be confronted with it again. It manifested as a tight jaw, gritted voice, forced composure.

She decided she owed him an honest reply.

"I do not see us as . . . marrying."

He gave a quick, "Ha!" that deflated her.

"Did I ask you to? I don't recall. And if I did, I think it's a memory I would like to have. So please, remind me."

That sucked the air right out of her lungs. Look at her, being so presumptuous that a man like him would fancy a woman like her. Fancy her so much that he'd want to wed her! She'd been so preoccupied with how he didn't fit into her image of her ideal life partner that she'd never considered what his intentions might actually be.

"No, you didn't propose," she said, now feeling annoyed. Was it with him? Or with herself, because, dear Lord, was that a shred of *care* she was experiencing? It was some sort of emotion that manifested its presence physically, in the region of her heart. But while they were asking the hard questions and getting to the heart of the matter, she had a question for him. "But tell me this: What other reason would *you* have to pay attention to *me*?"

"Are you one of those women blind to her own charms?"

"Not at all. I just don't think my charms are ones that appeal to a man like you."

"What do you mean by that?"

"You are interested in sport, and such, while I am interested in more intellectual pursuits."

She was not tall, and leggy, and blond, and bosomy. She did not cling or hang off his arm. She couldn't flirt or simper if her life depended on it. She was not Arabella Vaughn.

She also refused to consider herself deficient because she wasn't those things.

"According to you, Lady Logic, we have nothing in common and have no future together. And yet you have not exactly rebuffed my overtures to you. I did not drag you against your will to a mathematics lecture or to a boxing match or behind the hedges at Lady Winterbourne's garden party. I certainly didn't drag you into my study and ravish you against your will. In fact, I think you sought me out. I wonder why. Perhaps, since I am not intellectually inclined, you can explain it to me?"

The heat rose within her with every word he spoke. She felt like she was being chastised—probably because she was. She felt an overwhelming surge of emotions—ones she couldn't stop to identify because her heart was pounding, the orchestra was playing, he was looming, and he was looking at her like that. Like he cared. And she felt, among a million other things, the same.

With a vague notion of wanting to figure this all out later, but not wanting to lose him now, Claire did the only thing she could think of. Usually she had more inspired, intellectual thoughts than this. But really, her brain had only one idea. She acted upon it immediately.

She kissed him.

Her kiss shocked him, like a left hook he didn't see coming, but far more pleasurable on contact. Mostly. This kiss was tortured because he wanted it, but didn't want to want it.

Confounding. Woman. She made him *feel* things. She made the machinery of his brain start whirring and churning. She made the fury rise up within him, even though he was guilty of deception, too. She had lied to him—why? Days ago, he could understand. But now?

Well, it was because women always went from

point A to 107 with barely a stop in between. They had kissed a few times, so she assumed they would marry, and she didn't wish to marry him, but she kissed him anyway. So much for the logic and rationality she prided herself on.

Which was fine because that wasn't the reason for his interest at all.

The wager.

He shouldn't say anything about the wager. Though it would answer all of her questions about what he saw in her—at least, at first. But what had started as a dare had transformed into something else and he didn't know how to make sense of it, let alone explain it.

But Fox knew this: a small part of him did not want to win because it meant changing her, and he was falling for her just as she was. When or how or why this happened he could not say, either.

Also, it was hard to speak when they were kissing.

This was her answer.

A kiss.

Her hot little mouth on his. And this was no mere innocent, awkward, tentative *do-you-like-this?* kiss. They'd done this a time or two now and she'd already figured out just how to wreck him.

Her hands slid over his arms, his muscled arms. His chest. His every nerve snapped to attention, ready to feel every sensation and to transit it to his brain. His heart. The locked box in his stomach with all the feelings.

She pressed herself up against him, her breasts crushed against his chest. He nearly growled in the back of his throat.

All this, in a bloody darkened alcove. At Almack's.

With a woman who said she hadn't wished to marry him.

A woman who prided herself on being intelligent and logical.

But he understood now. He had an effect on her. It was the effect he had on all the women. For all her spectacles and equations and whatnot, she was just a woman.

Lady Claire Cavendish, of the brilliant mind, wanted him purely for his body. She cared nothing for the contents of his brain or his heart. Not even the contents of his bank account or the prestige of his title.

Women had often gone mad before for his muscles, his touch. His wealth and title were a boon. This business with Lady Claire, then, was nothing new. It was the way things had always gone with him and women. Fox ought to be glad that everything was back to normal after Arabella.

The truth was, he was not glad. Or relieved. He was troubled because this should have been everything and it wasn't enough. He wanted more, more than she was willing to give and perhaps more than they could ever be.

This realization struck him suddenly. His heart stopped beating, blood stopped pulsing through his veins, air ceased moving in and out of his lungs.

In this space, the truth revealed itself: they were madly attracted to each other and yet wildly incompatible. They could never be together, especially once she discovered the real reason he had originally pursued her. Fox now understood what she had been trying to convey.

There was no point in any of this, then—other than for him to try to change her so he could win a bet. But he no longer wanted to change her. He didn't want to lose the wager, because he didn't want to lose his dog. But he also didn't want to lose *her*—it wasn't possessive so much as not wishing to wreck something unique, beautiful, and true.

There was no point in any of this.

No matter what, he could not win.

He had played a dangerous game and was about to lose everything that mattered.

He stopped the kiss. His organs resumed their vital functions.

He stepped aside. Space between them was necessary if he wished to form and articulate a sentence.

"You have made things very clear. Thank you. I bid you a good evening."

Mowbray ought to have been looking for a bride of his own—that was why eligible gentlemen endured Almack's—but instead he spent the evening socializing with the pretense of observing Fox and Lady Claire.

He'd heard the rumors of their time spent together. He'd seen the beginnings of her transformation. He watched, transfixed, as he finally caught them together.

Mowbray watched Fox approach Lady Claire, standing off to the side of the ballroom.

He watched them converse. Was it tense or passionate? He could not tell. There was blushing. Eyes flashing. And then he watched them, hand in hand, quickly slip off to a secluded corner.

"Excuse me," he murmured to the group of people he was pretending to converse with. Then he followed.

And then, around a darkened corner, he witnessed the inconceivable sight of Fox kissing Lady Claire. Not any kiss, no. The kind with heat, passion, and real feelings. The kind that had Mowbray backing away slowly, feeling like the worst sort of creep for seeing it. The kind of kiss that plainly revealed that Fox wasn't just about a wager, that Arabella was about to lose him again, and that Mowbray was about to part with his prize racehorse and the winning streak he'd been on.

That is, unless he could chuck a wrench in the machine.

Chapter 14

Later that night, at White's

Fox quit Almack's and proceeded to his club, where he discovered that there was still no escaping the Cavendishes. Somehow those vexing, confounding, upstart American women had managed to infiltrate White's, haven of the aristocratic British male.

"Ah, so this is where the party is," Fox said dryly as he strolled in and pulled up a chair and collapsed into it. His friends Darcy, Rupert, and Alistair Finlay-Jones, recently returned from the Continent, were seated around a table, starting a game of cards. They had smartly avoided the marriage mart that evening. "I was at Almack's earlier, dying of boredom. And sobriety."

Actually, he was tortured with lust, possibly lovesick, confounded by the mind of an otherwise logical female. But he wasn't such a fool as to say anything about that to his friends, who would never let him hear the end of it.

"Were you expecting otherwise?" Darcy inquired in that dry Darcy-way of his.

"I had promised Francesca I would escort her." He turned to Darcy, whom Francesca had been keen on seeing that evening. "In fact, I noticed *you* weren't there."

"I had an urgent matter to attend to," he murmured. Fox eyed his friend, wondering if he was keeping a secret.

"Still drying off from your spill in the lake?" Fox asked, thinking that the more they talked about Darcy and his American girl, the less they would discuss Fox and his American girl, he reasoned.

Not that he had an American girl. She had made that very clear. She was too busy having imaginary affairs and dances with the Duke of Pythagoras and Lord Rhombus.

Alistair perked up at the prospect of Darcy doing something as uncivilized as fall into a lake.

"What did I miss?" Alistair asked.

A lot. And that was just last week. But Alistair had spent the past six years traveling and had only just returned. Fox took a long swallow of whiskey and wondered where to begin.

"You won't believe it," Rupert began with obvious delight, and he proceeded to explain.

There was little detail given to the rowboats, the race, and the collision and far too much information regarding the aftermath.

Fox was, unfortunately, forced to remember how he spent those moments: in a little rowboat, with Lady Claire, all to himself. Speaking of dragging her off to his lair where he might have his way with her.

Which he did, in a manner of speaking, just the other day.

She'd probably just been ogling the strength of his muscles, the masterfully athletic way he handled the oars. He was probably just some handsome, ignorant brute to her. Then again, he had been admiring the way her breasts swelled over her bodice, promising a wicked, wonderful handful for a man.

Which he confirmed. Which he wanted to experience again.

He had not been lusting over her way with an equation.

Shit, was that . . . empathy he felt? Was he, good god, obtaining greater understanding about something deep and meaningful? He was irate that she thought of him only as a prime physical specimen and not a person with feelings, and yet all he did was lust after her and plot ways to change her. He hadn't thought of her as a person in possession of *feelings.*

Fox took another swallow of his drink, shoved such thoughts from his mind, and focused on the conversation at hand.

"Fancied a swim, did you?" Alistair quipped, good-naturedly teasing Darcy, who was not often—or ever—teased.

"If that's what we're calling it these days," Rupert replied.

"I overheard Fran and her friends gossiping about it," Fox said, coming back to the conversation. He was the only one who could get away with calling Lady Francesca "Fran." "They were going on and on about Darcy here, in his wet shirt. Giggling like schoolgirls. It was horrifying."

Nothing terrified him. Except for giggling girls.

It occurred to him that he'd never once heard Lady Claire do something as missish as giggle. She was probably physically incapable of it. This prompted a pang in the region of his ~~heart~~ lungs.

"It has been said by some that Lady Bridget swooned right into Darcy's waiting arms," Rupert said, laughing. Darcy merely lifted one brow.

"She wasn't swooning. She was thrashing about in the water, attempting to swim," Darcy said, sounding painfully bored.

"And then you clutched her to your chest . . ." Fox said dramatically, mockingly.

"And she gazed into your eyes . . ." Rupert added.

"I couldn't very well let her drown," Darcy said.

Alistair was laughing heartily. "Let me guess. She swooned in your arms once you rescued her from an untimely demise."

"I daresay she swooned," Rupert said. "I was there."

"And they say ladies aren't much troubled by sexual feeling of any kind," Fox remarked dryly.

"My regards to the women in your life if you believe that," Darcy replied.

He certainly didn't believe it tonight. Not after being nearly ravished by Lady Claire Cavendish in an alcove. At Almack's. She had pressed her mouth to his, licked the seam of his lips, teased him into opening up to her.

She wasn't drunk, either, for he tasted her and he knew that her desire was real, and not just champagne induced.

Women were definitely troubled by sexual feelings. Fox had known, and confirmed it.

And now he was, too. Bloody hell.

"Sod off," he retorted. A long sip of alcohol was needed.

"My, how the mighty have fallen," Alistair murmured, glancing at his friends. "I go away for a mere six years . . . and come back to find Fox here in a snit over a woman and Darcy gallantly rescuing young ladies at garden parties."

"I don't know about you gents, but I came here to win all your money at cards and drink obscene amounts of brandy. I have no intention of gossiping like schoolgirls," Darcy said.

Fox raised a glass to that.

And with that they began to play in earnest.

But even this did not provide the escape he sought. Fox was reminded of the night he explained the rules of vingt-et-un to Claire, moments before she sat down and proceeded to win nearly every hand, and not by beginner's luck, either. It was by the sheer intellectual force of her "lady brainbox."

He lost that hand. Then the next. He didn't have her brilliant brain. Or, tonight, even an ability to focus. Everything reminded him of her, starting with the cards in his hand and the probabilities he couldn't calculate.

He could never compete. He could never compare.

He was in a deplorable state of angst when Mowbray sauntered by, drink in hand, cravat askew, nose red with drink.

Fox glanced up at him and swore under his breath.

"More wagering, Fox?" Mowbray said cuttingly.

Fox gave him a look reserved for insects that

were crushed under his boot and said, "I'm not in the mood, Mowbray."

Mowbray did saunter off, but not without a knowing look that Fox's fists itched to erase.

"What is that about?" Darcy asked.

"Nothing," Fox said sharply.

"It's obviously something," Alistair said.

"Allow me to clarify: it is about nothing that I'm going to discuss with you lot."

"It has to do with a woman," Rupert said.

This was greeted by low whistles and raised brows and murmurs.

Fox did his best to ignore them and instead focused on the cards in his hand. Sense was not made. He did his best to try to recall what cards had been played, and how to calculate odds, like *she* did, but that made his head ache and took all the fun out of the stupid game.

Drink. Scowl. Think. Repeat.

The numbers on the cards swam before his eyes—brandy at work. He could not make sense of them. He was supposed to be playing a game. Winning a wager. He was supposed to be feeling the thrill of the chase and the excitement of competition, yet he felt only bewildered. She had flummoxed him, so completely that he knew neither heads nor tails, hearts nor diamonds. Not how to win, nor even how to play the games.

His friends could have his blunt in the pot.

Mowbray would take his dog. All he wanted was an end to this madness. He wanted life to return to normal. Fox wanted *before* and if he couldn't have that he wanted an end to this torture.

Finally, he set down his cards.

"I'm out."

Chapter 15

Lucien Kemble returned to the stage at Covent Garden last night, to the sighs of his adoring female fans. But many in the audience were also hoping to catch a glimpse of fallen society darling Miss Arabella Vaughn. She did not attend.

—FASHIONABLE INTELLIGENCE,
THE LONDON WEEKLY

The next day, Durham House

If Claire hadn't been kissing Lord Fox, if she hadn't been so distracted by her wanton and wanting thoughts for him, if she hadn't been so preoccupied with a *man*, if she'd just had her priorities in order (family first, men last), if she hadn't disregarded the rules of proper behavior and common sense to passionately kiss him in the middle of Almack's . . .

Well, then, maybe what happened next wouldn't have happened . . .

Perhaps disaster could have been avoided . . .

If only Claire had been more sensible and attentive . . .

But first, the facts.

Whilst Claire was ravishing Lord Fox in an alcove, she was not paying attention to her youngest, most troubling sister, Amelia, who had managed to evade the duchess and find an opportunity to disregard propriety and cause a terrific scene. First, she feigned a faint to avoid dancing with a gentleman. In the process, she was discovered to be without shoes. At a ball. Like some backward, heathen, savage *American*.

What happened next only made the situation worse.

It stood to reason that if Claire had been paying attention to Amelia, instead of writhing against Lord Fox and claiming his mouth for a wicked kiss, none of this would have happened.

Lesson to Claire: pay more attention to her family, less attention to her own wild passions.

That lesson was reinforced the next morning when it was discovered that Amelia was missing. Gone. At large. Presumably alone. Possibly lost.

Her bed had not been slept in.

Claire abandoned all and any thoughts of Lord Fox and what she had done to him in an alcove.

Once the family realized Amelia was missing—when she did not come down to breakfast, as she was never known to miss a meal—they searched the house from top to bottom. This took some time, as Durham House was on the large side of massive. She was not anywhere to be found and she hadn't left even the slightest clue as to where she might have gone or—shudder—with whom.

Afterward the family gathered in the drawing room to determine their course of action. Expressions were grim and the mood was tense. James wanted to hire Bow Street Runners to fan out over London in search of Amelia, while the duchess urged discretion. It wouldn't do for Amelia to be publicly disgraced; the whole family would certainly be ruined then.

They had such precious little social capital as it was.

But Claire didn't care about that right now; she only wanted her little sister back, safe and sound, so she could hug her fiercely and yell at her tremendously about what a fright she'd caused them. She would apologize, too, for being so distracted and putting herself first.

Eventually a plan was determined—who was searching when and where and with whom and when the Runners would be called. Bridget had gone off with Lord Darcy for a ride in Hyde Park and to hopefully spot Amelia.

James had stormed out to alert the Bow Street

Runners and to walk every street in London himself, if necessary, in search of Amelia. Claire could almost imagine him calling out her name, like she was some lost puppy. But he couldn't, because discretion was essential. If the ton discovered her absence, there might be no recovering from the scandal.

Claire found herself alone in the drawing room with the duchess.

Alone in this massive room—in which their house in Maryland could fit, comfortably—with a fearsome woman determined to marry them all off.

This required extensive social machinations—which were just equations that Claire did not understand. There were introductions and dancing and calling hours and finer points of etiquette to learn. There were also factors to consider that Claire couldn't be bothered with—things like lineage, social connections, titles, wealth. Little thought was given to compatibility, whether it was a meeting of minds. Or hearts. Or other parts.

The thought of which made Claire turn red.

The duchess only wanted what was best for Durham, the dukedom.

But Claire wondered if that pressure to wed had sent Amelia running. Amelia had been under so much pressure to tame her wild spirit, to mind her manners, to smile more—but not too much. She wanted to explore the city, but the duchess had insisted on paying social calls instead.

Claire had found her own way to avoid the duchess's machinations for marriage; perhaps this was Amelia's way of doing so. Still, if only she'd done so without causing a scandal.

She should have guided Amelia more.

And given her a respite from the marriage machinations. Claire should have taken her little sister with her to the boxing match. Or skipped a session with Ashbrooke to take her to Vauxhall. She ought to have stayed by her side at Almack's instead of ravishing Fox in an alcove. She knew better; she had just been selfish.

"I am sorry," Claire said, when everyone had left and she was alone with the duchess.

"What do you have to feel sorry for?" the duchess asked after a sip of what had to be her eighty-ninth cup of tea that morning. "There is no need for *you* to apologize."

But there was. She thought of the hours she spent performing calculations, debating what an analytical machine could accomplish beyond simple functions, and not minding her family. There were those stolen moments with Fox, one after another—and the embarrassing number of minutes she spent lusting after him in her thoughts. She long ago stopped counting the minutes.

"I have not been as attentive to my sisters as I usually have been," Claire confessed. "As I ought to have been."

"You are not their mother," the duchess said softly.

This was true. But it was also not true.

"But I have been, in a way," Claire said. "I have spent so long taking care of them and acting as if I was. And I promised our mother that I would ensure they are happy above all else. I feel responsible for the lot of them. And I have to see that they are settled, and safe, and secure before . . ."

"Before?"

"Before I focus on myself. I have been all wrapped up in my work with Ashbrooke and Mr. Williams lately. This business with Amelia has made me realize it."

"Hmm." The duchess sipped her tea. "And Lord Fox."

"I don't know what you mean."

"Claire, you are too smart to be deliberately obtuse and to apologize for things that are not your fault."

Well. That caught her attention. No one ever spoke to her thusly.

"Furthermore, you don't need to raise them alone now. I am here."

"They don't like how you are raising them. I'm not sure I like it. You're changing us. You're making us be people we are not, and pushing us toward a life we are not ready for."

Their very natures were being restricted—James was not a man to sit around with ledgers and account books all day. Bridget, much as she wanted to be, was not a waifish, simpering creature. And Amelia—she was a wild pony who had gotten out of the pen this morning. Claire was terrified for her, but also knew she was born to roam and explore.

And the duchess was urging her to think about herself. Urging her into the oncoming path of Lord Fox. Though that seemed over and thus a moot point.

"I want the same thing for them as you do, Claire. I want them to be safe and secure." The duchess paused. And sipped her tea. "And I want the same for you."

Claire wanted more than that though. She wanted to be challenged intellectually. She wanted to follow her passion and be encouraged to do so. She wanted heart-pounding, stealing kisses, a can't-live-without-you kind of love. How could safety and security compare to that? She knew her siblings felt the same way.

But how to explain this to Her Grace? Claire decided now wasn't the time to try so she only said, "That is very kind of you, Duchess."

Now if only one of them knew who could give her all those things . . . Mr. Williams? Fox?

She thought again about last night. Fox couldn't be the one for her, could he? Mr. Williams challenged her thinking regarding mathematics, but Fox certainly challenged her and her expectations of her life. He indulged and encouraged her passions, all of them. That is to say nothing of the heart-pounding and stolen kisses.

She must have looked very troubled indeed, for the duchess reached over and patted her hand.

"We will find Amelia. And we will ensure that this does not ruin her."

"Thank you."

That *we* was everything. For the first time, Claire started to consider and feel that perhaps the future happiness of four people didn't rest only on her shoulders. She didn't love the duchess's insistence that they all be wed, immediately, to boring, respectable people, but she did appreciate that she didn't need to be the one forcing the issue and finding spouses for the lot of them.

"I daresay we'll have Bridget betrothed to Darcy in no time," the duchess remarked.

"But she hates him!"

"For a very smart girl, you are very foolish when it comes to matters of the heart." The duchess said this kindly, but it still stung.

Because of last night . . .

Because it was true.

"Hate is passion. Love is passion. Sometimes people confuse the two." And with that, the duchess rang for more tea.

Later that afternoon

"I cannot stand waiting around anymore," Claire said after hours of sitting around in the drawing room with the duchess and Meredith, sipping what seemed like all the tea in England and China and speculating about Amelia's whereabouts.

While they were busy with embroidery, Claire had tried to keep her mind occupied and nerves steady with a particularly challenging problem for the paper she was writing with Mr. Williams. Eventually she set down her pencil in defeat; if numbers and logic couldn't engage her, then very little could.

She might as well go out for a walk to help calm her thoughts—and look for her sister.

"I think I should go out," Claire said, standing. "I shall take a walk around the neighborhood and see what I can learn. Maybe I will find Amelia lurking in someone's stables."

"I'll join you," Miss Green said quickly.

"I'll just sit here with this pot of tea and my nerves," the duchess said dryly.

"You should lie down, Your Grace," Miss Green said softly.

"I cannot."

Claire noted the paleness of the duchess's face, the lines of worry increasing on her brow. She was beyond worried. Like a mother.

They had arrived at her doorstep merely weeks ago—at her instance—and it had been a rocky start, a battle of wills between three American girls used to running free to do as they pleased and one of the towers of London society who wanted them to be perfect English girls who made her proud.

Or to be safe. Welcomed in society. Secure in their futures.

Somewhere along the line, they had ceased to be merely charges, projects, vessels through which more Durhams would be created, and they had started to become something like family.

The duchess cared, like a mother. Claire would never stop fiercely loving her little sisters but having one more person to love them, one more person to care, one more person to be responsible for them . . .

Well, the air quite left her lungs.

It meant that perhaps there was a little more time for herself, a little corner of her heart that could be claimed by another?

"Yes, I definitely need some air."

* * *

With shawls, gloves, and bonnets all arranged, Claire and Meredith stepped out onto the Mayfair streets. Claire blinked at the bright day, after a morning ensconced indoors, preoccupied with worry.

Meanwhile, the world went about its business as if nothing were amiss—carriages rumbled by, pedestrians walked along at varying paces, everyone in motion. The sky was blue one moment, then cloudy the next, as if rain might be imminent. This only added a sense of urgency to everyone's movements.

"Where do you think she's gone?" Meredith asked.

"Tourist attractions, most likely," Claire said. "That's why James sent the Runners to places like Vauxhall, and Astley's and the British Museum. It's my fault—I should have taken her to see the Tower instead of calling hours. I should have insisted the duchess allow her some fun."

"Do you think she'll be all right?" Meredith asked, worried. "She doesn't know the city well."

"True. But she at least thinks well on her feet and knows how to make friends." Claire said these things because they were true and hoped it would be consoling. But Amelia was also Trouble and a magnet for more of it. "But, oh, Meredith, I am so nervous!"

"Aye, and anyone can tell just by looking at you. Let's slow down." The two ladies linked arms and Meredith set the pace. A slow, leisurely sedate pace as if they were idle ladies of leisure who had nothing to do but pass the minutes of the day and who were not at all threatened by an imminent rainstorm. Meredith smiled. "And now let's chat amiably as if we were talking about nothing more than pretty dresses or handsome men who bring terrible bouquets of flowers."

This brought a little laugh from Claire.

"Handsome men are nothing but trouble," Claire said.

"Truer words were never spoken," Meredith agreed.

The two women exchanged a glance, and Claire wondered if Meredith had more to say about *that* or if she wanted to question Claire. She didn't feel like raising the subject.

They had walked through Berkeley Square and then onward to Bond Street because no one would ever question two ladies of their station strolling along Bond Street, looking in the windows of all the finest shops.

"What are the chances that we'll find her here?" Meredith asked, a bit skeptical.

"Almost nil. Amelia doesn't have the patience for shopping," Claire replied with a faint smile. "But I don't exactly feel like wandering into Seven Dials."

After a few blocks of strolling along London's most fashionable shopping street—and hopefully conveying that absolutely nothing was amiss with the Cavendish family—Meredith and Claire made their way to Green Park, at the south of Mayfair.

Claire thought they might see Amelia there—perhaps she'd be interested in the horse guards or just the greenery instead of being stuck inside a drawing room all day. Claire was glad to be out-of-doors searching for her sister instead of sitting around inside, tying herself in knots. Now if only they could find her . . .

Claire was so intent upon finding Amelia that she didn't pay any mind to a tall, broad-shouldered man striding in her direction. A handsome hunting dog trotted alongside.

And then there he was—Lord Fox, standing in front of her with a polite smile that didn't quite reach his eyes. Meanwhile, her breath didn't quite make it back into her lungs.

Of course not; things between them—if there was a thing between them—were uncertain. Like the weather today—cloudy, then sunny for a moment, then cloudy again as if it couldn't decide what it wished to do.

"Hello, Lady Claire. Fancy seeing you here," Fox said, with a tip of his hat and a faint smile. "Miss Green, always lovely to see you as well."

Meredith inclined her head in greeting and

Claire murmured a hello. Just seeing him added to the knots in her stomach.

"What brings you out on a gray day like today?"

Oh, just in search of my sister, who has gone missing. We hope to find her alive and well and before the ton finds out and scandal ruins us all.

"Oh, Miss Green and I just fancied a walk," Claire answered lightly, as if people fancied walks on gray days with rain imminent all the time. Well, this was England after all. Rain was always imminent.

She spied Stella, his dog, and an opportunity to change the subject. "And I suppose you are walking Stella?"

"I could have a footman do it, but I rather enjoy a good brisk walk." It was clear the dog did, too. "Certainly more than correspondence or other lordly matters."

"I can imagine."

"As you know, I'm not the sort to sit behind a desk."

"I know," she said softly.

"But you are."

Yes, she was. Brainy Claire Cavendish, who stuck up her nose at those who didn't share or appreciate her interests, such as sitting behind a desk puzzling through increasingly complicated problems that may or may not have a bearing upon the world. She deserved to be thought of as such, given how much she had perpetuated the notion, even if she started to realize she didn't care for it. That wasn't all she wanted to be. She was more, wasn't she?

Claire gave Meredith a look that said, *I need a moment alone with him; please help a friend out and develop a sudden fascination with the shrubbery.*

Meredith obliged, and developed a sudden fascination with the shrubbery.

"About last night . . ." Claire began. Thunder rumbled in the distance. She rubbed her temples—so much had happened last night, and so much of it was her fault. It logically followed she must try to fix things, or at least make amends with Fox. Because even though she didn't see a future with him, she did care for him. "I'm confused about my feelings for you. But that is all secondary to the fact that I must remain focused on my family right now. They need me."

"Of course. I understand." His mouth was set in a grim line. Was his male pride affronted? She wondered if perhaps he did care for her, too. Why did that make her heart skip a beat? "But, Claire . . ."

Before Fox could say anything, another gentleman strolled toward them and interrupted. He seemed vaguely familiar, though she couldn't quite place him. Then again, she never did pay much attention to introductions.

"Well, well, well," the stranger said. "Look

who we have here. What a lovely chance encounter."

He glanced from Fox to Claire and back again with a grin that made her feel distinctly unsettled. She was glad when Meredith wandered back over to stand by her side.

"Mowbray," Fox said flatly, by way of greeting. Then he performed the introduction. "Lady Claire, may I present Lord Mowbray."

"I'm a good friend of Fox's," he said, despite what Claire thought was evidence to the contrary. Fox certainly didn't seem pleased to see him. There was another rumble of thunder. "It's a pleasure to make your acquaintance finally. Of course your reputation precedes you."

That caught her attention. "Oh? What do you mean by that?"

"Oh, you know," he said with a laugh. "That you might start a math lecture at any moment or embarrass us with your American manners. That you are, shall we say, an original."

For a moment, Claire was stunned. She knew people thought these things and whispered them behind her back, but no one outright said them to her face.

"Unless Fox here has transformed you and no one has noticed," Mowbray added casually. "But I daresay someone would notice a woman Fox suddenly decides to pay attention to."

Transformed?

Suddenly decides to pay attention to?

Claire slowly turned and lifted her gaze to Fox to see if his expression would reveal the truth about the conclusion her brain—her very smart lady brainbox—was coming to.

"Mowbray, if you don't mind, we were just—" Fox said, trying to get rid of his friend.

"Fine day to be out walking, is it not?" Mowbray mused, not taking the hint that his presence was unwelcomed. "Especially with such a fine dog. Has he told you all about this dog, Lady Claire?"

"Mowbray . . ."

"Yes, he has," Claire replied. "He raised her from a pup and trained her himself. Now she's the best hunting dog in England."

"Now, if you'll excuse us—" Fox cut in.

"I bet he'd hate to lose her," Mowbray said, looking at Fox.

"No one is losing her," Fox replied.

The men stared at each other, some fierce and silent battle of wills taking place. The tension between them was palpable. Something was going on, something she didn't understand, but something about her. She hated not understanding things.

"What is this about?" Claire demanded.

"He hasn't told you?" Mowbray laughed. "Fox, don't tell me you've been leading her on this whole time."

Leading her on?

"Mowbray . . ." The warning in his voice was unmistakable. It was punctuated by another low rumble of thunder.

"Tell me what? What is going on?"

"It was the stupidest thing, Lady Claire," Mowbray said. "Fox here wagered he could make you the darling of the ton in just a fortnight's time."

Mowbray laughed heartily.

Fox closed his eyes, as if pained. As if he just wished she and Mowbray and this conversation would go away. As if it were all true.

And with that, everything clicked into place. She recognized the feeling of everything adding up, an equation working out, a number being divisible evenly—but without any of the satisfaction or sense of accomplishment.

How could she have been so stupid?

Claire took a step back, needing to either sit down or flee entirely. A strange, unpleasant heat was creeping along her skin. It was the burn of humiliation.

She, who prided herself on being so smart, had been completely oblivious to a vast scheme involving herself. Her body. Her heart. That lummox Lord Fox—of all people!—had played her for a fool.

She *knew* they didn't make sense together. She knew it, and carried on anyway, blinded by lust and driven by a hope, deep down, that perhaps she wasn't the odd future spinster the gossips made her out to be. She wanted to be angry at Fox—and she was—but there was no denying that she had ignored the facts and her instincts.

Because of him, she had betrayed herself.

But a wager—that he, Mr. Popular, could transform her, Future Spinster and Social Outcast, into a darling of the ton was certainly reason enough for him to pursue her.

Claire turned to face him, furious.

"Is this true? Am I a bet?"

But she didn't need to ask. Guilt was etched into his features. If she were more charitable, she would say she detected sorrow and regret as well, but she wasn't feeling charitable at the moment.

She felt like a fool. She was a woman who prided herself on logic and intellect and yet allowed herself to get swept away by a charming, muscled man. Like all the other silly females she'd always felt so superior to.

She watched as Fox swallowed hard and finally said, "Yes."

Yes, she was a wager.

Yes, everything between them had been a lie.

"And you were so confident that you could *change me* that you wagered your beloved dog?"

A beloved dog who stood loyally at her master's side, oblivious that her fate hung in the balance. The poor *dog's* future happiness was at stake because of Fox's idiotic choices. Or Claire's wearing of spectacles and propensity to speak of subjects other than the weather.

"Yes." His voice was rough, like he was trying hard to keep the emotions out of his voice.

Like it pained him.

As it should.

What had he been thinking to make such a bet? He probably hadn't been thinking. He probably let his male pride make the decision, rather than reason.

Because reason would have told him he couldn't possibly succeed. Morals might have told him he shouldn't even try.

"That sounds terrible when you say it," Mowbray remarked, shaking his head sorrowfully. "But it seemed like innocent fun at the time . . ."

"Sod off, Mowbray." Fox turned on his so-called friend. Even Mowbray wasn't oblivious to the fury emanating from his rather large and strong friend.

"I didn't mean . . ." he said, hands up and backing away. For once, Mowbray took the hint and removed himself. Not a moment too soon. But the damage had already been done.

"Claire, it was a stupid mistake and I am sorry. More sorry than you can know."

"Because you have lost your dog."

"No, it's not just that—"

"Because you have lost."

"No, that's not what I mean to say—"

"What do you mean to say? What can you possibly say?"

"I made a mistake in making the wager. But we share a connection, Claire. Can we not forget and start over?"

Fox turned to her. Reached out to touch her sleeve. Days ago, moments ago, she might have leaned into the touch. But that was before she knew she was just a game. Or worse: that she discovered she had been infatuated with a man who gambled the things he loved on trying to change another. For fun. For sport.

Her heart, her body, her very essence, wasn't sport.

"No."

Claire turned and walked away. Meredith, bless her, fell in step immediately. But after ten paces—ten furious paces to the ever increasing rumble of thunder—Claire stopped, spun on her heel, and stomped back.

Fox hadn't moved.

She marched right up to him, not caring at all how he was so big or strong or handsome or that people were walking and watching and whispering things like "Who does she think she is anyway?"

"I knew we didn't make sense together."

That was when the heavens opened up and the rain burst forth, soaking them both in a minute.

On the street, as Claire walks away

She *knew* they hadn't made sense together. She *knew* it was odd that a man like him should take a liking to a woman like her. But he had introduced her to Ashbrooke and she enjoyed kissing him, so she ignored that missing variable throwing off the entire equation.

She didn't think.

And that was precisely the thing: usually all she ever did was think. She was very good it, it excited her, and she was fortunately in a family and position where she was at liberty to do so.

But Fox had revealed to her that she was more than just her brain. Her body—living, breathing, pulsing with pleasure—needed attention, too. He showed her what she was missing, and gave her what she needed.

And now he was gone. She had been made a fool. Well, this was the last time that she listened to her body's wanton desires instead of her head.

But there was an acute ache in the region of her heart and it could only mean one thing: she actually cared about Fox. He had tied her up in knots, swept her off her feet, taken over her brain, and wormed his way into her heart.

The truth of this wager clarified so much. What an inconvenient discovery. What a terrible thing to know. She had cared.

She had only been a game.

On the street, after Claire walks away

Fox was left to wrestle with a problem on his own. This was a state of being he usually avoided at all costs. But as he stood in the rain and watched Claire and Miss Green walk away, it was clear to him that this was a disaster of his own making. It was all his fault. And somehow, he had to fix it.

Stella nudged his hand with her nose, reminding him that they were idly standing in the rain on a city street and they were a pair who moved with purpose. They did not stand about, pining after a woman, in the rain.

What next, poetry? Tears?

His Male Pride would have none of that.

His Male Pride had had enough say though, and done enough damage. It had led him to this moment, where Fox loitered in the rain, and faced the stunning realization that the best thing that had ever happened to him was walking away.

Not that Lady Claire was a thing. She was not a toy or a pawn; he saw that now that as she stormed down the street and, unbeknownst to her, dragged his heart behind her.

Yes, his damned heart.

He had feelings after all.

Feelings that were inconvenient and ill-timed and, nevertheless, hammering away in the region of his heart. It pained him that he had hurt her. It pained him that he had lost her. Yet he was aware it might not even compare to the pain and humiliation she must be feeling right now.

Damned Mowbray, who had all but assured Fox lost the wager with that devious reveal. Damned Fox for agreeing in the first place.

Stella nosed at his hand again, reminding him that perhaps they ought to go seek shelter if they weren't going to hunt and kill something. After returning Stella home—while it was still her home—he set off once more. When one was faced with losing a woman and a dog, there was only one thing to do: hit something.

Later that afternoon, Durham House

When Claire and Meredith returned home, Amelia was still missing and there wasn't a clue as to her whereabouts. Shortly thereafter, Darcy escorted Bridget home. They were also soaking wet. There were baths to be had, fresh dresses to be donned, more tea to be drunk, and more and more trips to the window in the vain hope that one would see Amelia traipsing along the street toward the house.

The minutes ticked by, the tension within the family increasing until it seemed like they would all break into a thousand pieces, to be scattered all over England.

"You'd think the Runners would have found

her by now," James grumbled as he stood and strolled over to the window. He was too on edge to sit, so he paced around the drawing room, like a frustrated caged beast, terrifying everyone with his black mood.

"They did say they might have seen her at Vauxhall," Bridget pointed out.

Indeed, an hour ago a Runner had come by with a report that their sister might have been sighted but she had caused a scene and ran away. That *did* sound like her.

"Idiots didn't follow," James grumbled.

Claire watched her poor, tortured brother, and was reminded of all the nights he stayed up with sick horses or set off across the countryside in search of one that had escaped the paddock. He didn't give up on who or what he loved.

"Your Grace, I wonder if you all will be dressing for the ball this evening," Meredith asked.

It had clearly slipped the duchess's mind, which underscored the gravity of this situation. In the weeks that Claire had known her, the duchess never forgot something like a social engagement or what one said a dozen years ago that caused a scandal.

"Oh, that's right . . . Lady Carsington's affair," the duchess said, shaking her head. "She told me in no uncertain terms that she is counting on us to attend, though I don't see how we can, unless Lady Amelia deigns to arrive . . . Right. Now."

There was a moment of tense silence. No one moved. No one breathed. Everyone waited and hoped to hear the sound of the door opening and Amelia's footsteps.

Nothing.

"Very well," the duchess said wearily. "We must attend, though we'll tell everyone that Lady Amelia is ill."

"I'm not going to a damned party while my sister is missing," James said flatly.

Both Claire and Bridget nodded their heads in agreement.

"I cannot pretend to be happy and socialize while she's at large," Claire said. Fortunately, no one pointed out that she was never one to pretend to be happy about socializing. Between Amelia and Fox and his horrid wager, Claire was certain she did not need to go out tonight, or ever again.

"Of course I understand, Duke, but we must keep up appearances," the duchess said, but James spun around, his expression thunderous.

"Don't call me 'Duke,'" he said sharply. "I am a person. *James.* Not a title. I am a person who is terrified for the fate of his beloved sister. If I am going to leave this house, it will be to keep searching for her, not to be the entertainment at some batty old woman's party."

"I am in no mood to go out, either," Claire said. She could not bear to face the ton right now—how many, she wondered, had known about the wager? Would they all be gossiping about her behind their fans or to her face? She wanted to believe that she didn't care what they thought, but that was before a man had hurt and humiliated her.

Claire glanced at Bridget, who paused from writing in her diary to shake her head that no, she didn't wish to go out, either.

"Very well, I shall send our regrets to Lady Carsington," the duchess said. At that, Meredith stood to fetch the duchess's writing things. "But we cannot hide forever. We will have to face society eventually."

Later that afternoon, Horse and Dolphin pub

At this early evening hour, there weren't too many men hanging around at Bill Richardson's place. Most lords had gone home to dress for an evening out or had retired to the club for a late-afternoon drink before the night ahead.

Fox had Richardson to himself. Good. He needed a proper fight. One that would make him forget that he had possibly just lost his beloved dog and a woman for whom he actually possessed feelings.

Real, complicated, messy, loving, lusting feelings.

Fox had adored Arabella—she was beautiful, his social equal, his perfect complement. And that had been that. They seemed to match, like little knickknacks on a shelf.

But he and Claire seemed to fit together like puzzle pieces; strangely shaped, but they clicked together just right to be greater together. Already he felt incomplete without her and regretted the loss deeply.

Such were his thoughts whilst in the ring with Richardson, and they had nothing to do with keeping a close eye on his opponent, anticipating his next move, or planning his own.

This was how people got hurt.

"You're distracted again," Richardson warned, fists raised. "I can see you losing focus."

"I'm not—"

His protest was cut off by Richardson's fist connecting solidly with his jaw. Fox staggered back. He lifted his hand to the sore spot where he'd been hit. He thought of Claire's furious expression.

I knew we didn't make sense together.

"I'm not even sure if you're still in the game," Richardson taunted.

"I'm here," he said through gritted teeth. But again, he thought not of the recent hit to his face, but the stunning pain of Claire discovering that she had been a game to him. Or at least she had started as such—and now?

"Are you?" Richardson taunted him now and really went after him, lunging forward, darting to the left—no, the right!—throwing a swing here, a jab there. Usually, Fox would have loved the surge of adrenaline from this sustained attack, and shut out everything but him and his opponent and this moment.

Today, he couldn't stop thinking of Claire and the mistakes he'd made, and so he took one too many hits. He raised his fists to cover his face and started looking for a way out.

"You know the game isn't over until one of us is knocked down or thrown off our feet," Richardson taunted. "Are you on the ground or off your feet?"

No. Yes.

Fox knew what it felt like to be knocked off his feet before crashing to the ground. It was Arabella jilting him. He had lost his equilibrium, his sense of secure standing in the world. It felt like Claire discovering the wager. He felt like he was falling and could only brace himself for the inevitable crash.

"I'll ask you again," Richardson growled. "Are you on the ground or off your feet?"

He was still on his feet.

The match was still on.

The game was still in play.

There was still time. The wager wasn't technically lost until the evening of the Cavendish party and he had a day or two at least. He had not lost yet.

The realization struck like a fist to the chest. Oh—wait, that was actually Richardson's meaty fist connecting solidly with his solar plexus, blowing the wind right out of him.

He had to play hard until the end.

This realization renewed him. Fox drew himself up to his full height. Richardson smiled, a flash of white teeth, as he realized something had changed in his opponent. Fox darted to the left, threw a punch, missed, but tried again. And again.

The fight, which might have been over in a minute, stretched out now as the two opponents put everything into it.

Because here was the thing: Fox did not lose.

Or did he?

And yet, as they went around and around throwing punches and dodging hits, Fox realized that he did not *want* to win. To win the wager with Mowbray was to lose a lifetime with Lady Claire and that would be the real prize.

Lady Claire, just as she was—with spectacles and speaking words he didn't understand—was lovely. That was the woman he had fallen for and who dragged his heart behind her as she walked away. That was the woman he was endlessly sorry to have hurt when he really wanted to sweep her into his arms and kiss her for hours (and maybe more; very well, definitely more).

But how on earth was he to convince her that he wanted *her*?

Richardson took one last swing, his fist connecting solidly with Fox's face. He had only one thought as he went down: if he really wanted to win, he would have to lose the wager.

Chapter 16

The haute ton is asked to believe that Arabella Vaughn has an aunt in Bath, whom she was visiting, rather than attempting a failed elopement with actor Lucien Kemble.

—Fashionable Intelligence,
The London Weekly

The next day, Durham House

Mercifully, Claire's prayers were answered and deals with God had been accepted. Amelia arrived home late the previous night, intact and looking no worse for wear. But something about her had changed. She was quieter and more withdrawn—or perhaps she was merely exhausted after a day of adventure. Whatever happened, she was *not* telling. It was, the Cavendish siblings agreed, the first time Amelia kept a secret in her life.

"Now that Amelia is home safely—" the duchess began at breakfast the next day.

But all eyes turned to Amelia's empty chair.

"Has someone checked on her this morning?" Claire asked. "I think someone should check on her."

"You already did. As did I," Bridget pointed out.

"Frankly, I have half a mind to station a maid and footman outside her door and window," James added.

"You are the duke," Miss Green pointed out. "There is no stopping you."

James caught the eye of a footman standing by and merely nodded. The footman left immediately.

"How ducal of you, James," Claire said. "Perhaps you're suited for this role after all."

Ducal or not, he scowled mightily at her. For that brief second, everything was back to normal. Just brother and sister, teasing at the breakfast table, never mind runaway siblings and the humiliation of a broken heart.

"As I was saying," the duchess began. "Now that Amelia is returned to us, we must focus on ensuring that word of her adventure doesn't capture the ton's attention. And of course it would behoove us all to ensure we have allies, should there be some whiff of scandal."

She looked up from the newspapers spread out

before her and gave a pointed look to each one of the Cavendishes. It was an argument they'd heard before: if they married well in society, they would have powerful families to help smooth their way toward social acceptance. Her motives were even deeper: if the sisters wed Englishmen, James was more likely to stay and assume the duties of the title, rather than hightail it back to America.

"Duchess, I think this pressure to wed is what sent Amelia running," Claire said. And, she thought, what motivated her to repel suitors with talk of math or to use Fox as a distraction. In her own way, she, too, was running.

"I cannot help the way of the world. I can only try to ensure you all find happiness in it. And I daresay you would all be happier with proper matches than being cast out from society."

The duchess faced three skeptical expressions. The thing was, they knew what it was like outside of society and it was *fine*. They were at liberty to follow their passions and be familiar with each other. There were fewer rules to follow. It was trying to fit into society's strict little boxes that seemed to be the problem.

But telling that to the duchess had thus far proven fruitless.

"Bridget, you have a potential suitor in Rupert."

"I suppose," Bridget said. Then she took a large bite of toast so she wouldn't have to answer further.

"And, Claire, Fox has been pursuing you . . ."

"There will be nothing between Fox and me," she said sharply. Too sharply. It attracted notice—a few raised eyebrows and curious stares. Claire shrugged and sipped her tea.

She was firm in this. Her brain would once again override her heart (or other parts of her that desired more and listened to logic even less). She would not give herself to a man who had made a sport of trying to change her, who dallied with her but didn't want her true self, with her spectacles, passion for numbers, and quirky, scandalous family.

But the duchess's point was not lost on Claire. This quirky, scandalous family was pushing the ton's limits of acceptability. She might not give a fig for herself, but she would not stand in the way of her siblings' future happiness, no matter the cost. If she would not use Fox as a cloak of respectability and a way to deflect scandal, she would have to do something else . . .

Her family's happiness depended on it.

Later that morning, in the drawing room

Thoughts of saving her family from scandal and ensuring their future happiness were on Claire's mind—even whilst entertaining a call from Mr. Williams. They had planned to meet to review her initial draft of the paper. She would have postponed the meeting, but in the madness surrounding Amelia's "adventure" and that wretched business with Fox, she had quite forgotten.

And so, Claire found herself in the drawing room with Mr. Williams, trying to focus.

"Your note on how the machine would work out Bernoulli numbers is fascinating, but I think we should further discuss the table you provided."

"I relied on Ashbrooke's own formula when creating it."

"I might have discovered one or two errors in it that will require correction before we could publish," Williams said. Claire paused for a moment, not accustomed to making errors. But she wasn't surprised—she had been so distracted of late.

"Of course, let us review it."

And so they reviewed it, extensively, going over each line of the table and revising some of the calculations with pencil on paper. Her mind became focused and she got lost in the numbers . . . for a little while. Then she heard Amelia's voice in the hall, and remembered what a precarious position the family was now in. She was reminded of the events of yesterday, particularly the acutely painful revelation that she'd only been a bet, a game, to Fox.

She wanted to hate him completely, but that

logical and reasonable part recognized that if it weren't for his encouragement she wouldn't be working on this paper with Mr. Williams right now.

"Lady Claire?"

Mr. Williams. Yes. He was speaking to her. Asking a question. She had been lost in thought.

"I apologize, Mr. Williams, I have been distracted by family matters."

"Yes, of course," he said consolingly. "I heard your sister was ill. Has she recovered?"

"Yes, she is on the mend."

"Now about this sequence here . . ." Mr. Williams began, and the conversation about the numbers and perfecting the paper continued for another quarter of an hour. Claire managed to push thoughts of Fox and family out of her mind and focus. It was a blessed relief to feel free of all that and concentrate only on numbers that followed clear rules and formulas.

"I think the paper is almost ready for publication," Mr. Williams said, once their work wound down. "There is one other consideration as well. We must determine which name to publish it under."

"I have yet to make a decision whether it shall be under Lady Claire Cavendish, or simply 'C. Cavendish,'" she said.

"You should claim credit for your work," Williams said. "None of this hiding behind an initial."

"I would like to, but I must consider my family," Claire replied, thinking of what the duchess had said, and thinking that she didn't want her siblings to settle in matrimony because their brainy sister shocked the ton by authoring a mathematical paper.

"We have some time before you must decide," Mr. Williams said. "But you deserve credit, Lady Claire."

"Thank you," she said softly. Their eyes met. There was no denying they shared a connection—one that went beyond a shared interest in math, and one that could deepen if given the chance.

"I hope we can celebrate the publication together," he said. "And continue our friendship."

Mr. Williams placed his hand on hers. It was warm and soft, and his touch was pleasant enough, but she didn't feel the same spark and slow burn of desire she'd felt from simply being near Fox, let alone how she burst into flame when he touched her.

This suggested that it wasn't just that her body's desires had been neglected at the expense of her brain, as she'd thought. She had to acknowledge that it wasn't any touch she wanted, but Fox's.

It was plain to Claire that she would have some decisions to make: between her wish for publicity for her ideas and her wish for her family to avoid scandal and to find happiness and between her brain, her body, and her heart. But this was an equation she had no idea how to balance.

Later that afternoon, in the stables

Most of the time, brothers were a bother. They were rude and annoying, masquerading as "protective," and occasionally revolting. But occasionally they could be helpful, such as when one was in need of advice on dealing with males.

Presumably. Claire had never asked James for romantic advice before, not having had any romantic entanglements previously. Even in America, young men were more interested in girls that flirted instead of ones who spent parties doing sums in their head.

She found James in the stables, the first place she looked. Despite the best efforts of the duchess, he still spent as much time as possible escaping the pressures of the dukedom to care for the horses. But since the horses were very well cared for by the grooms and stable hands, Claire suspected James just liked being near them and in an environment that was somewhat familiar to home. No matter whether in England or America, horses smelled like horses and didn't care about one's station in life.

More specifically, she found him in a stall, brushing down a beautiful chestnut mare.

"I need man advice."

"Not you, too," James groaned.

"Who else has been here seeking man advice?" Claire wanted to know.

"The duchess," James said dryly. She huffed and rolled her eyes. "Take a guess, Claire. You are the smart one."

"I know," she said. Except that she had been so very foolish. But now that her wits were no longer addled with lust, she could resume being intelligent. "Part of what makes me smart is that I accept the facts and follow them to their logical conclusion."

"What upsetting conclusion have you come to?"

"I might have fallen for Lord Fox."

This was the most she could admit to herself, *love* being too strong a word. But after a perfectly amiable visit with her previously defined Ideal Man, with everything she'd ever wanted in reach, and complicated feelings for Fox that wouldn't quit, she had to consider that this is what had happened.

James started coughing. Violently.

The horse stomped one foot impatiently.

"The one known mostly for his prowess with sport and less for his wits?"

"Yes. Precisely. That one."

She could scarcely believe it herself. James paused in brushing the horse. "Didn't see that one coming."

"Neither did I." Claire began to pace as much as one could in a stall with a rather large horse and another full-sized person. "But we had struck up a sort of friendship, which turned somewhat intimate."

James's response of *"La la la la"* merited a withering glare.

"I am a very cerebral person," she continued. "But we shared a profound physical connection that showed me what I had been missing by focusing exclusively on intellectual matters."

James closed his eyes now and said, loudly, *"LA LA LA LA LA."*

"Why are you making that noise?"

"Because I don't want to hear about my sister having physical connections, profound or otherwise, with men. For a smart girl, Claire . . ."

"Oh, shush. It turns out he had wagered that he could make me popular." She stopped pacing and starting concentrating on not crying. One tear might have escaped. "His attentions were not real. They didn't mean anything. I was just a game."

"I'll call him out."

"You'll do no such thing. He'll murder you."

"Thank you for the vote of confidence."

"Fox is a gifted man with regards to athletic pursuits, whether it is fencing, boxing, shooting, rowing, wrestling—"

"All right, I get it," James muttered. "You've made your point."

"But his talents are entirely beside the point. I learned about the wager, confronted him, and he just said, 'Yes, it's true, terribly sorry.' He said he was sorry for the whole affair and he should never have engaged in such a scheme. He said we ought to forget the whole thing ever happened. But I cannot. I am hurt and furious and even more furious that I am hurt."

"What does he stand to lose?"

Claire stared at her brother, bewildered. What did that have to do with anything?

"His dog!" And now she wailed. Because a man had wagered an animal over her. This upset her in so many ways—that he played so carelessly with a living creature's existence. And surely she was at least worth an enormous sum of money or a hunting box in Scotland. Not something low stakes like a pet.

"So, probably the thing he cares about most in the world," James said.

She hadn't thought of it like that.

Claire remembered seeing the way he looked at the dog and explained how he'd bred, raised, and trained her himself. She saw the way the dog looked at him, like he was the sun, moon, breakfast, lunch, and dinner, too. In other words, everything.

And it wasn't altogether unlike the way this particular chestnut mare was nuzzling her brother as he fed her sugar cubes likely pilfered from the breakfast table when the duchess wasn't looking.

"Well, he must have been awfully sure of himself," Claire muttered, even more furious that he thought changing her would be *easy*.

"I suppose," James said with a shrug. "But I can assure you he is probably very sorry about the wager, then."

"He's not supposed to be sorry because he'll lose the wager, but because he'll lose me."

"Maybe he is. I'm assuming you stormed off in a dramatic fashion, breaking his heart."

"What makes you think I am the sort of woman who does that?"

"All women are, given the right circumstances. Such as finding out a man they like wagered a dog that they could make her into some stupid, simpering miss."

"I came here for comfort and I am not being comforted."

James heaved a sigh, the sort he did when he felt like he was being plagued by women, particularly his sisters. This was a fairly regular demonstration of exasperation.

"Since it's you, I shall provide some logic. If you like him, and you think that he cares for you, your course of action is simple: be with him."

"Why do men always simplify things?"

"Why do women always complicate things?"

"That was not the advice I came looking for."

"Well, it's the advice I have. Here's a question for you, Claire. Do you think you love him?"

Love? Well, she took a step backward and found herself up against the stable wall. She didn't know about love—she'd never experienced the romantic version herself, and Claire wasn't in the habit of reading poetry and gossiping about boys with other girls, either. She didn't know love from Adam. And yet.

There was something in her—something stubborn and fiery and determined—that wasn't yet done with him. She had not kissed him enough, she supposed. But she also didn't know him as well as she might, and she wanted to. She wanted to see if he was sorrier about losing the bet or losing her.

But there was something else as well.

"My dream man just called. We discussed the various complicated problems of the analytical engine for a quarter of an hour and he praised my brilliant intellect and insightful mind. We are going to publish a paper together. This is everything I've ever dreamt of. And the whole time my thoughts kept straying to Fox. Particularly kissing Fox."

James closed his eyes and covered his ears. "LA LA LA LA LA."

"You are a duke. Surely dukes do not cover their ears and shout nonsense words in the middle of conversations."

"But I am also your brother. And here is my worldly man advice to you: put your brilliant brain to solving the problem of Lord Fox just as you would with any other math problem."

That was hardly advice at all, but it set the machinery of her brain in motion.

"I must find the formula . . ." Claire murmured, after giving her brother a quick thank-you before returning to the house. She must break the problem down into solvable parts. She must solve for *x*.

X being whether Fox was sorry to have lost her because he had fallen for her, or whether he was sorry because he was losing the bet and losing his dog to Mowbray.

A mad—but oddly logical—idea was occurring to her.

If she did become popular, then the wager would be won.

If the wager was won, there would be no reason for Fox to pursue her unless he wanted to. It was the only chance for this possible thing that might be love to develop.

Even if she didn't manage to win the wager for Fox—and make no mistake, this was almost entirely in her hands—it would benefit her family.

Claire was arriving at the logical conclusion

that she would have to do something she never imagined: become one of those girls she always scoffed at. The ones who sat patiently to have their hair styled, who cared about dresses and jewelry, who flirted and talked only of gossip and the weather. It was possibly her only chance at happiness.

* * *

> *Well, here is something this author is shocked to report: Lady Claire Cavendish and Lady Francesca DeVere were seen shopping on Bond Street together.*
>
> —FASHIONABLE INTELLIGENCE,
> *THE LONDON WEEKLY*

Claire went to great lengths to ensure this embarrassing errand went unnoticed and unremarked upon. The last thing she needed was an audience before she was ready.

First, she read the sporting section of the newspaper to learn when there was an event that Fox would more than likely be attending, that is, not at home. It so happened there was a horse race that afternoon.

Next she borrowed a rather large and atrocious bonnet from the duchess, the better to obscure her face.

Miss Green waited in the carriage, on lookout.

The butler, thankfully, was quick to open the door and usher her inside where he took her card, looked at the name, raised his brow, and went to see if Lady Francesca was at home to Lady Claire.

The odds were not high.

The two women hardly cared for each other. Frankly, Claire thought Francesca the sort of poisonous woman who gave other women complexes about themselves. She was certain that Francesca didn't spare the slightest thought for her, and if she did, it was certainly not a favorable one.

But no matter.

Lady Claire had her priorities in order. She had to ensure that wager was won, and if she was to have a prayer of doing so, it would be because Lady Francesca deigned to help her.

The butler showed her to the drawing room.

Lady Francesca appeared curious, in spite of herself.

"I know we don't really care for each other," Claire started as she took a seat.

"Is this really how you are going to begin?" Lady Francesca asked, shocked. "Shall we not sip our tea and converse about mutual acquaintances first?"

"Lady Francesca, we are both intelligent women in a world that wants us to be stupid and silly if we even speak at all. Can we not be honest and direct with each other?"

Lady Francesca gave her a long look as if to

discern that yes, Claire was serious. "All right, then."

"Your brother—" Claire began.

"—is an idiot," Francesca finished.

Unfortunately, Claire could not entirely deny that. "He has also made a wager. With Mowbray." Francesca groaned at the mention of the name. "He wagered that he will turn *me* into the darling of the haute ton by the time of my family's ball, in just two days' time."

"Thus proving the validity of my previous statement," Lady Francesca replied.

"I hope you mean that as a statement upon his foolish wagering and not the impossibility that I should be transformed into a darling of the haute ton in a mere two days' time."

"I already knew about the wager." Francesca dropped that casually into the conversation and followed it up with a sip of tea. Claire was left to contemplate whether she ought to feel embarrassed to know this whole charade had had an audience.

"He's known for foolish choices," Francesca added. Now Claire was left to contemplate whether she was one of those foolish choices.

Yes, Fox was a fool. He didn't always make good choices. But somewhere along the line, Claire had started to see that he was also kind, in possession of his own talents and interests, and not the ignorant lummox she'd initially supposed him to be. And so, she didn't quite care to hear Lady Francesca speak of him thusly.

She wondered, idly, if his sister had always made clear that she was the brains of the family and he wasn't and so he didn't try . . . But that was neither here nor there at this point.

"It so happens that I have developed a certain fondness for him," Claire said softly.

"To each her own, I suppose." Lady Francesca shrugged and managed to do so elegantly. No wonder Bridget was fascinated by her.

"I should like to ensure that he wins," Claire said, returning to the matter at hand and the reason for her visit. "And for that, I shall need your help."

"That's a bit rich. Why should I help you? Your sister is attempting to steal my intended."

"Darcy? Bridget despises him."

"Is that so?" Francesca was clearly skeptical. In fact, Claire now wondered what Bridget was up to and with whom and why this stranger might know her own sister's heart better than Claire did. This only renewed her determination. She *had* to become popular by the time of their party.

"She fancies his brother, if you must know," Claire said. At least, that was the last update she'd heard from Amelia, who regularly read Bridget's diary. Lady Francesca turned away, clearly skeptical.

"I'm still not sure why I should help *you*."

"Think of it more as helping your brother. Your foolish but still somehow lovable brother. And if not him, then that poor dog who will have to go live with a vile rake like Mowbray."

"Oh, dear Lord," Francesca cut in. "I will help you, for the sake of my idiot brother, but only under one condition. No more sentimental nonsense and no one is to know about this."

Claire bit her tongue, knowing better than to point out that was two conditions. With Lady Francesca's assistance, she might have a chance at winning after all.

Chapter 17

The most sought after invitation in town is of course the one to the Duchess of Durham's soiree, to be hosted with the new duke and his sisters. Some are hoping for success, others eagerly await more missteps, and more than a few are curious about Lady Amelia's sudden illness and miraculous recovery.

—Fashionable Intelligence,
The London Weekly

The duchess had determined that a necessary component of the Cavendish siblings' education and entrée into society was hosting a ball. Not just any ball, either, but one that would showcase their wealth, the prestige of the title, their transformation from poor provincial relations from the former colonies to darlings of the English aristocracy.

It was quite a task.

One they were not up for.

Or were they?

The Cavendish sisters spent more time than usual preparing for the evening. First, there were naps and baths before the real preparations began in earnest. Their exceedingly fine gowns had been pressed and draped on the bed, ready to be worn with silk stockings and delicate shoes. Their hair had to be done *just so* in intricate coiffures that necessitated hot irons and ribbons and strands of pearls. The whole process took hours. Hours!

Once ready, Bridget and Amelia entered Claire's bedchamber without bothering to knock. Claire, standing before the mirror, turned at the sound of rustling silk and squabbling sisters.

"How do I look?" Claire asked them.

"See for yourself," Amelia replied, flopping on the bed without a care for her dress and the hours that went into pressing it free of wrinkles. "You are literally standing in front of a mirror."

"If you haven't noticed, I cannot see because I haven't got my spectacles on."

"Then put them on," Amelia said, staring up at the ceiling.

"I cannot," Claire replied. "Or rather, I will not."

"Then how are you going to manage all night?" Bridget asked. As far as Claire could tell, she was looking at herself in the small mirror on

Claire's vanity table. "Oh, I do hope you won't be stumbling around and bumping into people and things. We're supposed to be Elegant Ladies."

"I'm not sure how it'll work, but it must."

Venturing out without her spectacles was the height of idiocy. But she wanted Fox to win the wager and Lady Francesca had told her in no uncertain terms that it was essential to the success of her plan. She wanted to protect her family. She wanted the ton to talk about something other than how scandalous they all were. If she had to remove her glasses, subject herself to fashion and simper all night, then, by God, she would do it.

"Now can you just tell me how I look?"

She couldn't quite see and she really wanted to. Claire turned around to face the direction of her sisters' voices. There were soft coos.

"You look beautiful, Claire."

"And don't take this the wrong way, but you don't look like . . . you," Bridget said.

"Excellent," Claire murmured. That was the whole plan. She wasn't going to look like Claire Cavendish, lady mathematician, but Lady Claire Cavendish, darling of the haute ton.

She was going to win that wager for Fox. She would give him exactly what he thought he wanted. She calculated it was the only way to reveal what his true feelings were, and the best way to test her own.

She turned back to the mirror. Her reflection

was blurry to her eyes, but she knew what was revealed. A pretty young lady in an exceedingly fine gown—selected by Lady Francesca—cut low, to better enhance her breasts, and decorated with tiny sparkling beads that caught the light and presumably would catch gentlemen's eyes.

More importantly, it was worn with confidence.

Francesca had drilled her on the importance of acting as if she were an esteemed duke's sister, and heiress, a sought after woman of brains and beauty. She was *not* to think of herself as a quiet girl from the former colonies and now a social pariah in London society.

Claire's hair had been styled differently than usual. Instead of her simple coiffure, her maid had done an elaborate something on top of her head. There were wispy tendrils that did look pretty, even if they got in her way. Francesca had advised her on this particular style and insisted that she was not allowed to blow stray strands of hair out of her face. She was to smile placidly, even if she was bothered by them.

Claire couldn't see how she looked without her spectacles, but she remembered Fox's reaction when he saw her without them. She had taken his breath away.

How silly that a pair of *glasses* could make such a difference in how the world perceived her. It wasn't, perhaps, that they changed her appearance so dramatically, but that without them she appeared more normal—simple and not complicated.

Tonight, Claire looked like any other pretty girl. She vowed to act like one, too. She would walk with tiny, elegant steps and keep her movements restrained and delicate. She would laugh gently at supposed-to-be-amusing *bon mots*. She would discuss the weather without mentioning the different types of clouds.

To be clear, she was doing this so that she could win Fox's wager for him. She was not doing this to win his affections. He would have to love her as she truly was, or not at all.

That evening, at the ball

The ballroom at Durham House was overflowing with guests. It had been ages since the duchess had entertained, and with the general scandal that had been the entire Cavendish existence in London—the ton turned out, in force.

Lord Fox was among them. He had no illusions about how this evening would proceed—he would lose the wager, Mowbray would win, and Claire would go on to solve real problems in the world with her genius brain when she was free of distractions like him.

He knew he would lose because he had made no overtures to Claire since his deception had been revealed. He had not tried to explain himself, woo her, or beg her forgiveness. Groveling wasn't going to be a sufficient way to prove that he was sorry and that he had changed since the night he made the wager. She had made him a better man.

His plan was to lose, spectacularly, and to sacrifice his beloved dog and his Male Pride. His plan was to subject himself to Mowbray's gloating and glee. His plan was to show Lady Claire, in the only way he knew how, that he did not want her to change, that he loved her, just as she was, spectacles and unfashionable dresses and all.

Losing was a strange feeling for Fox and losing deliberately was almost unfathomable. Thus he was in an unfamiliar and uncomfortable state when Mowbray approached.

"Good evening, friend."

"Mowbray." Fox gave him a curt nod. He wasn't so sure *friend* was the word for them anymore.

"Tell me, how does it feel to lose, Fox?" Mowbray asked. Of course he assumed he won, after that deuced unsporting stunt he pulled by telling Claire about the wager. "I know it's a new feeling for you."

Fox wanted to grab the man by his cravat and throttle him and rage that he didn't even know losing. Mowbray, being a person with misplaced priorities, would think Fox cared about losing this wager. In truth, Fox was discovering—the hard, aching way—that he cared about losing Claire.

Fox also wanted to issue some devastating set-down in reply. But he deserved all the taunting that came his way.

"It was a stupid and unsporting wager, Mowbray, one we should never have agreed to."

Mowbray's reply was lost in a sudden buzz and hum in the ballroom, the collective murmur of hundreds of people witnessing something sensational.

Fox turned and looked, but it took him a moment to register the sight before him. It was Lady Claire, as he had never seen her, never even imagined her. He scarcely recognized her in that fancy, sparkly dress with her hair done differently and her spectacles stashed away somewhere.

This was not the woman he knew.

What had she done?

It took a moment of dreadful confusion, but Fox finally understood.

A grin tugged at his lips; *she had just changed the game.*

Fox straightened, exhaled slowly.

"You tell me, Mowbray. How does it feel to lose?"

He inclined his head in the direction of Lady Claire and the sensation she was causing. People were staring, murmuring, gossiping—but also smiling and welcoming her. Fox watched from a distance as the guests ate it up. Mowbray stared, slack jawed.

That was not the Lady Claire Cavendish they had known and ignored. The woman who had just arrived was a revelation. She was beautiful, yes, and they could see it now that she removed her spectacles and softened her coiffure and simpered.

She moved differently, too. Her steps and gestures were hesitant and delicate, as if she were asking permission for even the slightest movement.

The Claire he had fallen for moved with a purpose, quite at odds with this fragile, oh-do-help sort of way that aroused a man's chivalrous and protective instincts, including his own. It took all his self-control not to lunge through the crowds to clasp her hand and hold her close.

Lady Claire smiled demurely. A smile that conveyed *I am so delighted you are here. I am so anxious to please you. I do hope you like me.*

It was not her usual sphinx-like smile, which suggested *I know things you don't know.*

Fox knew two things: he had won the wager. But he had lost the girl.

Claire couldn't see a damn thing, but she was still painfully aware that everyone was staring at her. She wanted to shout, *It's still me! Was this transformation really so great?*

She was not an unkempt person. She did not wear dowdy clothes or maintain a slovenly appearance. She simply did not usually go the extra mile—an hour spent doing her hair was an hour not spent on more intellectually stimulating pursuits. So she wore whatever dress the maid picked out, she kept her hair simple, she wore her glasses so she could see, and she stormed through life with her priorities in order.

But not tonight.

Tonight, she tried. More than tried. Endured.

She had slipped on her glasses for a peek in the mirror and even then she barely recognized herself.

Hair, done in an elaborate, twisted, curled, towering arrangement. It had taken two maids, hot tongs, papers, ointments, and the direction of Lady Francesca. For extra effect, a strand of diamonds and pearls had been threaded through so every time she moved her head, it sparkled. All this because she was the sister of a wealthy duke, by God, and everyone should know it.

There were audible gasps when people saw her. *Audible* being the key word as she could scarcely see anything. There were vague, blurry shapes of humans in the vicinity. Splotches of color to indicate a dress, dark patches to indicate a gentleman.

Names and faces were beyond her.

Moving had become a high risk endeavor. So she kept her steps delicate, her movements small, and as a result had perhaps finally achieved the ladylike comportment the duchess was always striving for them to acquire. She felt rather like a newborn fawn, learning to use its legs.

Between the reduced vision and the uncomfortable shoes she wore (but they sparkled!), there was no chance of Lady Claire breaking the rules and moving about the ballroom unescorted. The thought of her finding the card room and attempting to play was laughable. She would stand right here, and be seen and not heard, and would be at the conversational mercy of whomever came by.

She wanted to fidget—wring her hands, tap her foot, that sort of thing. She did not fidget. She repeated *epitome of grace* in her head a thousand times instead.

She reminded herself why she had done this.

Because it would set an excellent example for her sisters. With her great adventure, Amelia had demonstrated that she very badly needed a positive role model to emulate. Furthermore, it would give the ton something else to talk about when it came to the Cavendish family. This, then, was her gift to them. She hoped it bought them all time to find their true happiness.

Because she wanted to publish that paper

under her full name and an improved reputation with the ton would lessen the potential scandal.

Because she wanted to know what would happen between her and Fox once the wager was no longer a factor.

And, oh, because that adorable dog should not live with a dissolute rogue like Mowbray.

Reasons. She had them.

Claire sensed a man approaching her—but she instinctively knew it wasn't Fox. This man wasn't as tall, wasn't as wide, and seemed to have a woman on his arm.

"Lady Claire, you look beautiful this evening."

She smiled in recognition. "Ashbrooke, hello. And I presume that is Her Grace?"

"Claire, can you see anything without your glasses?" the duchess, Emma, asked, sounding concerned.

"Not a thing. But don't I look beautiful?"

"You do," Emma agreed hesitantly.

"That is," Ashbrooke cut in, "until you are black and blue in the face after walking into a pillar."

"That is an excellent point, Your Grace. Which is why I plan to stand right in this spot for the duration of the evening. Unless, of course, a gentleman should escort me for a turn about the ballroom."

"Lady Claire, what is this about?" She caught a

vision of Ashbrooke gesturing generally toward her person. "This isn't you."

"A man, of course," Claire said flatly.

"What I presume you cannot see," the duchess explained, "is the look of incomprehension on my husband's face. If I might attempt to describe his expression it might be *but I thought you were smarter than that.*"

Claire gave a little laugh.

"Indeed," Ashbrooke agreed. "But anyway, I was going to tell you when we met next, but I cannot wait—" Here, he launched into a detailed description of a new line of thinking for the analytical engine, which solved a critical problem they'd been grappling with. It made her heart sing to hear about it, to think about it, to be discussing with Ashbrooke, inventor of the difference engine. How far she had come!

"How very impressive, Your Grace," she murmured, even though she wanted to corner him and ask a thousand questions. But tonight, she had to be on her Best and Most Ladylike Behavior and that meant she was not to discuss math. Not even with a duke.

"I'll explain it in more detail when we next meet. And wear your glasses, you don't want to miss anything."

Claire forced a smile to remain on her lips as they walked away even though that one interaction had caused a little crack in her heart. She did not want to pretend to be someone she was not. She did not want to hide her light under a bushel.

But she was determined to see this experiment through to the end. Thus, Claire kept up the charade. She expressed her hope that her guests were enjoying themselves. She laughed politely at terrible jokes. She made excuses for Amelia's "illness" and "recovery." She commented upon the weather. She repeated all of it for what felt like a thousand times.

Though Claire couldn't exactly *see* the reactions, she could hear them and it sounded like murmurs of approval.

Claire had expected Fox to find her, and it felt like an eternity before he finally did. She could tell it was him standing before her, even without her glasses, by the size of a dark splotch in her line of vision, and by the way his mere presence made her heart beat in a ridiculous rhythm.

"What. Is. This." His voice was a low rumble.

"I do not know what you mean," she replied lightly.

"You have bits of sparkly stuff in your hair."

"Those would be diamonds."

"And where are your glasses? Can you even see a damn thing?"

His concern and distinct lack of enthusiasm thrilled her. It probably shouldn't, but it did.

"I cannot, but I have no need to see. A lady is

not to go about the ballroom unaccompanied, so if I move from this spot it will be with an escort, whom I have every faith will not lead me straight into a pillar."

Then Fox did the strangest thing.

He knocked on her head. Rapped his knuckles on her skull, without a care for the intricate styling of her hair that he was disrupting. An hour of her life, for naught.

"Hello, is anyone home in there?"

Claire wanted to laugh and cry in equal measures. He was seeing through this to the real her, seeking her out and saying nothing about the wager. He wasn't happy with this show she was putting on.

Fox took a step closer and clasped her hand.

"May I have the honor of this dance?"

"What does my dance card say?"

"It says Lord Fox for every dance." He didn't even look.

"That cannot be true."

"Well, you can't see to argue with me now, can you?"

And so, they waltzed. It was their first time dancing together. He had been right; dancing with him was like flying or, she could perhaps imagine, making love. Claire was not a good dancer, but he was and he didn't allow either of them to make a misstep.

"Why are you doing this?" Fox asked softly after a moment.

"Doing what?" Claire tried her best to do a simpering laugh.

"Don't. Not with me," he said softly, which didn't make the request any less forceful.

"I am doing this so you can win your wager. I should think that was obvious."

"Ah, you're still a spitfire even when you're all trussed up like a proper young lady."

"It's quite a challenge to truss myself up like this, I'll have you know."

"Well, don't do it on my account. I'm not some pitiful maiden who needs you to come to her defenses."

But . . . he *was* going to lose if she hadn't done this. He was going to give up his dog. He didn't seem like the kind of person who just gave up and lost when things didn't go his way. And it wasn't just done on his account—she needed to do this for her family.

"You were just going to lose?" Claire couldn't keep the incredulity out of her voice.

"Yes. *This* doesn't exactly feel like winning," he murmured.

"What is that supposed to mean?"

"I don't know. But I know what winning feels like—the surge of exhilaration and joy, the feeling of triumph, like all the pain and sweat was worth it—and it doesn't feel like this."

"After all the trouble I've gone to . . ."

"I never asked you to."

"You couldn't possibly like me the way I truly am. The way I was."

The way I still am, deep down.

"What makes you so sure of that?"

"We're just so different, you and I . . ."

She wished she had her spectacles on so she could read his expression.

"Now I may not be terribly smart here, Claire. But I wonder if what you're trying to say is that *you* can't like *me* the way I am."

"I don't know what you mean," she whispered. But she did. Oh, she did. Fox, proving himself to be more astute than she imagined, gave voice to the innermost thoughts she barely acknowledged to herself.

"I don't know a rhombus from a Pythagoras. The only kind of pi I care about is the pie one eats. I need pencil, paper, ten minutes, and a whiskey to perform even the simplest calculation. I'm happiest when I am sweaty, breathing hard, and on the verge of injuring myself in pursuit of athletic glory. You want a man like Benedict Williams to match wits with. But do you think marriage and what happens between a man and a woman is all math problems and intelligent conversations?"

"No." Her voice was just a whisper. He had opened her eyes to that.

"Frankly, I don't know, either, though in this I probably know better than you, Miss Know-it-all."

She deserved that. And she felt her skin warm as she thought of all that he knew about what happens between a man and a woman and how she wanted him to show her. "I haven't been married—I was jilted, as you know. As *everyone knows*. My Male Pride was wounded and now I'm here because of a wager I made when my pride was suffering. Can't say I'm terribly sorry about it, to be honest, because I got to discover you. But do you know the truth, Claire? I don't feel like I have won at all."

"You really know how to make a woman feel terrible."

"I also know how to make a woman feel pleasurable. But only if she says yes."

The following day, at the home of Arabella Vaughn

After their chance encounter at the boxing match, it had become something of a habit for Mowbray to call on Arabella. Mowbray had helped her return to London and her father had reluctantly taken her back into their home while Arabella and her mother plotted her return to society.

It would be no small task—to elope was scandalous enough. To do so with an actor was breathtaking in its madness and nearly impossible to live down. Their only hope was in Arabella reuniting with Fox. If he were to renew their engagement and demonstrate that he had forgiven her, then it was hoped that the rest of the haute ton would follow suit.

But Mowbray wasn't optimistic about the success of this after what he saw at Almack's, to say nothing of what he witnessed at the Cavendish ball.

"He's bloody done it again," Mowbray griped. "He's won."

He leaned against the mantelpiece in the Vaughn drawing room and gritted his teeth. There was no denying that Fox had won the wager—all the London papers were crowing about what a *revelation* Lady Claire Cavendish had been.

He had no idea how Fox had gotten her to agree to such a swift and sudden transformation after Mowbray had deliberately tried to ruin things between them by telling her about the wager.

"I told you he wins at everything," Arabella said from where she lounged and pouted on a settee. Mowbray had filled her in on the wager as a way to explain the items in the gossip columns linking her former intended with the least likely woman imaginable. "So I don't know why you are surprised."

Mowbray wasn't sure how to put into words

for Arabella that it was his turn, his time, to step from behind the shadows and into the light, from second place into first.

"I didn't think he had a prayer of succeeding with her," he said.

"No one did. No one does," Arabella said. "It can't last."

But Mowbray wasn't sure about that. Perhaps she ought to know that her chances of winning with Fox weren't assured, either, also thanks to Lady Claire.

"Did you know I saw them kissing?"

His gaze flitted over to her, now sitting up straighter on the settee. She was paying attention now.

"You did not see fit to mention that," Arabella said icily.

"At Almack's. They had stolen away for a moment."

"He's a tremendous flirt. I'm sure it means nothing."

"But what if it does, Arabella?"

She was silent for a moment and he longed to know the thoughts behind those big blue eyes. His gaze drifted lower, to her mouth, pressed in a firm line of worry over Fox.

Mowbray knew he wanted to kiss her and make her forget about Fox. He wanted her to want him instead. He had a title, a fortune of his own. He could bring her back into the fold of society, could he not? Mowbray's heart was pounding as his brain was whirring . . .

And then, she spoke.

"You just want him to lose at something for once. And I need to win him."

"Yes . . ." Where was she going with this? Her eyes sparkled wickedly and, oh, what a devilish smile on her lips.

"Well, then, I have a plan."

Chapter 18

It is confirmed Miss Arabella Vaughn is still Miss Arabella Vaughn and not Mrs. Lucien Kemble. But this author still has not been able to confirm the existence of her aunt in Bath.

—FASHIONABLE INTELLIGENCE,
THE LONDON WEEKLY

Lord Fox's residence

By all accounts, Fox had won the wager.

Stella was slumbering at her preferred patch of sunlight in his study, blissfully unaware what a cruel fate she had dodged.

Arrangements were being made to transfer Zephyr from Mowbray's stables to his own. Fox didn't particularly want or need the animal, but Mowbray refused Fox's "charity" and "pitiful" offer to let him keep the horse. Fox understood a thing or two about Male Pride, and so he shut up and accepted his prize.

And yet, he didn't feel the thrill of triumph because in winning the wager, he had wrecked Lady Claire. The woman who had confounded him, transfixed him, and seduced him was gone and in her place was just another nice young lady. The papers were all raving about her transformation. They said things like:

> *At the family soiree, Lady Claire Cavendish proved to be a revelation. With her new look and elegant manners, she's a rival to any young English Lady. This author does wonder what inspired the dramatic transformation. Could it be a man? Or perhaps it has something to do with her sister's sudden illness and even more sudden recovery.*
>
> —FASHIONABLE INTELLIGENCE,
> *THE LONDON WEEKLY*

They did not mention her intelligence, or her work with Ashbrooke and the Royal Society, or any of the unconventional and interesting things about her. They did not know about her quick retorts, the wicked way she kissed a man, that she was the one woman to bring him low, and that his heart ached for how she had changed and what he was missing. She was now just another lovely English lady, as if they needed any more of those.

One of those English ladies interrupted him. Lady Francesca strolled into his study, unannounced and uninvited.

"Why are you brooding? You won the wager. You have your dog, and a new horse, and presumably your Male Pride is soothed."

Yes, but he didn't have the girl. But that was not something one said aloud to one's decidedly unromantic sister. Instead, Fox said gruffly, "I'm not brooding."

Francesca scoffed. Dusk was falling and he was sitting alone in dwindling light with a glass of brandy. She pressed on, not even dignifying that with a response.

"Are you not happy with my work? I have performed a miracle. In fact, some of the papers are calling it a miracle. All for you, dear brother."

"I only asked you for advice."

"Yes, and so did she." That caught his attention.

"She enlisted your help?"

"You don't think she suddenly knew what to wear and how to style her hair, do you?"

He hadn't thought about it. Fox had only noticed that the authentic, original girl he'd fallen for was gone, replaced by some generic version. It was one thing for Claire to take on the transformation, another to enlist the help of Francesca. It had to mean something, that.

But his mind kept returning to one truth: "We have wrecked her."

"I thought you wanted her to be popular. I have helped you make her popular. You're welcome." Francesca finished this with a pout.

"She transformed herself—"

"—with my assistance."

"In spite of me. Or to spite me. Either way, it's not good."

"I see what has happened." She nodded sagely. "You have fallen in love with her, spectacles and all. Now you want her back, just as she was before your silly wager. But only after weeks of insinuating she was too odd and unfashionable."

"Yes. Is that too much to ask?"

"I have no idea," Francesca said with a shrug. "But I do know that you have quite a bit of wooing ahead of you if you are to try."

Of course he had to try—and not because of his Male Pride or some bloodthirsty need to win—but because he put two and two together and figured that he needed her in his life, the real her, to be happy. And he thought maybe she might feel the same way.

Calling hours, at Durham House

Wooing was not something Fox had ever had to put much effort into and he hadn't wooed in some time—not since Arabella, ages ago, and she hardly made it difficult for him since they both seemed to recognize that they ought to be together for practical reasons, such as their looks complementing each other.

But wooing Lady Claire was different.

Wooing her after everything they'd gone through thus far would require dedication, careful planning, and flawless execution. Experts were consulted. His valet advised on what a contrite gentleman should wear when courting (*not* the purple waistcoat). Francesca told him in no uncertain terms that he should arrive with a massive bouquet of flowers.

Expensive, fragrant hothouse blooms were procured.

"Dear brother, are you nervous?" Francesca said with a laugh as she saw him in the foyer on his way to calling hours.

"Why can't you say something supportive like 'Just be yourself and she will return your affections'?"

Francesca made A Face.

"All right, now I am nervous," he muttered before stepping out of the house and toward his awaiting carriage.

Wooing was a sport he was unpracticed in, with a woman who defied everything he thought he knew about women. Yes, he was nervous in anticipation not of a game or a battle, but of laying his heart bare.

* * *

In the drawing room at Durham House, the duchess sat on a grand chair, like a throne, overseeing all, particularly three Cavendish sisters seated in a row on a settee. Lady Bridget was eyeing the biscuits longingly, Lady Amelia looked like she wanted to launch sugar cubes with a spoon to the far side of the room or in the faces of these suitors, and Lady Claire had a placid, vapid smile pasted on her face.

Ah, so Lady Claire was still carrying on with her Perfect Lady and Society Darling routine.

And the men—the drawing room seemed to be swarming with them—were eating it up. There was an assorted lot of second sons and fortune hunters in the room, and many were directing their addresses to Lady Claire, who seemed to be encouraging them with pretty smiles and a tittering laugh.

Bloody hell, he had created a monster. Seeing her thusly renewed his determination to love her so much she felt she could be the Claire he met who talked about math to deliberately get rid of fools like these.

"Lady Claire, how good to see you." He bowed.

"Good afternoon, Lord Fox."

She smiled and batted her eyelashes. Which were not magnified behind a pair of spectacles. He fought a scowl.

"These are for you," he said, handing her the flowers. He was pleased to note they dwarfed every other bouquet in the room and pleased that they were probably large enough for her to see without her glasses.

"Why, thank you. They are beautiful."

She handed them to a maid and returned her attentions to her callers, who were all chattering away about some new theater production or other. Fox, not often having the attention span to sit through the theater, had nothing to add.

So he changed the subject.

"Lady Claire, how fare your studies?"

For a second her eyes lit up, and a second later that spark was gone.

"I'm sure no one here wishes to hear about the simple studies of a young lady," she said with a little laugh.

Fox caught Lady Amelia rolling her eyes and frankly wished to do the same. He raised his brow at her, as if to ask, *What has gotten into your sister?* She shrugged her shoulders in response.

Bridget gave up her internal battle and popped a biscuit in her mouth.

"When I saw Ashbrooke, he told me you were collaborating on a paper."

"You heard the lady, Fox," some young buck drawled. "No one is here to talk about dry, boring stuff such as that."

"We're here to discuss light things," Claire replied. "Did you know Eversleigh has a horse racing at the big event in three days' time?"

Fox didn't know or care who Eversleigh was, but he was suddenly immensely competitive with him.

"Best of luck to you. My new mount, Zephyr, will be running as well."

"That's the one from Mowbray, isn't it?" This, presumably from Eversleigh. "How'd you get him to part with her?"

Claire's expression darkened, because in spite of her stupid act, she probably correctly surmised how exactly Fox came into possession of the horse. Fox decided a change of subject and scenery was the best course of action. Perhaps if he could get her alone, they could have a proper and honest conversation.

"Lady Claire, would you care for a turn about the garden?"

"I would love a turn about the garden," Lady Amelia quickly replied.

"He's not asking you," the duchess retorted. "Lady Claire, it would be rude to refuse his kind offer. Do stay in view of the windows though."

Claire smiled tightly, politely, and said, "I would love a turn about the garden, Lord Fox."

In truth, she would love a turn about the garden. Keeping up the ruse of a Perfect Lady was exhausting, especially in the company of such superficial gentlemen as the ones packed into the drawing room. At one point she would have lumped Fox in with them, but now she knew better.

He might make foolish wagers, but he was kind. He had passion, talent, and dedication for the things that interested him. He wasn't just some idle lord.

They linked arms and he escorted her toward the doors to the garden, where they would have the privacy to speak freely, though she still felt the need to keep up this act. She had her reasons, and they didn't entirely involve testing Fox.

"Careful now," he said as they walked through the French doors to the garden. "I wouldn't want you to walk into anything."

"But I thought you liked me without my glasses."

"I do. I just don't want anyone else to see you thusly. But I also like you with your glasses. You are beautiful to me, Claire."

Ba-bump went her heart. This is what she had wanted to hear from him, now that he hadn't any excuse to say it other than it being his true feeling.

But she heard him earlier—he had Mowbray's horse (he had wagered a horse for her!) and presumably had then kept his dog (he had wagered a dog over her!). The reminder of this lessened any inclination she had to make this easy on him.

So she cooed like a silly female and said, "Oh, Fox."

It came out sounding like a missish swoony sigh.

"Claire, what the devil are you doing?"

"I am being perfect and popular," she replied, forcing a lilting laugh. "I thought this is what you wanted, so I cannot imagine that you'll have a problem with it now."

"I do have a problem with it now. As I did the other night. And as I will do if you continue."

"And yet you accepted Mowbray's horse."

He turned to face her. Those green eyes of his darkened as they gazed deeply into hers.

"I was prepared to lose. I wanted to lose, if it meant you stayed *you*."

Her heart skipped a beat or two. That was something else she had wanted to hear. But this from a man who prided himself on always winning? She couldn't quite bring herself to believe it so easily.

"So says Mr. I Win at Sports and Women All the Time."

He paused. And in that silence, her heart skipped another beat. Because he was so serious in the way he looked at her, like she meant something—no, everything.

"You changed me, Claire."

"You changed me, too."

There was the obvious change in her appearance and her feigned Perfect Lady demeanor—but that was all just an act.

And in publicly disavowing one of her passions for the sake of this ruse, she was confirming that her studies were essential to her happiness. She would not give up her work.

His kiss had woken her up to the truth that there was more to her than her brain . . . she possessed a body with desire and capable of giving her pleasure. He helped her realize that she needn't choose between her head and her body and that passion was passion and should be celebrated.

She would refuse to compromise, to live with only one or the other.

"I am sorry, Claire, if I have turned you into this—" He waved his arm in the general direction of her frilly pretend self.

"Are you?"

Her heart was beating hard, slow and steady. Her nerves were sparking to attention because Fox had that effect on her, especially when he was looking at her like that—green eyes glimmering, a gaze full of love.

"I am sorry. I am not as smart as you, Claire. I do not think things through with logic and reason. I am driven by my Male Pride and a competitive spirit. Occasionally, it leads me into trouble, but that's passion for you. But sometimes, it leads me to you. I cannot entirely regret it."

This was the moment where she wanted to launch herself into his arms and kiss him senseless. Her every nerve, every beat of her heart, was crying out to connect with him, body and mind and soul. She might have done, were it not for the very good reasons she had to keep up this Perfect Lady routine.

Later that night, Durham House

The hour was late, but Claire was still awake and working on the final edits for her paper on the analytical engine. On her desk, beside the candelabra, was a stunning bouquet of hothouse blooms.

By day, she kept up the ruse of Perfect Lady—stumbling around as elegantly as possible without her spectacles and having conversations about not much at all. There was a lot of smiling and some simpering.

But at unfashionable hours—before noon, mainly, or late at night—she would meet with Mr. Williams, and occasionally Ashbrooke, to continue progress on their paper. She had reworked the table with the Bernoulli numbers until it was perfect; Mr. Williams had inked over her pencil marks and Ashbrooke had reviewed it once more before approving it. She just had a few more notes to write and then the paper would be off to the printer.

With her name on it as the author.

And *that* was the other reason she kept up this Perfect Lady nonsense. Yes, she wanted to test Fox's feelings for her when only his heart and happiness were on the line, and after calling hours she was on her way to trusting him with her own heart.

But she also wanted to ensure a positive reception in society for herself and her sisters when the paper was published, crediting herself as the primary author.

It might be scandalous, but a good reputation would help with that.

Being well behaved might be a way for her to find her own happiness without wrecking her siblings' chances.

The hour was late, and Claire set down her pencil and paused to inhale the lovely, fragrant flowers. Fox had said all the right things today, but she knew the true test would be how he would react when she put her spectacles back on and published this paper for all the world to see the thought and work of Lady Claire Cavendish.

Two weeks later, the basement of Durham House

Fox had continued to court her with flowers, and walks in the park, and waltzes in ballrooms. Claire kept up her ruse, finding it harder and harder to be anything but herself. But there was so much on the line, like the future happiness of herself and her siblings, and so she simpered.

And just like that, everything had changed. Lord Darcy proposed to Bridget (again) and this time she accepted (hurrah!). Not only was her future secured, but thanks to her impending marriage to one of the most respected men of the haute ton, the family now had connections that could see them through possible scandals.

Scandals that, say, involved Lady Amelia. She recently accepted the proposal of one Mr. Alistair Finlay-Jones, who clearly adored the wild and impulsive Amelia. It was something to take note of. Amelia hadn't had to shrink herself to fit into a little box labeled Perfect Lady in order to find love.

Now with both her and Bridget's futures secured, Claire could breathe a sigh of relief. And put her spectacles back on.

She could also raise a glass, having something of her own to celebrate. It might be a scandal. But it was definitely something she was proud of—her paper had been published, with her name on it. Mr. Williams had sent a copy over that evening.

It necessitated a meeting of the Cavendish siblings in the kitchen, at midnight, with cake and champagne.

"To Claire, for finding a willing audience for all her brilliant thoughts about math," James said, lifting his glass in tribute to her.

"To Claire, for publishing your paper for all the world to read, including Amelia, who now has something to read other than my diary," Bridget added.

"To Claire, for setting a wonderful example for her younger sisters and showing that certain rules should be broken," Amelia added.

"Thank you all for your support and encouragement. It means the world to me." With tears of happiness in her eyes, Claire raised her glass. The four siblings toasted to her accomplishment.

The moment was perfect except for one thing—she wished Fox were here to share it.

Chapter 19

Miss Arabella Vaughn was spotted shopping on Bond Street. She was overheard declaring a need to find something fabulous to wear to Lady Westbury's ball. This author is quite keen to see what sort of reception she'll receive—if any—upon her return to society after a scandalous failed elopement with an actor.

—FASHIONABLE INTELLIGENCE,
THE LONDON WEEKLY

Lady Westbury's ball

Tonight Lady Claire was nervous. For the first time, she would be entering a fabulous and fierce London ballroom with an open heart and a wish for love. It was easier and far less terrifying when she didn't care at all what anyone thought; when she could stand off on the sidelines and practice sums in her head or get a spot of amusement out of lecturing dissipated young lords; when she could push them all away before they could push her out.

The comments she overheard as she milled about in the crowds didn't help, either.

"She's wearing her spectacles again," some nameless, faceless girl remarked loud enough for Claire to hear.

"I wonder if it's because she knows there's no point in trying to win Lord Fox anymore."

Why was there no point? Claire developed a sudden fascination with a potted palm and lingered to eavesdrop.

"Now that Arabella Vaughn has returned. She is here tonight."

What? When? Why?

"Do you think he'll take her back?"

No. But wait, maybe? Why had Claire waited so long?

"How can he not? They are so perfect together. Did you see the dress she's wearing? It's the first stare of fashion."

Claire couldn't care less about seeing a dress; she had come tonight with an idea of seeing Fox. Seeing what it was like to let herself feel for him, love him, perhaps even say the words.

Seeing because she was wearing her spectacles again. She had made her point with the wager, had ensured her sisters' futures were secured, published her paper, and it was now time for her to see to her own future happiness. Starting tonight. If she wasn't too late.

And if Lord Mowbray didn't delay her even more.

"Lady Claire, good evening." Mowbray stepped in front of her, bowed politely, and tried to kiss her hand.

"Mowbray, good evening."

"Lady Claire, I was hoping to have a chance to speak with you tonight. I do feel I owe you an apology." This was unexpected, and thus intriguing. Also, true. "Perhaps we might step out on the terrace?"

"I'd rather not."

"Perhaps you might favor me with a dance?"

Claire prepared to decline—she hadn't had a chance to fill in her dance card with fake names, for precisely a moment like this—when the duchess interrupted them.

"Ah, Claire, there you are! Good evening, Mowbray."

"Your Grace, it is wonderful to see you. I was just asking Lady Claire if she might do me the honor of a dance."

"Of course she will."

And that was how Lady Claire found herself stuck in a quadrille with Mowbray. It went without saying that this was not how she'd hoped to spend the evening—avoiding Mowbray's smarmy smile, trying to remember all the steps to some English dance requiring many steps and turns and this and that, all in formation.

And it was while she was stuck dancing she became aware of a murmur in the ballroom. Claire looked, and saw Arabella Vaughn. And she overheard more comments.

"She's so beautiful."

"A vision."

"An angel."

"A *fallen* angel," someone said cuttingly.

Or a woman's worst nightmare, Claire thought. Because Arabella Vaughn wasn't just a vision of beauty by any measure and undeniably gorgeous, she was here in the ballroom, having returned to society and, one assumed, planning to regain her former glory. Including Lord Fox.

Claire saw him, too, turning to leave the ballroom.

She watched Arabella thread her way through the crowds, heading in the same direction.

Out of the ballroom, away from prying eyes, together, alone, and perfect . . .

Mowbray's grip on her hand tightened. He gave her an icy smile. Her instincts screamed at her to flee. Her brain reminded her that she was in the middle of dance, in full view of the ton, and that to storm off now would cause an excess of talk that might undo all her hard work of the past fortnight.

"You don't want to keep true love apart, do

you?" Mowbray murmured in a way designed to intimidate her into meekly accepting the situation. "You don't want to cause a scene, do you?"

She didn't *want* to. But she would. Because it was high time that she listened to her heart.

"Mowbray, you've meddled enough. You simply must find something else to do with your time," Claire said. "If you'll excuse me, I have something better to do with mine."

Tonight Lord Fox was nervous. He, a grown man of three and thirty, was actually nervous for a ball after having attended thousands (it was probably thousands). But to be fair, he was in love.

And he was a bundle of pent-up desire and frustration that no amount of boxing, fencing, or riding could diminish. Fox wanted Claire, needed to feel her, lose himself with her, bring them both to great heights of pleasure. It was all he could think about.

Something had to be done.

Sweeping her off her feet, to start. He'd been wooing her for the past fortnight and tonight he had some notion of stealing away with Lady Claire and saying something devastatingly romantic that made her fall for him the way he'd fallen for her—to his surprise, in spite of his preconceived notions, and irrevocably.

But that all went to hell before the evening had scarcely begun.

Mowbray had asked to meet him for a quick word—so Fox lingered at the appointed time and place, a corridor just off the foyer, anxious to conclude this portion of the evening so he might find Claire.

His heart leapt at the sound of a woman's footsteps approaching. He turned and—

Her. It was Arabella Vaughn. In all her honey-haired, long-legged glory.

Her. His former intended and the woman who once upon a time set his heart aflame, but no longer.

She strolled toward him, the silk of her skirts swirling around her long legs. Her long slender arms outstretched for him.

"Hello, Fox." She murmured his name with her plump red lips. He bowed in greeting and she dipped into a slight curtsy, lingering on the drop so that he might have a moment to gaze down her bodice. He recognized her old tricks—and that's what they were, tricks.

"Arabella. You're . . . here."

When she'd eloped, he assumed he would never see her again, and certainly not in polite society. His mind had been so wrapped up in Claire he'd never imagined this moment might occur. This was an encounter he had not prepared for.

Feeling vaguely stunned, he didn't protest when she linked arms with his, and after determining that no one was paying attention to them, she guided them farther into a darkened corridor off the main foyer.

"I've missed you, Fox." His eyes had barely adjusted to the dim light. But he thought he saw her pout.

"I thought you were married."

"Haven't you read the gossip columns? I have not wed." She leaned in close and murmured into his ear. "I made a silly mistake. But now I see that we belong together."

Fox had a sudden recollection of Lady Claire in the rain defiantly declaring, *I knew we didn't make sense together.* He didn't know why this memory surfaced now, or what to make of it.

He closed his eyes and tried to think—and tried to shut out Arabella's flowery perfume and the heat of her body near his.

"You're not going to snub me now, too, are you?" She pouted. Then she leaned in closer. He felt her breasts brush against his sleeve. "Not after all we've been through together, Fox. Remember that rainy afternoon in Norwood Park?"

She was trying to seduce him with her nearness, her perfume, the promise of her lips, and the memory of what was once.

"Arabella—" He did not mean to snub her, but

he didn't mean to shag her in a corridor at a ball, either.

"I thought I could always count on you, Fox. You promised that once."

This was true. He had promised that once. And she had promised to be true to him. But those promises had been broken. He wasn't sorry. Suddenly she was too close and her perfume was too strong.

"That was before you jilted me to elope with an actor." He removed her arms from his person—she had somehow wrapped herself around him, like a vine—and stepped to the side.

"We all make mistakes. What about forgiveness?"

"I have forgiven you." Fox said this automatically because it was the polite thing to say.

But the moment he said the words was the moment he realized the truth. She had hurt him and made him question everything, sent his Male Pride into a downward spiral, but he didn't hold it against her. If anything, he was grateful because if she hadn't left him, he never would have discovered Claire. And she . . . she was a woman who pleased and confounded him, challenged and enchanted him. She was the one he wanted.

"I have forgiven you, Arabella, but I have also realized that we do not suit after all."

Arabella scoffed. "Of course we do. Are we

not well matched in temperament? Do we not enjoy the same things? Waltzing at balls, spending the day at the races, long rides at Norwood Park, parties with all of our friends."

Damn, they did enjoy all the same things. Even more confusing, Fox didn't know if Claire enjoyed those things as well. Or if it even mattered.

"Not to mention the things a lady wouldn't mention . . ." she continued. "We make a striking couple, the perfect couple. Everyone says so."

That memory surfaced again, of Lady Claire in the rain. *I knew we didn't make sense together.* Maybe they did not make sense together, but he knew they fit together and complemented each other. He knew this deep down, even if no one would say they were the perfect couple.

The thing was, Fox no longer cared what anyone else said.

"Arabella, no."

He tried to remove her arms from around his neck.

"This isn't about that American, is it? The one you've been squiring around for that wager?"

"Her name is Lady Claire Cavendish. She's quite lovely when you get to know her."

"Get to know her? Oh, please. You won the wager, what else is there to do with her?"

Everything. Marry her. Love her forever and ever.

He conveyed all that with a sharp look; he

would not have anyone casting aspersions on the woman he loved and his future bride.

"Oh. You must be joking."

He was the opposite of joking. This, too, was conveyed with another pointed look.

"You're *not* joking."

"Arabella, this isn't something that we need to discuss."

But it was as if he hadn't spoken at all. She gave him a coy smile and draped her arms around his shoulders again.

"Then I'll just have to change your mind."

And then she leaned in and tilted her head up to his. He saw those plump lips of hers coming closer, closer, closer to his for a kiss that would wreck him and not in a good way.

Fox turned his head.

Arabella's mouth crashed into his cheek.

And he saw Claire.

Beautiful Claire with her spectacles on, taking in every last detail of his inadvertent treachery. Her spine was straight, but her hands were anxiously clasping the fabric of her skirts. She was bothered. Very bothered.

"I thought you were smarter than this, Fox. To fall for what is so obviously a trap. Unless you wanted to?"

"Claire. It's not what it looks like—"

He started to protest as he tried to disentangle himself from Arabella's grasp. Goddamn, the woman was worse than ivy and seemed to have as many arms and legs as an octopus, all of them wrapped around him and ruining everything.

"But it is," Arabella cut in. "You had your fun with him. Or he's had his fun with you. Not that you seem very fun, from what I've heard. But now that's over and I'm just reminding him of how good we were together." She turned to him and gazed into his eyes. "And how good we can be again."

"But you jilted him," Claire pointed out logically. Always Claire, with the logic. And morals. That was his girl.

"Can't a woman change her mind? Besides, but I'm not dead. If you understand my meaning," Arabella said with another coy look and very unnecessary wink.

"I *am* known for my powers of comprehension. If you'll excuse me."

With that, Claire turned with a swish of her skirts and stalked off, dragging his heart behind her. Not unlike that day in the rain . . .

"Claire—" Fox called out after her, but he didn't want to shout and draw attention to himself, with Arabella once again tangled around him, and Lady Claire, who cared for her reputation. This was not a scene that the ton needed to feast upon.

"Fox . . ." Arabella pouted.

"Get *off* me, woman."

Arabella looked stunned at the sharpness in his voice. But she finally relented.

"Fox, darling, this is madness."

"I'm not your darling."

"Fine. But *you* can't possibly be chasing after *her*."

There was no mistaking the derision and disbelief in her voice. It was that attitude and expectation of who belonged with whom, based upon such superficial qualities like looks or popularity, that had nearly kept him and Claire apart.

The difference between Claire, who once shared that sentiment, and Arabella, is that Claire opened her heart and mind. He knew Arabella never would.

This was no longer his problem. His heart felt lighter at the thought.

"Yes, Arabella, I am chasing after Lady Claire Cavendish and I don't care who knows it."

Chapter 20

Fox called out after her. "Claire, it's not what you think."

Claire raced down the darkened corridor.

Fox rushed after her, leaving Arabella behind forever. She called out after him but he let her voice echo in the hall as he rushed away from her toward the woman he really wanted.

It didn't take long for his long strides to catch up with Claire's brisk little steps.

Fox reached and clasped her wrist, hoping to stop her from running away. She spun around and glared up at him with such a vulnerable but furious expression that, if it didn't break his heart, certainly hammered a few cracks into it.

"Claire, I can explain," he said, using his most rational, logical, let's-be-calm voice. He had learned it from her. "She came after me. I did not pursue her."

"How wonderful for you to always have women throwing themselves at you. Always. Forever. I would not wish to live in fear of finding my husband in darkened corridors with other women."

"Not always. Not forever. Not anymore. Not now that I have you."

Fox pulled her close. There were mere inches between their bodies—he would swear he could feel the heat of her hurt and anger radiating off her—but it felt like oceans separated them.

They'd been so close. Happiness had almost been in reach. But he saw now that he'd been set up: he'd fallen for Mowbray's plan to meet, Arabella's seductive scheme to get him back. He saw now that he was lucky to be free of the woman he'd one called his betrothed and the man he once called a friend.

They were a small price to pay for a future with Lady Claire. If she would have him.

"You don't *have* me," she said coldly.

"Please, Claire."

She placed her hands on his chest. Could she feel the pounding of his heart? Could she feel his lungs constricting and refusing to work? Could she feel the tension in his chest as every muscle was coiled, taut, tense, waiting for her judgment?

* * *

Claire pushed him away and walked briskly down the corridor, needing to get away. Her heart had been so full and her hopes had been so high.

She was so mad that Fox had fallen for what was clearly a trap set by a pretty girl, with long legs and honey blond hair and a mouth that promised all kinds of wickedness.

And she was so mad at herself because actually seeing the infamous Arabella Vaughn in the flesh, all tangled up with Fox, made Claire feel so provincial and inconsequential, so odd.

She'd worn her glasses tonight. Her badge of intelligence and honor, now that she was no longer trying to hide herself or change herself to win a wager or a man. She hoped he wanted her—brainy, not-quite-a-seductress, but loving—her.

She thought he might.

But just when she thought she knew him—really knew him, the contents of his character, the goodness of his heart—she was confronted by that awful sight of Perfect Lord Fox with Perfect Arabella being Perfect together.

Well, it was perfectly awful and humiliating and she just wanted to get away from all of it.

But Fox was hot on her heels.

"Claire, wait . . . Please."

It was the *please* that gave her pause. She turned to face him.

"I know what I saw," she said stubbornly, jutting her chin out. "I saw you and her, the perfect couple, all tangled up."

"You're wrong," he said flatly, and she laughed.

"In case you haven't noticed, I'm wearing my glasses tonight. I know what I saw."

He took a step toward her.

She took a step back.

"I know you think you know everything, Claire. But in this, you don't."

"Oh?"

"Oh." He took another step toward her. Claire took another step away and found her back up against the wall. Fox loomed large before her. Her heart started to pound.

"What you saw was Arabella toying with me, trying to get what she can't have." He spoke softly, but surely. "What she'll never have. Because I want another woman. You, Claire. You're the only one I want. I'm sick of all this talk of matching and perfect couples and what society says. None of it matters. The only thing I care about is you and the connection we have together."

Fox took another step closer and she had nowhere to go. She was acutely aware of a mere inch or two of space between their bodies and that her traitorous body ached to close the distance.

"You're the one for me," he whispered. Fox placed a palm on either side of her head and leaned forward. "I don't care what anyone says. Except for you."

God, she wanted to feel his weight on her, his mouth on hers, but he kept that distance between them. Then he started speaking, murmuring low in her ear, words for only her to hear . . .

"I was devastated when Arabella left me, but now I'm so glad. I thought nothing of making that stupid wager, but I see now it was the smartest thing I've ever done. Tonight was a test and I know in my heart that I passed because she was offering me anything and I only want you. I want to be with you, Claire. Tonight. Tomorrow. Forever."

Her knees were weak.

Her heart was pounding.

It was then that he kissed her. A slow, tantalizing promise of pleasure forever and ever if she would just say yes. If she would just open to him, trust him, give herself to him, open her heart and kiss him back.

"You can't just kiss me and . . ."

Whatever Claire was about to say would have to wait—there were voices farther down the darkened corridor. Fox was not going to secure her hand in marriage by something as low and devious as allowing them to be caught in a compromising position. He tugged her through the nearest open door, into some dimly lit parlor that was empty, thank God.

Then he shut the door.

And locked it.

"Apologies for the interruption. You were saying, 'I can't just kiss you and . . .'"

"You can't just kiss me and make everything fine."

"Is that a dare?"

She inclined her head.

"Why is everything always a game with you?"

"That is just the way I am. Just know that in this game, though, I'm playing for keeps. I may have won the wager—all thanks to you—but I didn't win your heart."

Claire reached for the door and glanced over her shoulder. "You want my heart?"

"Yes. I want your love and your smiles and your exasperated sighs because you're smarter than me, and your sighs of pleasure that only I can give you because I am beginning to know you and I am dedicated to learning what makes your heart beat fast, what takes your breath away, and what makes you cry out in pleasure."

Claire turned, her back to the door.

She didn't say anything.

The silence was deafening.

His heart was pounding so hard he thought it'd burst right out of his chest.

Finally, she smiled. A coy, dangerous smile. "Well, then, show me."

He closed the distance between them in a few

brisk strides and pulled her into his arms. His mouth crashed down on hers. He kissed with everything he had—with his love for her, with his fear of losing her, with his desire to kiss her everywhere, every morning, noon, and night for the rest of their lives.

And then, by some miracle, she kissed him back.

"Oh, you . . ." she whispered. "You . . ."

"Yes . . ."

She reached for his shirt, grabbing fistfuls of fabric and pulling it apart, and ripping the fabric.

He grinned.

"I want to see you. Feel you."

Her little palms splayed against the bare skin of his chest, roaming, caressing, possessing.

"I'm yours," he whispered. "All yours. Now. Forever."

Her reply was a kiss. With her kiss, she told him *yes*. She opened to him and their tongues tangled, a delicate give and take and taste. He nibbled her lower lip. She threaded her fingers through his hair, bringing him closer to her.

He pressed against her, feeling the soft vee of her thighs against the hardness of his cock.

This kiss didn't end. Fox traced hot kisses along her neck, and she moaned softly. He skimmed down the sleeves of her silk dress, pushing the fabric aside. He lavished attention on her breasts, taking the dusky pink centers into his mouth, teasing gently until she couldn't contain her own soft moans.

Claire slid her fingers along the waistband of his breeches. He was already hard but somehow became harder still.

"I want you. I need you."

This time it was her turn to whisper, "Yes . . ."

And then, because he knew she loved his strength and muscles and because their future happiness was on the line, he lifted her up like she weighed nothing. She wrapped her arms around his neck and her legs around his back and held on to him.

Never let me go.

Faintly in the distance, there was the sound of the orchestra playing and hundreds of people enjoying the party. Here, though, there was nothing but the sound of their frantic breaths, and the rustling of fabric as it was ripped and pushed aside.

With his fingers he found her sensitive spot and began to stroke in a slow and steady rhythm as she writhed against his hand. He clasped a handful of her hair and kissed her while still teasing her with his fingers, bringing her higher and higher, as the pressure built inside of her.

Pressure building from the way he enveloped her in those strong, muscled arms of his, holding her close like he never wanted to let go.

Pressure building from the way his hands,

skimming up her legs, pushed her skirts aside. His fingertips lingered around her garters, where the stockings gave way to her soft, bare flesh.

"More . . ." she moaned. "More of you."

Fox slid one finger, then another inside. She moaned and clung to him. Nothing, *nothing* would make him stop now—not until she cried out in pleasure.

"You're so wet. So ready."

"Yes . . ." she gasped. She slid her hand along his breeches, her palms skimming the hard length of him and he issued a low groan.

"More . . ."

"More?"

"Yes?"

"Yes."

Hearts pounding.

Frantic kisses. Frantic unbuttoning of breeches.

He slowed as he entered her, wanting to savor every second of this moment . . . as much as he wanted to be inside her, be one with her. Now. Forever.

"Oh, yes." Claire let her head fall back as Fox filled her up. He held her in those strong, muscled arms of his. She clung to him, burrowing her face in his neck to breathe him in, or turning her head to kiss him, taste him.

He moved within her in a steady rhythm that seemed designed to drive her wild. Every thrust made her gasp. Every time he groaned in pleasure she wanted to sigh.

They were one now. One, fused together, connecting, needing, giving, taking, and wanting. Hearts beating as one. A tangle of arms and legs and kisses and whispers until he didn't know where he ended and she began.

The world was reduced to her. And him. And that exquisitely torturous pressure building within her. The heat started in her core and started to spread. Her skin felt hot. Her breath was caught. Her heart was pounding, pounding. He was thrusting, steady and relentless. And when she didn't think she could take so much pleasure anymore, she didn't.

She cried out as waves of pleasure pulsed through her.

He captured the sound with his mouth for a kiss.

He groaned and his mouth closed around her shoulder as he came with a few last, passionate, possessive thrusts.

They held each other in the aftermath.

Hearts were still pounding.

Breaths were not quite caught.

Words still unspoken.

Chapter 21

The next day, Durham House

When a man is ready for the rest of his life to begin, there is no point in waiting, which is why Fox was seen on the doorstop of Durham House at the earliest possible hour.

He was swiftly granted an audience with the duke in his study.

Durham stood to greet him and Fox noticed mud on the duke's boots. It was one thing in the country, but in the city . . . It wasn't the sort of thing that wouldn't help the rumors, but it oddly improved the man in Fox's opinion. Showed he was the sort of man who wasn't afraid of a little dirt and activity. Perhaps they might get along.

If Fox didn't bungle the reason for his call.

After a polite interlude of small talk—of horse races and boxing matches and nothing to do with women—Fox finally started to get to his point.

"The reason I'm calling is that I would like your permission to wed Lady Claire."

The duke appeared skeptical, perhaps slightly murderous, which gave Fox pause. He came here to do things properly—ask permission, propose, et cetera—not duel. He did not want to duel. For one thing, he was exceptional at pistols *and* swords and didn't fancy doing an injury to his hopefully future brother-in-law.

Before he could finish the sentence, there was a knock on the door immediately followed by the door opening. It was the sort of perfunctory but pointless knock done by someone who was intent upon barging in with or without permission.

Lady Bridget came barging into the library, oblivious to the fact that people were trying to have a potentially life-altering private discussion.

"Oh! I didn't mean to interrupt, but I was just looking for my diary . . ."

"You lost it again, Bridge?" The duke rubbed his temples wearily. Fox was starting to sympathize with the duke. He had an estate to run, society to conquer, and these sisters . . .

"How can you be so careless after the last time?" the duke asked. "That was nearly a disaster."

"Well, it turned out well enough," Lady Bridget said smugly.

"Well enough indeed," Fox agreed, no thanks to his own sister, which he decided not to mention at present.

"Aren't you going to look for it?" James asked. "And I don't want to know why it would be lost in *my* private study."

"Oh, right. Yes. I'm searching for it." Lady Bridget made a show of searching for it on the bookshelves and, oddly, under the chair cushions. James sighed wearily. A moment ago, Fox had been a tight ball of nerves but now he was beginning to enjoy himself.

This family was ridiculous in a funny, wonderful way.

"You didn't lose it, did you?" the duke asked. "You are just using that as an excuse to come and eavesdrop on this private conversation. A private conversation between two gentlemen about business," James reminded her.

"Why do I suspect that this business has to do with Claire?" Lady Bridget asked. "Are you about to propose to her, Lord Fox?"

Yes, if he could get blasted permission first. He was spared from answering by the interruption of another sister.

"Who is about to propose?" Lady Amelia asked.

James just groaned and dropped his head in his hands.

"Sisters. A man has no peace when he has sisters. I give up. If you want her, Fox, she's all yours. If you don't, please consider taking her off my hands."

"That's a fine way to talk about your sisters!" Amelia admonished.

"Your beloved sisters," Bridget added.

"Who have endured so much to support your ducalness," Amelia said.

"It was your idea to come here," the duke replied to the lot of them.

"You were the one who inherited."

"Not on purpose."

"What is everyone arguing about?" Enter the duchess.

Her Grace, the notoriously terrifying Duchess of Durham, swept into the library and surveyed the scene: a guest besieged by her nieces and nephew. Her eyes narrowed when she caught sight of Fox. They narrowed in the way of a marriage-minded mama's in the presence of unmarried gentlemen of rank and fortune, such as himself.

"Lord Fox, how do you do. It is a pleasure to have you call upon us," she said graciously.

"Thank you, Duchess. I am actually quite enjoying the company."

"Though after witnessing this display, if you

wish to pretend there was some other reason for your call, then I completely understand and will not hold it against you," the duke said.

"I find it charming actually."

The duchess just smiled.

"I suppose you wish to see Lady Claire, but I'm afraid now is not a good time," the duchess said.

"She's with the Duke of Ashbrooke," Bridget said.

"And that crashing bore, Benedict Williams," Amelia said, making a face.

"She's presenting her paper to the Royal Society," James said, beaming with pride. "It was just published."

"We were just on our way out to attend and to show our support," the duchess added. "Would you care to join us?"

The Royal Society

Love did strange things to a man, like make him eager to get to a meeting of the Royal Society of Numerical Things That Make No Sense to Normal People.

Fox and the Cavendish family arrived just as the doors were closing and the meeting about to begin. He had some idea of striding up to the lectern where she stood and making a grand declaration of his love and dropping to one knee to propose as soon as possible.

But the duchess stopped him.

"Not yet," she murmured. "Let her have this moment."

And so he took a seat for Lady Claire's lecture and was pleased to see that she was herself again. Her hair was pulled back simply and she wore a plain but elegant dress, because this wasn't a ballroom and this wasn't a demonstration of ladies' fashion. She wore her glasses.

After an introduction from Ashbrooke and Benedict Williams, she presented her paper, speaking eloquently and passionately about things he absolutely did not understand. He caught something about how the digits on the cogs of the proposed analytical engine could represent things other than mathematical quantities. This did not make any sense to him but he loved that it made sense to her, and even got some murmurs of interest and heads nodding around the room.

And so she spoke, at length, and though he didn't follow what she said, he was happy to sit there to watch and listen.

He must be in love.

It was the only logical conclusion to why he was enjoying a math lecture.

Finally, she concluded and took questions. After addressing the concerns of the man in the front row, replying to a point from the man in the blue striped waistcoat, answering a question about the table of Bernoulli numbers (whatever those were) from the gentleman on the left, she shuffled her papers together and said, "Thank you for your attention. If there are no further questions—"

Fox raised his hand and said loudly, "I have a question."

Claire felt her hands tremble as she shuffled her papers together. Fox was here! She had seen him arrive with her family and she'd been aware of them sitting quietly in the back, and probably bored to tears, but making a forceful demonstration of their support, which she appreciated tremendously.

And now he had a question.

After everything they had been through together, and the pleasures of the previous evening, she had a good idea what his question would be. It would not have anything to do with the analytical engine's design or function or math at all. But it was a question she was keen to answer.

He smiled and strolled down the center aisle toward her.

Yes.

He reached for her hand and gazed into her eyes.

Yes.

Then Fox dropped to one knee. In front of the entire Royal Society.

She felt breathless. But Claire rationalized that if there was ever a time to be breathless it was when one was about to wholeheartedly accept a future one never imagined, but one that was just right anyway.

He clasped her hand. Fox kneeling was practically as tall as Claire standing, so she could look straight into his green eyes and see all the love and desire for her shining there.

"Claire. From the moment we met, I knew you were different from all the other women I had known. Mainly because you weren't the slightest bit interested in me."

Here, she laughed. There were a few soft chuckles in the crowd as well.

"I was intrigued. And I have never stopped being fascinated and confused by you, overwhelmed and impressed. You challenge me and surprise me. You and your brilliant mind, your kind heart, your wicked kiss."

Here, she blushed. And a few eyebrows were raised.

"I don't know anything about what you just spoke about, but I do know I could listen to you talk about it all day. I know that in an odd way, you and I complement each other. I know my own heart, and my own mind, and I know that I want to spend the rest of my life with you. I hope you'll make me the happiest man in the world and agree to marry me."

Here, tears started welling up in her eyes.

"Yes."

Claire launched herself into his arms and said it again. "Yes."

The crowd applauded and cheered, reminding them of their presence at what had to be the most romantic thing to ever happen at a math lecture.

"Wait, I'm not done." Fox reached into his pocket and pulled out a pair of spectacles that he pressed into Claire's hand. "I'll still get you a ring, of course, but I wanted to give you these. Because I want *you,* Claire. Not any other woman, and not you trying to be like other women. Just you."

With that her heart skipped a beat. That was love. That was happiness. And she knew with absolute certainty that Fox was the man for her, because he challenged her to be better and supported her endeavors, because he set her aflame with his touch. He was kind and knew how to kiss a girl. And because there were some things a woman just knew, and she knew they would make each other happy.

"I love you, Fox."

"I love you, too, Claire. Say 'yes' again."

"Yes! A thousand times, yes."

"Just a thousand?"

"Multiplied by a thousand . . ." And she started to explain how to get that number to infinity, but found herself momentarily distracted. Her lips found his for a kiss that promised forever.

Epilogue

Norwood Park
Kent, England, 1837
In the drawing room

"I find this equation to be particularly beautiful, as it relates all of the most fundamental constants in math in one line," Claire explained to the children crowding around her—her two sons and daughter, as well as some children from neighboring estates—for a closer look at Euler's equation as she had written it on a sheet of paper. "Now who can tell me what they are?"

Little voices piped up, followed by the sound of chalk scratching on slates as they diligently copied what she had written.

Many were aghast that the marchioness herself had taken to teaching the children their math, but as Lord Fox would proudly point out to anyone who would listen, who was better qualified to do it?

Really, there was no one better.

And no one who enjoyed it more.

Just as there was no one better than Fox to teach the children to ride, fence, swim, play cricket, or risk their precious necks in various outdoor adventures.

Claire didn't entirely mind; it provided her with quiet time to focus on her rewarding work, which included more collaborations with Ashbrooke and other Royal Society members.

Speaking of the other notable, engaging, all-consuming collaboration of her life . . .

Fox strolled into the drawing room just then, all tall and brawny and sweaty from a ride around the estate. Her husband was loath to miss a day's ride when they were in the country, especially since James had gifted him with a splendid horse from his stables.

For a moment, she paused in the lesson to take in the way his breeches clung to his powerful thighs, or the way his jacket stretched across his broad shoulders. Except for the streaks of gray in his hair and slight crow's-feet when he smiled, the man had hardly aged at all.

She did quite like seeing him like this: hair tussled from the wind, eyes bright, a slick sheen of sweat on his skin that'd she like to lick off, from head to toe.

Fox caught her eye over the heads of the children. His green eyes sparkled and she crossed her legs, knowing *exactly* what he was thinking.

It had nothing to do with Euler's equation.

Which she wasn't exactly thinking about, either.

"There is cake in the kitchen and kittens in the barn," he said.

The children fled.

Fox gave her a wolfish grin.

"Hello, my lady wife."

"Hello, you, Lord Interrupter of Lessons."

"What were you working on, my princess of parallelograms?"

"Euler's equation. I was just explaining that this equation contains all the most fundamental constants of math in one line. 1, 0, pi . . ."

"Pie?"

"Not that kind." She rolled her eyes at the joke he'd been making for *years* now.

"Speaking of math, fancy calculating the angles of our bedsheets?" Fox asked with a mischievous grin.

"Now tell me how you would do that?" she replied with an arch of her brow and a hint of a smile on her lips. "And I insist that you show your work."

His reply did not involve numbers.

It involved a kiss on the stairs leading from the foyer to their bedroom. A soft press of his lips to hers as he swept her into a close embrace.

Even the merest brush of her husband's lips against hers never failed to make her pulse quicken. And, Claire noted with a sly smile, make her husband harden.

His calculations included an interlude up against the wall in the corridor, her back pressed against the wall as Fox's hands skimmed along her curves, from her hips and waist to her breasts—all now rounder, now fuller, but no less appealing to him.

She felt him hard against her. Tasted the salty sweat on his neck. He was wild and active and passionate, this man of hers. She sighed into his shirt, eager to remove it and feel his warm, bare skin against her own.

"Me plus you," he whispered, pressing a kiss to her neck.

"Plus privacy," she murmured.

Once in their bedroom there was a cascade of clothes, falling from *his* body to the floor. The jacket went first, then the shirt, then Claire hummed her appreciation. He paused, standing proud, as she indulged in a long, lusty look at him. The afternoon light highlighted the planes and ridges of his muscles, barely hidden beneath a smattering of hair on his chest.

The breeches and everything went next.

"Now you, my lady."

Claire sauntered across the room to him, enjoying the desire for her plain in his eyes.

"I might need your assistance. Or shall we ring for my maid and wait?"

Fox spun her around so fast she couldn't help but start laughing. He went to work on the buttons of her gown.

"I miss the dresses you wore when we first met. The fashions then were easier to get you out of."

"I would think you prefer *no* dresses."

"They are best on the floor, aren't they?" He eased the fabric away from her body and she sighed from the sensation of being unbound, and in anticipation of the pleasures yet to come. Then, in a low voice, he murmured, "And then I get to see you like this. Still so beautiful."

There was no hiding the appreciation in his voice.

"You're not so bad yourself," she said coyly, turning to face him, her gaze flitting from his lips, to his chest, to his arousal jutting out, hard and wanting her touch.

"I know."

"So modest."

"I can see the appreciation in your eyes."

"You can see it in every woman's eyes. Young ladies still swoon when you walk through a ballroom."

"But I only have eyes for you."

Claire glanced away from her husband to the bed. "What were you saying about calculating the angles of the bedsheets?"

"Me plus you plus privacy . . ."

"Plus love . . ."

"Plus lust . . ."

"Plus this kiss."

And there was just kissing after that. Deep, passionate kisses that set her body aflame with wanting. Claire tugged Fox closer and he rolled above her, treating her to that thrilling sensation of his weight atop her. She tasted the salt on his skin as she teased him with her tongue. He lavished attention on her breasts until she was gasping for breath.

After all these years together, he knew exactly how to tease her and please her. Fox expertly stroked her clitoris, intensifying her pleasure. She rolled over and returned the favor, taking him in hand, and then in her mouth, knowing just how he liked it.

"Me plus you," he whispered, pulling her to straddle him.

Claire felt him hard at her entrance, and then sighed as she felt him push inside her. What followed: sighs and moans of satisfaction. Touch and taste and all the senses working in concert to bring them both to the heights of pleasure. There was a tangle of limbs and a tangle of bedsheets until she wasn't sure where she ended and he began. They were one in love, in life, in pleasure.

Me plus you.

Such a simple equation that added up to something better than she could have ever imagined.

Author's Note

The inspiration for Lady Claire Cavendish is the real life Ada, Countess of Lovelace, who is widely considered the first computer programmer due to her work with Charles Babbage on his analytical engine.

After I wrote *The Wicked Wallflower,* in which the hero, the Duke of Ashbrooke, is inspired by Babbage and his work, quite a few readers wrote to me asking, "Where was Ada?" She didn't quite fit in that story, and she very much deserved her own. And so, Lady Claire Cavendish was created.

While their personal lives were quite different, I did give Claire the task of Ada's most significant contribution—translating Babbage's paper explaining the analytical engine, which grew to include her famous notes where she developed the first algorithm to be carried out by machine.

I have taken some liberties with dates (Ada would have been only nine in 1824, when this story takes place) in order to bring these characters and their work to life in a Regency romance.

For more on the research for this book and inspiration for the series, please visit me online at www.mayarodale.com.

Keep reading for an exclusive sneak peek at the fourth enchanting tale in *USA Today* bestselling author Maya Rodale's Keeping Up with the Cavendishes series

It's Hard Out Here for a Duke

Prologue

The Queen's Head tavern
Southampton, England, 1824

Some men were born to be dukes, and some men were James Cavendish, who despite being an undistinguished American, found himself in possession of an aristocratic title in a country he'd never before visited.

Back home in Maryland he was James Cavendish, the horse breeder and trainer of some renown around those parts. He was known as Henry's son, and the one responsible for three sisters who were endlessly trouble.

But here in England, he was the Duke of Durham.

Whatever that was.

Whatever that meant.

Or he would be, once he and his sisters completed their journey and arrived in London.

They had docked in Southampton this morning, would remain here tonight, and continue on to London on the morrow. James had sworn to himself that he would not be Durham until he set foot in London.

Oh, he knew that the title had passed to him the moment his father breathed his last breath, shortly after his mother had passed away. Or rather, he learned it a year later, when the Duchess of Durham's representatives had tracked him down and informed him of that fact.

But he had resolved that until he stepped foot in London, until he crossed the threshold of Durham House, he would be James, just James. An unremarkable, plain young man of no import or renown, just having a pint in a pub like anyone else.

His sisters—Claire, Bridget, and Amelia, each one more trouble than the last—had been settled in a room upstairs, happily having baths and stretching out on full beds after a long journey at sea.

James wasn't ready to sleep. Couldn't, really. More to the point, he wasn't ready to be alone with his thoughts. A tavern at night was an excellent place to be in that situation.

This particular tavern wasn't too different from the ones back home and he appreciated the familiarity provided by the same scuffed wood floors, rough-hewn tables and chairs, tallow candles. If he tried hard, he could concentrate only on the hum and roar of voices and tune out the strange accents. He could pretend he was at Faunces Tavern back home, that his friend Marcus would stroll through the door any minute, ready to regale him with some of his latest exploits.

James glanced around. Marcus wasn't here, wasn't going to be here, and James knew no one. There wasn't anyone he particularly wanted to know, either, except—

He noticed a woman. She sat primly at the bar, sipping from a mug, occasionally conversing with the barmaid.

She just happened to glance his way, giving him just a hint of doe eyes, high cheekbones, and full lips.

He caught her eye.

Then she looked away.

She wasn't looking at him. She wasn't looking at him. She wasn't looking at him.

He waited, wanting another glimpse.

Finally, she glanced his way again. The corners of her lips teased up into a hint of a smile and her gaze darted away.

Careful, this one startles easily.

James just leaned back against the wall, nearly empty mug of ale dangling from his fingers. He had all night to play this kind of game. Even if they did nothing but exchange glances across the room for the rest of the evening, he'd be happy. It distracted him from the things he wanted distraction from.

Their gazes connected again.

James just leaned there, drinking in the sight of her. He grinned and felt his heartbeat quicken.

She looked away.

She dared another glance.

He was still waiting for her to invite him over. Perhaps it would have been a smile, a wink, a something.

Eventually, she laughed at their little game. He couldn't hear her from where he stood and that was intolerable. When she held his gaze for a real moment, he knew he had permission to speak to her.

James crossed the room. Time seemed to slow. And then he was standing in front of her, his breath knocked right out of his lungs. She was beautiful and she was smiling prettily at him, just James.

The night just got better.